Cornered

"Get out here, Shumner," Leonard growled between clenched teeth. The footsteps continued almost immediately. Leonard wasn't going to wait for him.

The door to the only other stall in the bathroom slammed open, rattling Eric, who now leaned against the metal dividing wall, as close to the tiled back wall as he could get.

The power in his chest thrummed like a lawn mower starting up. He tried to calm it, afraid that Leonard would hear it in the powerful acoustics of a public bathroom.

The door to his stall shuddered, but it was still locked.

"E'm not gonna to wet for you, Shumner," Leonard said. He pounded a fist against the locked door. Eric stiffened. There was no way Leonard could get through that door. If he tried crawling under it, Eric could kick him in the face, probably re-breaking his jaw.

He prepared to do just that when the shadow of Leonard's legs shifted. But instead of ducking down to crawl under the door, Leonard reared back and struck the door with the flat of his booted foot. The entire stall shook. The metal door flexed, but the lock miraculously held.

The power in Eric's chest flared. The vibration spread down his arms and legs, feeling like the uncontrollable shiver of a sudden chill without the cold feeling. Eric felt himself falling backward, toward the stall's dividing wall. He stumbled back…

… through the wall!

When he blinked again, he was in the adjoining stall, his nose nearly touching the dividing wall and his butt against the half-open door of the stall.

His eyes widened.

What the hell had just happened?!

HEROES OF F.O.R.C.E.
BY ALEC GUNN

UNTOUCHABLE

ALEC GUNN

Untouchable

Copyright © 2017 Nick Marsden
All Rights Reserved
1st Print Edition
Published by Pencastle Publications
www.pencastlebooks.com
Cover and Interior design Copyright © 2020 Nicholas Marsden
ISBN: 978-1-7360973-0-4

Contents

Forward

This is a work of fiction.

This is also a book of alternative history. I've included several "real" people to ground the story and give it a certain feel. However, these representations of real people are fictionalized to the point that they can't possibly represent the real thing.

People like Al Gore, Chuck Grassley, Zak Williams, and others are merely around as sort of easter eggs for the astute reader to point to history or reality and see a glimpse of the alternate.

In this world, "Superheroes" have made war obsolete. Since Vietnam, the United States has used them to secretly prevent the major conflicts we know of in this modern age from happening. Just these changes have drastically altered who people are, or if they existed at all.

So if you are or know one of these people (Hiya, Chuck!), don't take offense at any changes to appearance or personality.

I've tried not to make any of them *total* dicks.

These strange events may have also altered some of our pop culture. I make several pop culture references in this book, some of which are "wrong". That is intended, so don't write me saying that Eric Roberts wasn't in Back to the Future.

I know (He's not really a bad actor, either. Sorry, Mr. Roberts.).

-Alec Gunn

<u>Prologue</u>

Washington D.C. - September 23rd, 2001:

12 days after the Incident

Do we need to watch this?" Senator Andrew Marshall asked, turning toward the President, who waited patiently at the far end of the conference table.

"Yes," replied, not the President, but a man with black-rimmed glasses and hair nearly as black and twice as glossy. Both matched the rumpled black suit he wore. The dark clothing only made his pale, waxy skin shine in contrast.

"And who are you again?" Senator Marshall asked.

"Edward," the man said, stabbing the power buttons on the TV and DVD player. "DSA."

Twelve men gathered in a dimly lit conference room that Senator Chuck Grassley insisted on calling the "war room." It might as well have been. Perhaps in the distant past, it had been used for such a purpose, but it had been decades since the last war – nearly 40 years since the last time the United States had engaged in any kind of meaningful conflict.

Marshall, the Junior Senator from Missouri, preferred the term "situation room." Even if what had happened in New York necessitated military action, who would they be fighting? Who would *do* the fighting? The US military was nowhere near the strength it had been in the Korea Conflict, the last time major military action had even been considered as far as Marshall knew.

"What is that?" Marshall asked, looking around the table to see if any of the others were familiar with the DSA. "Department of Special Administration?"

Edward cracked an amused smile at Marshall's guess, shaking his head. "You wouldn't have heard of it, I'm sure." He motioned toward the President, "Would you be so kind, Mr. President?"

President Albert Gore nodded his dark-haired head. "Department of Supernormal Affairs, Senator."

"Supernormal... FORCE? That publicity stunt?" The DSA must be the department under which the black ops "Field Operations and Reconnaissance Corps – Enhanced" was budgeted. What did those frauds have to do with New York?

Senator Marshall glanced from Edward to President Gore. Gore looked almost as sickly as Edward. The once-robust man now looked as if he would be ill at any moment. His dark hair had sprouted a thin layer of gray in the last week or so. They said the presidency ages you, but in just a matter of weeks? Gore had only been President for less than a year. Before the 11th of September, he'd been a fierce, determined man eager to press Congress on his agenda. Now, he looked like a sickly lion past his prime.

It was understandable with what he'd been through.

Edward inserted a DVD marked with a stripe of orange tape that said "CLASSIFIED: TSSCI." Top Secret: Special Compartmentalized Information was one of the highest classifications in the US Government. It was far from the highest clearance, but the highest were all very specialized and "need-to-know" on a case by case basis, organized by codenames. Until four years ago, FORCE had been a codename project known only to a handful of the highest administration officials, perhaps only the President himself. Most of the details of that project were still on a need-to-know basis. Until today, Marshall had never had a need to know.

The reason he was in this room at all, with three other much more senior Senators and a handful of Congressmen, was that he'd been tapped as a member of the Justice Committee into looking into the events in New York City two weeks ago. The first Senator to be named to lead that investigation, the Honorable Senator from New York, had killed herself a few days ago.

"Consider this your read-in, gentlemen," Edward began, "FORCE is – was – a team of special operatives with enhanced physical and mental abilities. This has been known to the general public for almost four years now since the previous administration chose to crack open the lid, so-to-speak." It was clear Edward had disagreed with that decision. "What isn't generally known is that FORCE has been active since 1963. Its first mission was to lead a raid into Hanoi in northern Vietnam to capture or kill the communist leaders of the regime there." Edward shrugged. "No one was captured."

Marshall nearly spoke up. A black ops team working unilaterally to topple foreign governments? Who the hell had decided that was a good idea? But, though he wanted to blurt these things out, he kept silent. It was as if his thoughts couldn't trigger his voice and lips. By the time he thought he might have said something, Edward was speaking again.

"FORCE was sent to New York City on an exercise. Shortly beforehand, documents were destroyed, so we are not sure–"

"Is that how you run your operation, Edward?" Senator Grassley cut in. "Are you not even aware of what your own people are doing?"

Edward didn't seem to realize Grassley was speaking, though he'd stopped to listen. He didn't make eye contact with the Senator. As soon as Grassley was done, Edward continued as if he hadn't been interrupted. "This is video obtained by the sole survivor of the New York Incident, FORCE operative codename 'Mental Block.' He was aboard the Sea Stallion that crashed into the Atlantic shortly after the explosion. The pilot and co-pilot both died of their injuries. Mental Block is still in the ICU as we speak, though I hear he will make a full recovery. He will be fully debriefed when he can be."

"What is this man's real name?" Senator Grassley asked. This time, Edward's eyes shifted lazily to the Senate Majority Leader.

"Above your pay-grade, Senator," Edward said shortly. Marshall's eyebrows rose. As the Senate Majority Leader, there weren't many people above Grassley's pay-grade. In this room, only one person was, and President Gore was keeping his mouth shut.

"I don't like this cloak-and-dagger shit," Grassley growled, glancing at President Gore. The President didn't seem to be listening to the exchange at all. His eyes were steady and unfocused. For his part, Edward ignored the Senator.

Grassley opened his mouth to speak again, he was getting noticeably annoyed at the black ops suit. Something Marshall could appreciate. He was beginning to feel the pang of frustration, too. They were in a private setting, all of them had been cleared to investigate this matter as a committee. There was no reason for the secrecy.

But instead of being intimidated or even considerate of the Majority Leader's position, Edward raised a hand authoritatively. Grassley silenced. Not with a growl or a sigh, but just closed his mouth and didn't make a sound. Edward nodded and pressed play on the video. Marshall narrowed his eyes.

Who was this asshole, and why was the President letting him walk all over his betters?

As the lights went down and a black screen with the words: "Operation 911" came on the screen, Edward said one last thing. "Everything you will see is from the perspective of the operative known as Mental Block. The only sound you'll hear is the communication channel shared by the team."

On the TV screen, the camera came on, showing the familiar ribbed bulkheads of a military cargo aircraft – presumably the CH-53 Sea Stallion Edward had mentioned. The interior of the aircraft was flooded with red light and shook violently. Only a large square of gray light, bleached out in the view of the body camera allowed any color other than red to show.

In the center of the compartment, three figures crouched.

The largest of them, a huge hulk of a man, gestured into the space between them. There was nothing there, but the big man pointed to something in the air as if there was.

This was Citadel, instantly recognizable as the leader of the covert "superhero" team called FORCE. Every one of the Congressmen in the room had been present when FORCE was revealed to the world four years ago. But as soon as they were presented to the public, they vanished again into the shadows. They were a covert operations team, after all. Still, Citadel wasn't a man you could mistake for anyone else. He was huge, standing at least seven feet tall, though he crouched now. He was also more than half as wide as he was tall, huge muscles bulged from his chest and arms. His black uniform had the sleeves torn off, revealing pale skin lined with thick veins over rock hard biceps and forearms.

If this was Citadel, that made the other two smaller figures Rumble and Jitterbug. With Mental Block, that rounded out the team.

"What are they doing?" Senator Grassley asked.

"Mission planning," Edward said. "Mental Block is projecting an image of their target into their minds, allowing Citadel to give a detailed briefing."

Marshall shook his head. All this telepathy, telekinesis, super strength bullshit was hard to swallow. Even if this team had supposedly destroyed an entire Texas town fighting "insurgents," the reports and images from that day were sketchy and possibly doctored. On the one day FORCE had been brought out into the lights of a media hailstorm, there had been no demonstration of their abilities. There was no proof that these abilities really existed.

"What target?" Grassley asked.

"You'll see."

Then, the red light vanished, replaced by a wash of gray, early morning daylight. At the top of the large square of light, a green bulb was lit.

"We're here," a soft voice said over the commlink, probably the pilot.

Mental Block moved, the camera rising and moving closer

to the door. As the camera's aperture closed to adjust for the increase in light, the New York City skyline came into view. It fell away below them as the helicopter climbed higher toward the top of two large towers that dominated the view.

The Twin Towers of the World Trade Center.

The helicopter approached and rose above the platform atop of the South Tower. This was where tourists would come to stand atop the world. The roof was surrounded by railings and wire to keep lunatics from jumping off. The small platform in the center might have been used as a helipad, but the CH-53 was too large for it. There would be no landing.

The members of FORCE gathered around the door. Citadel was the first to jump. It was a good thirty feet to the platform. Normally, soldiers would repel down ropes at this height. But Citadel merely stepped off the deck and dropped feet first. Mental Block's camera tracked him down. Citadel struck the concrete and steel platform flat-footed. His only nod of respect to the height from which he'd dropped was a slight bending of his knees. The platform cracked and buckled beneath his feet, absorbing the force Citadel's body should have absorbed.

Any normal man would have shattered both legs on such a stunt. By all rights, Citadel should have been rolling around on that platform writhing in pain.

"Jesus!" Grassley breathed.

But if Citadel's descent was spectacular, it couldn't compete with that of Jitterbug and Rumble.

Jitterbug wrapped an arm around Rumble's waist, and they stepped off the helicopter simultaneously, as if onto an invisible platform. Instead of falling to their deaths, they descended slowly.

"They can fly?!" Marshall blurted, incredulous.

"No," Edward said. "Flying is impossible, Senator. Jitterbug is merely using telekinesis to carry Rumble and slow his descent. She is using him for support. See how her foot is braced on his. She can't direct her powers onto herself, so she is directing them onto Rumble. The leverage is poor, so all she can do is slow their fall." Marshall shook his head, not really understanding any of that.

They landed softly on the platform not far from Citadel. As soon as they touched down, Jitterbug stepped away from Rumble, toward Citadel.

"You know what you need to do," said a hard voice through the comm-link. *"Get everyone clear."* Citadel raised his hand and half-waved, half-gestured toward the helicopter. Mental Block's body camera began to move away from the South Tower as the helicopter moved into position between the two towers.

"Mental Block is using his powers to influence the minds of the people inside the tower," Edward commented blandly. "It's standard procedure when civilians are involved. Unless Citadel's command was some sort of code they agreed upon ahead of time, Mental Block is evacuating the towers." Marshall glanced at Edward, who wore a smirk as if not believing his own words. What was he going on about now? A code?

"Jitter," Citadel's voice came over the comm again, *"Take position at the edge of the roof. I want to know when those missiles are incoming. Rumble and I will begin sweeping this tower."*

"Roger," replied a female voice – Jitterbug.

"Missiles?" Grassley asked. Edward sighed.

"We don't know. The mission brief and associated intel reports were destroyed just before FORCE left DSA Headquarters that day. We suspect Citadel had an ulterior motive for taking FORCE to New York."

Ulterior motive? Marshall almost laughed. If Edward's suspicions were true, Citadel was some kind of bastard. For what Citadel did, 'ulterior motive' was not sinister enough a phrase.

There was radio silence as Jitterbug moved away from the other two. She crossed the platform and leaped down toward the roof proper. Something was strange about the way she jumped. Her hands flung backward. She cleared the wire and suicide fence with ease. Again, it almost appeared as if she was flying. But instead of floating above the roof, she landed lightly on her feet. Marshall guessed she'd used her powers to push against the roof as she jumped, resulting in a leap an Olympic high jumper would have envied. She began a patrol at the edge of the roof, her eyes scanning the horizon.

Meanwhile, Citadel and Rumble moved toward the entrance of the stairwell. Instead of entering though, Citadel stood as Rumble crouched down. The smaller man laid a hand on the concrete wall and bowed his head. At this distance, it was impossible to tell what he was doing.

"More telepathy?" Grassley asked, despite all they'd seen so far, the Majority Leader's voice was still skeptical. That's why Marshall respected the man. Grassley didn't take anything at face value. A required skill for a politician.

"Something like that," Edward said but refused to elaborate. Marshall glanced at Grassley but saw no indication of the irritation he'd seen before.

Then, it became clear that Rumble and Citadel were arguing. They weren't using the comm channel, so there was no way to tell what they were discussing. Rumble repeatedly pointed at the floor, insistent. Citadel shook his head.

Finally, Rumble said something that made Citadel freeze. He put his hand to his ear to trigger the comm channel.

"We're going inside," Citadel said. The words stopped Jitterbug's patrol, and Mental Block's body camera shifted, easing out toward the open air outside of the hovering helicopter.

"What do you mean?" said a new voice, probably Mental Block. His voice had the inflection of an Arab. "That's not part of the plan. The building is being evacuated. We just need to stop the missiles."

"Sorry, Block. Jitter, do your best to divert the missiles. Put them in the water, not in the streets. Even this early in the morning, there will be people down there."

With that, Citadel and Rumble vanished into the stairwell.

"No, there's nothing I can do about it," Mental Block said through the comms as if answering an unspoken question. "Not if we want the evacuation to continue. Not everyone is out." The body camera was pointed toward the roof and Jitterbug who was staring up at the helicopter. Jitterbug seemed annoyed. As she returned to her patrol, her arms waved needlessly, as if she were arguing with herself.

The next few minutes passed in silence. Mental Block kept his camera trained on Jitterbug, who carefully scanned the skies around New York City.

"*Block!*" Jitterbug gasped into the comm, coming to an abrupt stop. "*Southeast. That's not a missile.*"

The helicopter rotated so that Mental Block's camera got a view of the approaching "missile."

The "missile" was an airliner racing toward the South Tower of the World Trade Center.

There was an audible shift among the people who were watching the video in the briefing room. Marshall realized he was holding his breath. He slowly let it out, trying not to whimper audibly. Though all of them knew how this would end, part of them hoped this video would end differently, somehow changing history, and making all of this horror go away.

Jitterbug flung out her arms toward the plane. The jet lurched, but it refused to be turned. Jitterbug slid backward across the concrete as if she were dragged backward by invisible ropes. Metal on the plane's nose and wings crumpled, but its forward momentum merely slowed. It didn't stop.

"*Jesus, Block,*" Jitterbug gasped, "*it's too big. I can't push something like that!*"

"*Use its aerodynamics against it,*" Block said. "*Turn it.*"

Jitterbug shifted her arms, setting them wider, then rotating them in opposite directions. The airplane lurched. One wing rose up startlingly, while the other dipped, following the movements of Jitterbugs arms. The plane wavered there. The pilot must have been trying to counteract the effect of Jitterbug's powers. Still, it barreled toward the tower. Then, parts of the wings appeared to bend. Jitterbug was fighting the force of the pilot's control, pulling the ailerons and flaps up. At the rear, the tail flap twisted. The jointed sections of the wings pulled at the plane, causing it to turn from its course. Scraps of metal sheared off the wings as the stress of the forces pitted against the structure began to break the plane apart. At the last minute, the plane rolled upside down, then vanished from the view of the camera.

The helicopter jerked around, pulling up and away from the crashing airliner. There was a flash and a curl of smoke at the bottom of the camera frame. When the helicopter righted itself again, Mental Block leaned out the side to get a view of the tops of the towers. They were much higher now, but it was clear that the towers still stood, untouched. A few blocks away, flaming debris littered the streets.

Jitterbug had saved the tower but killed hundreds in the process.

"God, that's a shit show," Grassley muttered in the briefing room.

"You know it gets worse," Marshall replied grimly. Unable to tear his eyes from the TV screen, he didn't see Grassley's reaction.

Mental Block moved back into the helicopter. Marshall tried to imagine what the man must be thinking. If he was at all human, he'd just watched hundreds, maybe thousands of people die in an instant. It wasn't a wonder why the man now seemed to be staring into space. Except for the shaking of the helicopter, the camera hadn't moved for quite a–

The Senator saw the dark object moving across the gray sky just moments before Mental Block shouted into the comms.

"Jitterbug! North Tower. Northwest. Another one!"

Mental Block once more leaned out to see if Jitterbug was reacting. She was. She sprinted toward the corner of the South Tower where the gap between North and South Towers was smallest though still yawned dozens of feet. What did she think she was doing?

She reached the edge of the building and pushed off with her feet. She must have pushed off with her telekinesis as well because suddenly, she was soaring through the air. If this wasn't flight, Marshall didn't know what was. Her hands were stretched straight against her sides, and her legs were straight, toes pointed.

Marshall's rear end slid forward on his seat. It was one of the most marvelous things he'd ever seen. How was it possible?

Then, long before reaching the other tower, Jitterbug began

to lose altitude. The camera jerked forward. For the first time, Mental Block's hand came into view, olive-brown Mediterranean arm reaching out toward Jitterbug.

But it wasn't Mental Block who saved Jitterbug. Instead, she flung her arms up toward the top of the tower. Marshall clearly saw her clench her fists and she ripped her arms back like she was doing a pull-up. Her body launched up into the air as if attached to a bungee cord connected to the North Tower. She cleared the edge of the tower by inches and tumbled onto the roof, accompanied by a collective gasp that rippled through the assembled officials in the briefing room.

After a brief pause, Jitterbug was on her feet. She limped, favoring her right leg. She'd been injured in the extraordinary leap, but she wasn't letting the injury stop her from crossing the roof of this building until she could see the approaching second airliner. The helicopter followed her movements. Either Mental Block or the pilot was now more interested in seeing the result of this second attack more than in keeping the aircraft safe.

Jitterbug flung out her arms toward the plane as she had the last. This time, however, the pilot was more successful in controlling the plane, preventing it from being turned over as the last had. The plane loomed closer and closer, pushing Jitterbug back across the tower's roof like she was an ant trying to stop the tread of a giant's toe.

Then, Citadel's voice crackled over the intercom.

"Exodus…"

At the word, Mental Block's camera jerked. Had the word been an abort code? If so, the pilot was pulling away swiftly and without question.

The Sea Stallion arced away from the city. Mental Block watched the city recede, the rest of FORCE and even the plane vanishing in the distance faster than Marshall would have thought possible.

A brilliant flash of light blinded the camera, turning the TV screen white. The white light faded, revealing a black cloud lit orange-gray by the early morning sun. The cloud rose above the horizon, obscuring the once-magnificent New York City skyline. It mushroomed up and out, pushing aside anything that stood in its way. Steel and stone shredded like tissue paper. Even the water of the Atlantic ocean roiled as the shockwave pushed outward from the island.

"Ya'Allah..." Mental Block breathed. *"He did it. The bastard actually did it."*

Then, the shockwave hit the helicopter, throwing the image on the screen into chaos as if the camera were being thrown across the cargo space by a bad football quarterback.

Finally, the screen went black.

The assembled Congressmen and the President of the United States sat in the dark, stunned to silence. When the lights came on, it was Edward who stood at the switch. He was the only one who seemed unaffected by the video. Marshall glanced at President Gore, who only stared at the blank screen, his emotions unreadable.

"That, gentlemen," Edward said, "Was how the United States lost New York City."

The room exploded with questions.

Alec Gunn

AUPrimeHistory: True Conspiracies

(Airdate: 9/11/2008)

INTRODUCTION

<Narrator over True Conspiracies intro graphic>

Tonight, on True Conspiracies, we cover the devastating events that changed the world and exposed the true horror of the Super-Powered Individual.

<Archive photo of New York City skyline, 1999>

New York City, the pinnacle of old American greed. The date? September 11, 2001. In the early morning hours, an explosion ripped through the Twin Towers of the World Trade Center in New York City. The blast, a triggered nuclear explosion, obliterated the majority of Manhattan and created a fallout zone miles in diameter.

<Archive footage of New York City, Sept 20, 2001>

Everyone knows the outcome, but how did the United States of America see its final days laid out in nuclear fire and radiation? What chain of events could result in such a terrible tragedy, resulting in the loss of millions of lives?

The truth was hidden in the shadow of black ops and secret government programs for over fifty years. The responsibility for this horror lies squarely in the hands of the government of the United States.

<Close-up: American Union Flag>

Only now, when the standard of the American Union flies over the capitol in Chicago can the truth be known. Only now, after the guiding light of President Andrew Marshall shines on the dark secrets of the previous government can we begin to piece together the facts that led up to that terrible morning. Only now, seven years after the event, can we complete the puzzle of the events of that day.

<Commercial Announcement>

September 8, 2017

The old man finished off the last dregs of the warm cola and made a face. He'd let it sit too long. It had been cold just an hour ago when he'd pulled it from his refrigerator. The warm morning sun had done the job of an oven on the shiny aluminum can. He crushed the can in one hand, then rolled it lightly between his palms until it was a sharp metal stick the size of a cigarette. He tossed it to the ground, where it speared the grassy dirt to half its length.

He looked up from the third such aluminum dart and peered across the street with sharp eyes through the screen of long gray hair he'd grown accustomed to over the last decade. He remembered to pick up the cardboard sign that leaned against his leg and faced it mostly toward the approaching cars.

It read:

Trying to make it through hard times. Anything helps.

His mind wasn't on the cars, though. He watched the corner between Park and Wall where any minute now, the kid he was waiting for would come around and pedal his silver-blue bike into the driveway of Marshall High School like he was running from something big and nasty.

For three years the old man watched. The pattern never changed. In the morning, the kid raced into school. In the afternoon, he coasted down the sloping drive toward the street and rode home at a leisurely pace. The kid had never noticed him that he could tell.

Even the parents dropping their kids off at school didn't mind his presence. Many were generous, giving him money and greeting him as they drove up or drove off.

"Morning, Buck!"

"Good Luck, Buck!"

It was almost funny, if they knew what he was, they'd be terrified. He would most certainly not be their friend.

Such was life in a small town, to Buck's fortunate advantage. In the Chaos Years, Ender, Oklahoma had been spared the worst of it. Ender had no real resources to take advantage of. It had been founded in the nineteenth century as a crossroads town. The coal trains came through here but rarely stopped. There wasn't even a station. McAlester, the big city about fifty miles north of here was where the coal came from. McAlester still bore remnants of its futile defense against looters and raiders that had nearly beaten it down before being liberated by Marshall's Coup. But Ender hadn't had to worry. There was nothing here worth claiming, even when the County Sheriff had turned its back on them.

There was a reason the founders had called it "Ender" in the first place.

For the five Chaos Years – years without security, without an economic system, without hope – people here had depended on each other. They'd learned to trust and respect each other in order to survive. If you couldn't be trusted, you didn't live here long. Ender didn't need police to enforce that particular rule.

Buck had arrived at a time when help had been needed. He'd pitched in, doing what he could to help out. He'd earned the trust of these people and became one of them, even if he didn't have a job or a home with a foundation. To them, he was a refugee of the New York event who hadn't been able to escape the Quarantine Zone with much of anything. He had the clothes on his back and an RV that he lived in at the edge of town. He did odd jobs here and there if asked. He was just a harmless old man to most.

Like a blue-silver streak, the Sumner kid's bike burst from the side street and banked right toward the driveway and a scattering of kids heading into school. His longish black hair fluttered behind him, and his gray-and-red backpack rumbled against his back, battering the boy in protest over the vigorous action of his body. He had skin just a shade darker than white. He was part Hispanic, on his father's side, though it only really showed in his midnight hair and slightly curved nose. He stopped pedaling when his bank was low enough to obstruct the motion. The brief pause in effort seemed second nature to the teenage boy for as soon as he was clear, his legs resumed their frenzied work.

It wasn't any sort of excitement that urged the kid to race into the school yard. He didn't love school. He just loved what lay in the other direction a lot less. Buck guessed he had a lot of anger and frustration to release before school started and piled stress on top of it, hence the furious pedaling.

It was a little sad.

When the kid was gone, Buck bent and plucked the rolled up soda cans from the dirt. The damned habit would get him killed one day. If someone saw him mangle aluminum cans with such ease – the least he could do – any trust he had earned with the people of Ender would evaporate.

He folded up the cardboard sign along its existing folds. The predictable rattle of the school bell called teenage stragglers to class. It would be several hours now before Buck would have a chance to check on the kid again.

It had become a habit to come out here and watch for any changes in the kid. He'd continue doing it until he'd seen what he needed to see. After that…?

The kid's time was growing near if it hadn't already happened. Would he be able to hide as successfully as Buck had? What would he become? What would he be capable of?

The possibilities were intriguing, but despite that, Buck had to admit something to himself.

He had no idea why he gave a damn.

Eric Sumner skidded to a stop just inches from the bike rack. The first bell sounded, spurring Eric to motion uncoiling the plastic-covered chain lock from the blue-silver center bar of the bike and winding it through the frame and the rack, being careful not to scrape the frame against the bare metal rack. He didn't wipe down the bike every night to let it get scratched out of negligence.

His legs were energized as he began walking toward homeroom. It was a good feeling, getting the blood pumping before having to sit on his ass in hard wooden seats all day. He could almost pretend he was glad to be at school.

It had been a long summer, he reflected. There hadn't been much to do and his family – just him and his mother, really – didn't really do road trips or vacations.

It wasn't like school was a reprieve from life. It was more like it amplified the suck. Here, he was constantly reminded that he was a loser. He wasn't a jock, he wasn't popular. He wasn't even a geek. He was a science nerd who didn't give a crap about fantasy, science-fiction, time-or-space travel or any of those things. It put him on a lonely fringe that somewhat overlapped with writers and the kids who spent their lunches drawing in sketch pads. Still, those kids usually had somewhat of a social life, even if it was playing Dungeons & Dragons in a dimly lit basement somewhere.

So, this being the second week of his second year of high school in a small town where he should know everyone just due to the law of probability, he walked through the halls of the school surrounded by strangers with familiar faces. He knew the names of most of them, but usually nothing more than that. He passed through the halls like a ghost, neither acknowledging the life around him nor being acknowledged by it.

He found his locker and got through the combination lock on the third try. You'd think they'd let the kids use the same lockers year to year, but no. New year, new locker, new lock combo.

He dug in his backpack and pulled out his lunch bag so it wouldn't get even more crushed than it already was. Dumping it into the lowest shelf in the locker, he dug out the two books he wouldn't need until the afternoon and put them on the top shelf. With his English Composition book and his chemistry book flopping around inside, he shouldered the backpack and slammed the door shut.

Two steps away from the locker, just a minute before the late bell would ring, Eric stopped dead in his tracks. Just two paces away stood Leonard Strange and his constant companion, Ken Hunter. Both were popular kids in the "jock" category. Leonard was one of the state's best runners on both the track and the football field, and Ken played nearly every sport they'd let him play: basketball, football, baseball, and even LaCrosse in the summers. He was tall and burly, more than sizable enough to intimidate anyone in the school.

But it was Leonard that had caused Eric to freeze. The older boy, a senior this year, had something against Eric. It might have been something Eric had done, or – most likely – it was just the fact that Eric was smaller than the All-Stater. Eric also didn't have any friends to back him up, so he was an easy target.

"Where you going, Sumner?" Leonard asked. "The bell hasn't rung yet. We got time to… talk."

At the sinister tone of voice, Eric's chest quivered. It was a strange sensation, a manifestation of his fear. Last year, Leonard had had Eric to himself all year.

He tried to stand up to the older kid, but that hadn't worked, no matter what the PSA's on TV said. Eric finally had to report the bully, but his status as a school football star and his father's position as the County Sheriff had protected him. In retaliation, Eric has suffered the worst beating he'd ever taken in his life. He didn't want a repeat of that this year

"What do you want, Leonard?" Eric asked. He straightened his back, tamping down his fear to appear calm and maybe even a little annoyed at the intrusion.

Leonard looked down at his own shoulder, picking some

imaginary thread on his blue and gold letterman jacket at the Varsity Football patch. His face was thoughtful.

"I'm running low on cash, Sumner," Leonard said, "What do you have for me today?"

"I don't have any money," Eric said, "And if I did, you wouldn't get it."

"I think I would. And I will."

Ken took half a step toward Eric. Despite himself, Eric took a step back, breaking his bravado. Both bullies grinned like wild animals who'd found weakness in prey.

Leonard clenched a fist and held it at waist level as he advanced. The first blow would be to the stomach. That was how it'd been last year. But before Leonard could reach Eric, a hand rested on his shoulder and pulled back on him. Leonard spun, lifting his fist up, ready to bring it down on whoever dared try and stop him. He froze when he saw the girl who restrained him.

"Come on, Lenny, let him go," the girl said. She stepped from behind Leonard. Kristin Matthews was one of the cheerleaders on the Junior Varsity squad. Eric guessed she was Leonard's girlfriend by the way she, an underclassman, addressed him as "Lenny."

The late bell rang, and Eric winced. He'd be tardy again, thanks to the jock brigade. He tried to find a way around Leonard while he was distracted, but Ken snapped his long fingers and pointed at Eric, a command to stay still.

Kristin looked back down the bend in the hall. "A teacher's coming, let's go," she said. Leonard glanced the same direction Kristin had looked and growled. He pointed a finger at Eric, an inadvertent imitation of his friend.

"I need some cash for the long weekend, Sumner. You'd best go get some before I see you again." He retreated down the hall with Ken and Kristin in tow. Kristin looked back at Eric and winked at him. Eric's chest fluttered again.

What was that about?

But he didn't have time to worry about it. He fled down the side hallway that Kristin had noted the teacher walking down. The teacher was Mr. Turner, his chemistry teacher.

"Everything all right, Eric?" Mr. Turner asked. Eric had Mr. Turner for last year's physics class as well. He liked the bespectacled man, who tried his hardest not to curse in class by using words like "poo" and "darn." Eric imagined the man was downright foul-mouthed outside of class. His skin was a dark-shade similar to the pictures of Eric's father, Steven Sumner, who was nearly full-blooded Hispanic, though his nose and eyes were something else. Indian? Persian?

"Yeah," Eric said, pretending to be out of breath. "Just running late."

"Better move your butt, then," Mr. Turner said. Eric grinned and lengthened his stride, doing his best not to run down the hall with a teacher present, not that Mr. Turner would have called him out on it.

Eric's favorite class was, of course, chemistry. Pretty much any science class was his favorite. Last year, it had been physics. Usually, it was an either-or choice at Marshall High, but Eric chose to do both. He hoped to get into the Advanced Placement versions of both classes over the next few years.

He sat in the front row, the only one to do so without showing up late to class. There was no one he would have wanted to hang out with, so he didn't have to worry about snubbing a friend. Sometimes, loneliness had its benefits.

"Last week," Mr. Turner started, "We spoke of elements, atoms, and the periodic table. Who can tell me what an 'element' is?"

He waited for a response that didn't come before looking at Eric. Eric smiled.

"An element is the simplest chemical substance. They can't be broken down any further."

"Technically, yes," Mr. Turner said. "They can't be broken down further chemically, but even elements are made up of something."

Mr. Turner drew a series of concentric circles on the board.

"Every element is made up of particles..." He turned to

the class and sighed. "I went through this last week people." He waited for another moment then turned back to the whiteboard. "Protons, Neutrons, and Electrons."

Mr. Turner poked at the board with his marker at each word, dotting the circles with points to represent the different particles in an atom.

"Now, we know all the elements in the periodic table right?" He looked over his shoulder with a grin. Eric glanced to his side and saw the horrified look in the student next to him, Thomas Byers, another science geek who wore black-rimmed glasses with some sort of science fiction logo at the temples. "Don't worry," Mr. Turner continued, "You won't need to have the whole thing memorized until next Friday for the chapter test."

A collective sigh whispered through the room. Eric had already memorized the Table of Elements. He had nothing else to do with his time, after all.

"But the world isn't just made up of simple elements, it's made up of combinations of elements. We'll get to this on a more practical level when we start our lab work, but for now, I want to talk about bonding." He drew another atom on the board, identical to the first. Then he marked both with an "O" for Oxygen. "There are two main types of bonds. Covalent Bonds and Ionic Bonds. On a basic level, think of a bond as a relationship. You all have friends, boyfriends, girlfriends, pets, family, whatever, right?"

Eric gulped at this question. Well, he had a mother.

"Think about a chemical bond as a type of relationship. A covalent bond is when two atoms share electrons. This is like when you and your best friend share clothes or music or whatever that makes your life complete. It's why they're your friend."

Eric squinted at the board as Mr. Turner went through a dizzying amount of changes to the oxygen atoms drawn there. Suddenly, they were connected by their circles, and the dots were all jumbled together. Eric tried to copy the diagram into his notes, but Mr. Turner was speaking too fast.

"The ionic bond," Mr. Turner said, "Is like that bad relationship we all get into at least once in our life. One partner takes something from the other, usually self-esteem, which causes the other partner to cling." He doodled two more atoms on the board, dotting them with particles and labeling them "Cl" and "NA": Chlorine and Sodium. "In this case, Chlorine steals an electron from Sodium, and they bond by magnetic polarity. It's a little like when good girls like bad boys. Opposites attract."

Eric copied that diagram in his notes, too. But he still couldn't understand how it all worked.

"This is bonding at the very basic level. But why do atoms bond in the first place? Why do we seek out people to share our lives?" He looked out over the class. No one answered. "Did anyone do the reading?" Eric looked down at his book. He'd done the reading, but he didn't remember anything about this.

Why did people look for friends?

Mr. Turner looked at Eric who usually had an answer. His eyebrows flicked up when Eric shrugged at him, shaking his head.

"The atoms seek to bond because they are unstable. They're missing something within themselves... Electrons."

The light went on in Eric's head. Of course, it was the stability issue. If the outer shell of an atom didn't have enough electrons, it bonded with other atoms to fill out the lack. Why didn't Mr. Turner just say that in the first place?

The rest of the class was much easier once Mr. Turner started working out the simple math in his examples. Once the detail emerged, the frustrating relationship analogy went out the window, and Eric was finally able to work out the logic of electrons, stability, and polarity.

The bell rang for the next class, and Mr. Turner had to shout out the homework assignment as chairs scraped against the floor tiles and students shuffled out of the room. Eric wrote the assignment down – a number of examples of bonding that he'd have to work out and label covalent or ionic – then he packed up his books and slung his pack over his shoulder.

He emerged into the hallway and nearly bumped into

someone standing in his way. He glanced up from the pink and white sneakers to find a gold-trimmed blue cheerleader's skirt and uniform. The sheer length of dark, bare leg startled him. His eyes landed finally on the brown, freckled face of Kristin Matthews.

He swallowed hard.

"You okay?" she asked him. Had she been waiting for him at the door? How did she know he had Mr. Turner for 3rd period? When he didn't answer right away, Kristin spoke again, "Chemistry, right? I couldn't follow half of that."

Eric stared at her. She'd been in the class. Kristin had Chemistry with him? A shuddering ran through his chest, and he took a deep breath to try and calm his nerves. What did she want? Maybe he should ask her?

"Listen," she said before his brain could make his mouth, throat, and tongue coordinate to make words. "I'm sorry about Leonard. He's kind of a dick." She glanced around self-consciously as she said the last, maybe thinking he'd appear out of nowhere and hurt her for calling him names.

"But you're his girl–" Eric was finally able to enunciate.

"God no!" Kristin said. "I'm just a cheerleader, and I've gotta make sure his ass can play tonight. We're playing Sanford." Eric shook his head, not understanding the reference. "Last year's champs," she offered. Eric gave his head a single up and down, pretending that he cared.

Eric didn't know if it was okay for him to start walking to his next class, but he did move away from the door, in case another class had to be let into Mr. Turner's room. Kristin moved along with him, effectively trapping him up against the wall next to the doorway.

"Well," she said, her own conversation falling flat on his silence. "I guess I'll see you around. I just wanted to apologize. Sorry." She moved away.

Eric watched her go and placed a hand on his chest. It felt strange there as if his stomach were growling, but it was up in his chest in the middle of his ribcage. Was he having a heart attack? Fifteen was a little young for that, wasn't it?

He moved through the hall toward his next class, algebra. As his mind strayed to reviewing the algebra work from last night in his head, he forgot about the strange feeling in his chest.

After algebra, there was lunch. Eric returned to his locker to drop off his books and retrieve his lunch bag. He never ate at the cafeteria. The food there was horrible, and he didn't have the money for it anyway. So, instead of trying to find a seat in the crowded room full of squawking teenagers, he took his usual spot at the concrete platform where the flagpole was mounted.

The American Union flag fluttered overhead, a rather uninspired conglomeration of the flags of the three former-nations that made up the AU: Canada, Mexico, and the United States. Technically, none of them existed anymore. They were all the AU, with the capital in Chicago. Less than ten years ago, the three countries had ceased to exist, and a huge federation had risen to take its place. There were still nationalist elements in each country that yearned for the "good old days." Mexico City was a hotbed of protest, while the three western-most states of the USA had broken off completely and declared themselves independent of the AU. Only Canada, the "controlling partner" so-to-speak of the AU had little problem with nationalists.

Eric sat under that flag, the only one he'd ever really known, and ate his lunch. Just as with the flag, lunch was an uninspired collection of tried and true items: a PB&J sandwich crushed by the weight of his books in his backpack, a bag of sealed air that also contained a few Doritos, and a "king-sized" bag of Peanut M&M's. Anyone looking at his lunch would quickly realize his mother hadn't packed it. Little care had been taken to assembling the sandwich, and M&M's weren't normally high on the list of nutritional snacks that parents included in lunch.

But, of course, there was no one around to judge his lunch choices. It was better that way. He ate the sandwich – the grape jelly was soaked through the smashed white bread, but that somehow made it better – and watched the street in front of the school. Old Buck, the homeless guy, was standing across the street, waving his cardboard sign at anyone who would look. Eric wondered why the guy chose the street in front of the school to panhandle. Was he a closet pedophile or something? He looked way too old to Eric's eyes. He had a thick gray beard and long stringy gray hair streaked with some dark color, black or brown. He looked fat, but that might have just been the huge coat he was always wrapped in. His figure was stooped, perhaps from some spinal trouble that kept him from working a normal job.

As Eric watched, a car slowed, and Buck approached it. Something was exchanged, and Buck retreated, stuffing the gift into one of the cavernous pockets of his coat. Eric hoped it was just money. He laughed at himself. What else would it be, drugs? His imagination was running away. He shook his head and finished up his lunch.

Too soon for his taste, the end-of-lunch bell rang, and Eric was forced to return to the world of people and education again.

The afternoon ride home was mellower than the ride to school. By three in the afternoon, Eric was beat. He just wanted to coast all the way home if he could. He rode through downtown Ender, a single street with a limited selection of businesses, including a Murphy's gas station, the 1st National bank, and a bowling alley called Ender Lanes and Lounge. If the bowling alley hadn't had an attached bar, the drunks of Ender would have to get their beer at the gas station or go to McAlester for a drink.

Eric hated that bar. It was one of the reasons he never went into the bowling alley. The other was that he really didn't have anyone to go bowling with.

After the clump of businesses ended, there were railroad tracks. Once a day, long trains of coal cars passed through Ender, either going to or from McAlester, a city built on the coal industry. It might have been cliché, but Eric lived on the other side of the tracks, where the "urban" part of Ender ended and the "rural" tradition ruled. After the tracks, there was a run-down motel that nobody in particular went to, then the private homes began. Houses about fifty years past their prime sat on large lots overgrown with brown grasses. Occasionally, a rusted piece of farming equipment sat in the corner of an ill-kept lawn. Why anyone would want to keep something like that for decoration was beyond Eric.

Eric's house was in a clump of more modern homes, forty years old instead of a sixty – with much smaller yards. They were connected in a cul de sac that dead-ended at the edge of an open field that might have once been a thriving farm. Eric had never seen crops growing on it. The field was overgrown with brambles and shrunken versions of old vegetable plants.

A twenty-year-old, red Ford Tempo sat in the driveway of Eric's house, parked at an angle to the garage for no apparent reason. Eric coasted his bike around it and stopped smoothly at the side of the garage. A quick trip into the garage through the large roller door and Eric had his maintenance kit. He wiped down the frame and checked the chain and gears for damage and grime. He'd have to clean out the chain and re-oil it this weekend. The dirt was beginning to crust on it. He tightened some screws and measured the pads on the brake calipers. He'd just adjusted the calipers last weekend so he wouldn't need to do that for awhile.

With nothing left to do on the bike, Eric reluctantly gathered his pack and stowed the maintenance kit back in the garage. He pulled the mail from the box, flipping through it slowly, marking with a sigh that it was mostly overdue bills. Only when he'd run out of things to do outside the house did he finally open the front door and step in.

The front door opened immediately to the living room. The huge TV, an old console thing, rested against one wall and the long couch faced it, occupied by the reposed form of an ancient-looking woman. Gillian Sumner wasn't really ancient. She was only in her thirties, but the skin under her eyes drooped, even when they were closed as they were now. The flesh around her mouth was wrinkled and sallow. She lay on the couch as if she'd slept there all night, half-covered by a thin blanket.

She wasn't awake, but she wasn't really sleeping either, not really. Her arm was extended over the edge of the couch, her hand hovering over the floor where a nearly-empty bottle lay on its side. She was passed out.

Again.

Eric turned off the TV in the middle of an old program that played every year at this time, sort of like It's a Wonderful Life at Christmas time. It was called "True Conspiracies," a documentary about the New York Incident and its aftermath. Eric hated it.

With the damned baritone narrator of the show silenced, Eric began to clean up. It wasn't just the bottle on the floor, which held whiskey. It was the four others, smaller and shaped like flasks on the coffee table. Gillian had gone all out today, probably after torturing herself with repeated viewings of "True Conspiracies" again. The drinking was always worst this time of year.

Sixteen years ago today, Gillian Sumner had been pregnant with her first-and-only child, living a happy life with her husband in a quiet little suburb of McAlester. Little did she know that in two days, while delivering the child she'd call "Eric," the world as she knew it would be ending. Five years later, she'd find herself raising a child alone in one of the worst periods of anarchy seen on the American continent.

She'd been strong in those times, but her strength was gone now, used up to survive those lawless days. Now, she was passed out drunk more often than not. Eric saw it as his job to make sure she didn't drink herself to death.

So the nightly ritual began. Eric called it "mine sweeping." He started in the living room, where the open bottles were. He gathered them up, most of them empty or nearly so, and carried them into the kitchen. He dumped the remnants in the sink and placed the glass carefully into the trash bin. Then, he began his sweep. The kitchen cupboards were first. The refrigerator, the oven, the dishwasher. Any place that could hold a bottle. He found three more bottles, all full. He dumped them out and put them in the trash with the others.

The rest of the house was trickier. It had taken him years to find all the places Gillian had to hide bottles. The back of the linen closet, between folded towels. Inside the toilet tank. Inside his mother's box-spring. The first time he'd checked there, he'd found hundreds of dollars of cheap booze. He'd never seen his mother so angry before when she found it empty the next day. But Eric never thought of just returning the booze to the grocery store or gas station or wherever she'd bought it. He always dumped it out and left the empties in the bin for her to find when she sobered up, an act of defiance to let her know how her drinking made him feel. Maybe if he did it enough, she'd see what it was doing. Maybe one day, she'd decide to stop.

But it was a task that was never really complete. Within a few days, she'd somehow get more. She always did. Eric had no idea where the money came from. Most of their bills were way past due. If the house wasn't paid for, they probably wouldn't have a place to live. A check came once a month from the insurance company that had held his father's life insurance policy. When Eric could get to the mail first, he made sure half of that was placed into his own account so it wouldn't go to waste. When he had to, he paid the bills out of that, which was why his bank account was nearly empty this early in the month. Last week, the electric company had tried to cut them off.

Eric finished the sweep and stood in the back hallway to the bedrooms, looking around trying to think if there was a place he'd missed. He couldn't think of anything, so he retreated to his room and dumped his books on his desk. Homework, then bed.

What else was there to do?

September 9, 2017

Eric woke up hungry the next morning. It was the first day of a long weekend. Monday was 9/11, Patriot's Day and a government holiday. It was also Eric's birthday. For some people, it might be cool to have a birthday on a holiday, but there were no celebrations on 9/11. It was the AU's Memorial Day, without the barbecues and picnics. Only bleak despair and memories that were far too fresh for most, especially those who'd survived New York. Even as AUPrime TV tried to spin the event as the birth of a great nation, an alliance of all of North America, there was no true joy to be had.

As Eric lay in bed, one leg bent and the other crossing it, his stomach rumbled. It really was his stomach this time, not the strange rumbling in his chest that had bothered him yesterday. He lay there and planned out the day. He'd grab what was left of the toaster waffles in the freezer, then he'd take his drawing pad to the park to practice his art assignment. They were working on figure sketches, and there would be plenty of people at the park today to use as models. He liked drawing, he was generally good at it, and it was relaxing. It was better than painting, which he found messy and not nearly exact enough for him. Too many broad strokes and generalities.

Something tickled his nose, and he sniffed. It smelled like

waffles. He pulled himself out of bed and dressed. He glanced at the clock. It was too early. She shouldn't be up yet, especially as passed out as she'd been.

Even so, Gillian was in the kitchen, sitting down to a plate of waffles. The same waffles he'd planned to eat himself. He knew exactly how many had been left, and they were all on Gillian's plate. She dug into them as he entered. She was wearing her bathrobe, the edges of her nightgown peaked out beneath.

"Morning, kiddo!" she said brightly. Eric's eyes narrowed. Where was the hangover and the surly growl?

He grunted a reply and turned to the freezer. He opened it and was surprised to see the box of waffles inside. Had he miscounted? He pulled it out and shook it.

Empty.

He sighed, crushed it, and tossed it in the wastebasket.

"There's pizza in there," Gillian said. "Go ahead and throw it in the oven. 375."

Eric shook his head. Pizza for breakfast was just... wrong. At least freshly baked pizza was. It didn't count if it was last night's pizza gone cold.

"No," he said. "I'll go out. I was planning on going out today anyway."

"I'm doing some grocery shopping today," Gillian said. She didn't seem to realize he was upset. "Anything you want?"

"Waffles," he said, then went back to his room to gather his things.

The lone gas station in town was a Murphy's. Its red and yellow stripes were almost identical to the Shell station in McAlester. Shell bought out Murphy's in the chaos following New York. Now, it was just Shell gas with the Murphy's name and logo on the side of the building.

Eric slid his bike next to a trash can by the front door of the station. He leaned the bike against the window and went inside. A guy not much older than he was stood behind the counter, flipping through one of the porno mags kept on a shelf behind him. He didn't seem to care that Eric had come in even though Eric tripped the sensor at the door that triggered what was supposed to be a friendly, welcoming chirp.

Eric ignored the guy in return and went down the snack aisle. He snatched a bag of Doritos from a shelf, then stood in front of the cooler considering the sodas. Chips and soda. All he'd wanted was those damned waffles. He must have been fuming in front of the cooler for too long because a voice called back to him.

"Everything okay, kid?"

Eric glanced up at the curved mirror above him and saw the clerk, his porno mag lowered to waist level. Eric scowled. Kid? If that guy was more than a year out of high school, Eric was a circus clown.

"Fine," he said. His anger bubbled up. Eric was a high school kid wearing a backpack on a Saturday. That didn't mean he was a thief.

He yanked the cooler open and grabbed the first soda he saw. Grape. He didn't even like grape soda, but he grabbed it anyway. He let the cooler door slam closed and went to the counter.

"Give me two of those breakfast things," he said, gesturing to the roller food. It was nasty stuff. Like fried food, only fried in some factory, probably in Cambodia or something. The food was prepared, fried, then frozen solid for a trip to America. Then, after being thawed two or three times, it was thrown between two heated rollers and sold to idiots like Eric for ten times the cost of making it.

The breakfast ones had something like eggs in them and bits of mystery meat that tasted like bacon. Of course there had to be some fake cheese in there to disguise the real taste. Then the whole thing was wrapped in a tortilla and called a taquito like it was Mexican or something.

"You gonna pay for them?" the clerk asked.

"Maybe," replied Eric. He reached into his pocket and dropped his debit card on the counter.

Only then did the clerk bag up two of the breakfast rolls and put them on the counter. He didn't take his eyes off Eric. He rang up the rolls, the soda, and the chips and threw the whole thing into a plastic bag with handles. After the transaction was done, Eric left. The growling in his stomach had moved from just behind his belly button up into his chest. He breathed deeply, trying to make room for the feeling there, maybe give it room to escape out his nose or mouth as he breathed out, but nothing he did calmed him.

Standing by his bike, he pulled one of the taquitos from the bag and bit into it. It wasn't a waffle, but at least it was hot. He hung the plastic bag from his handlebars and jumped on the bike. He pedaled furiously away from the gas station, letting his legs and the bike get him away from town.

Eric's bike took him to Saint's Drive Park, a neighborhood park that consisted of a flat field of grass, a small playground and a hill that was the best sledding hill – the only sledding hill – in Ender during the winter.

The playground was circled by a half-dozen benches. Eric liked to watch kids play, a reminder of what his childhood must have been like before his dad died. Saturdays, especially on holiday weekends when the weather was good, the playground was packed. Only one bench wasn't occupied. He made it so, parking the bike behind the bench.

Normally, Eric didn't like being around so many people. But he'd found that parents were too busy at the park to notice him. They were either freaking out about every little thing their kids were doing or ignoring the kids entirely and chatting amongst themselves.

He leaned back on the bench and started sketching what he saw, gnawing on the other taquito with his free hand. He started with the playset, a metal, plastic, and wood structure with two slides, a straight metal pole for sliding down and a spiral pole that Eric couldn't fathom its purpose.

Once the structure was drawn, he watched the kids. One, no more than three years old was reaching for the top of the spiral pole from the top level of the structure. His arms were just too short to get a good grip on the metal pole, but he tried anyway. Eric sketched that, showing the kid in his picture just able to brush the pole with his fingers. He considered sketching the inevitable result of the little boy's folly, a kid at the bottom of the pole with a cracked open head and a broken leg. He restrained himself.

A short woman approached the boy and reached up for him. She took him and placed him on the pole so he could wrap his arms and legs around it. She guided him down as he giggled around every curve.

Eric sketched the woman reaching up to the boy. He looked up again to see if he could capture her better. She had turned obliquely toward him.

It was Kristin Matthews.

He watched her interact with a number of children, his pencil moving non-stop. He traced her sharp nose and high cheekbones and tried to emulate her curly dark hair with cheap pencil lead. He used the lightest of touches to shade in her light brown skin and just a little harder to dot in her chocolate chip freckles. She was always smiling, the love she bore for these kids obvious on her face. Eric's skill with a pencil wasn't up to the task of curving her lips in just the right way. On his paper, her smile looked fake.

When he completed her face, he scowled. It wasn't right. He gave up and just watched her play, helping children up to the top of the playset or spinning them around until they burst out with shrill laughter.

Hi, he imagined himself saying to her, so, uh, you like kids, huh? he scrapped that opening line. It sounded like he was asking her if she was a pedophile or if she wanted to have his baby.

But what else could he say to her? He barely knew her. She was popular. She had friends. They'd all laugh at him if he even tried to talk to her. He was a nobody, which in high school was worse than a mass-murderer. You could get away with murder if you were cool.

Then, in a terrifying instant, Eric caught Kristin glance at him while she was sitting a three year old on the top of the slide. Her smile never faltered.

He buried himself into his sketchpad. The image of her face was burned in his memory, so he dumped it onto the blank page in quick pencil strokes. He didn't try to capture her smile this time, just drawing in her lips the best he could. It made her look cruel.

He flipped the book to a blank page.

Almost as soon as he'd decided to try something else – maybe draw one of the kids – she caught a kid at the bottom of the slide and slapped his butt as he scampered off toward someone who must have been his mother, approaching from the street. Then, she turned toward Eric and started heading his way. Her face was determined and serious.

He panicked, slapping the pad closed and jamming the pencil in his pocket as he stood. He rounded the bench to get his bike...

...and ran straight into Leonard Strange.

"You a kiddie-phile, Sumner?" Leonard said. He approached the bench Eric occupied from the direction of the street. He was too close now to avoid.

Eric reached for his bike and snatched it by the seat. He tried pulling it toward him, but Leonard caught it swiftly by the handlebars and yanked it away. The bike toppled to the ground beyond Leonard. The bag with his soda and chips broke on a rock, piercing the bottle and spraying grape soda everywhere.

"Dammit, Leonard," Eric said. "Aren't you getting sick of this?"

"Nope, are you?" Leonard said with a laugh. "I told you I needed cash for this weekend. Looks like you had some and you didn't share," he gestured at the broken bag looped around Eric's handlebars.

"You're not getting my money, asshole. You need to find an easier target." He took a step toward his bike, which would take him dangerously close to Leonard. But before he could even take a full step, his arms were grabbed and locked tight against his back. He was pulled back and would have fallen if not for the large, heavy body blocking his motion. A wicked laugh sounded behind him.

That would be Ken Hunter.

"I like you, Sumner," Leonard said. "I like a challenge. Besides, if I left you alone, what kind of example would that set for the others?"

Leonard wound back and slammed a balled fist into Eric's stomach. Eric tried to tense, to protect his insides, but he was doubled over just the same. He felt the roller food come back up into his throat, but he swallowed it. He wouldn't give the bastard the satisfaction of throwing up in front of him. The next instant, Ken yanked back on his arms while Leonard delivered another punch, just as hard. This one blew the wind out of his lungs, and he coughed for air.

"Stop it, Lenny!" Kristin cried. Eric looked through blurry eyes to see Kristin coming up on Leonard from behind. Leonard glanced back at her.

"You again?" Leonard asked. "I'm starting to think you've been playing us, Kris. Are you sweet on this lovable loser?"

"There are parents here, Lenny," Kristin said. "Do you want to get reported and kicked off the—"

Leonard's arms snapped out, punching Kristin in the face. As if she was a puppet with her strings cut, she crumpled to the ground. Her hand flew to her face as she looked up at Leonard in shock.

Horrified, Eric struggled against Ken. The queasiness and pain that had been building in his stomach from Leonard's punches moved up to his chest. He felt the shudder there again. His chest felt like it would rip off his body and jump away like a penny on a table during an earthquake. For the moment, the pain of Leonard's punches was forgotten. He jerked his body left and right trying to free himself from Ken's arm lock. His vision tightened into a tunnel focused on Leonard.

Leonard turned back to Eric, his eyes gleeful. Eric felt something in his chest snap as if it really had come apart. A bass note resounded like a concert speaker against his bones. Pain washed through his chest and arms, an intense ache that hit him like one of Leonard's punches. In the moment, Eric thought Ken had done something, maybe broken his arms. But he suddenly found himself free from Ken's grip.

He fell forward. Leonard's face rushed down the long tunnel before him. Eric brought his right arm around, seeing a blur of motion on that side as his fist came into view. Suddenly, the blurring stopped, and Eric's fist came into sharp focus, accompanied by another pain as if a hammer had been dropped on his right hand.

Then his fist made contact with Leonard's face. There was a crack as skin ripped and bone broke. Blood burst from a deep gash in Leonard's cheek. Eric's eyes widened as Leonard went crashing down to the ground, screaming in pain.

Panicked, Eric spun and saw Ken backpedaling away from him. There was a look of shock and fear on the tall boy's face.

"How'd you do that?" Ken demanded. "I had you!"

Eric didn't know how to answer that question. He'd just slipped out of Ken's hold somehow.

Ken shook his head. He watched as Leonard flopped about on the ground. The older boy's nose was bleeding in addition to his cheek. A disturbing red splash was forming in his left eye.

Kristin was rising from the ground, a shocked look on her face as her eyes zig-zagged between Eric and Leonard. She had a line of blood running out of her nostril but seemed otherwise unharmed.

Eric picked up his backpack, threw it over his shoulders and ran to his bike. He was on the bike and gone before any of the adults in the park could realize what happened and stop him.

Eric was exhausted by the time he got back to downtown Ender. It felt like he was pressing against some irresistible force every time he pedaled, but he was moving just as fast as he normally did. He wondered if the bike getting thrown around had done something to it, but he couldn't find anything wrong as he rode.

He found himself back at Murphy's before he stopped. He slid off the bike and checked its working parts, including the air in the tires. Everything was fine. But his legs felt like jelly. He was stressed, that was it. He'd just taken a beating and narrowly escaped. That was all. He just needed to rest a little, let his heart rate slow.

He sat on the curb in front of the store.

"Everything okay, kid?" a voice said behind him. Expecting the clerk from inside, Eric turned, ready to give the guy a piece of his–

Old Buck hobbled across the concrete, glancing at the bike and the shredded plastic bag hanging from the handlebars. The chips and broken soda bottle had come free at some part of his furious ride, and he hadn't bothered to go back for them.

"Yeah, I'm fine," he lied. Old Buck nodded. The big man limped closer, the hitch in his step starting at his hip. Laboriously, Buck crouched down and sat next to Eric on the curb. He reached into his coat pocket and drew out a can of Coke. He held it out to Eric.

"Eric Sumner, right?"

Eric froze in the act of reaching for the soda. "How do you know me?" Old Buck shrugged.

"Small town," he said. Buck never looked directly at Eric. His long gray hair and beard covered nearly all of his face. Only one bright eye of indeterminate color – what they called hazel at the eye doctor – was clearly visible behind the oily strands. What Eric could see of the man's skin was strangely shiny. "Something happened to you just now," Buck said. "I can see it. I know scared when I see it, trust me."

"Just a bully. I'm okay." Eric took the can. It was cold as if it had been pulled from a refrigerator not too long ago. Buck must have gotten it at the store just now. He popped it open and took a sip. Much better than grape soda. Buck drew another can from his huge pocket and copied Eric.

"Hmm," Buck sighed. The sound was something between the pleasure of the cola and doubt in Eric's words. "How old are you, kid?"

"Almost sixteen," Eric replied. Why was he talking to this man, a homeless stranger who might be after more than just conversation? This was the guy who hung out in front of the middle school all day, after all.

"It's been a long time since I was sixteen," Buck said with a wistful smile. "But I remember enough to know that things change very fast at that age. It can be too much to take in sometimes." Buck's one visible eye twinkled as it fixed on Eric. "I know a lot about those changes."

Buck drained his soda in one pull and crushed the can between his thumb and forefinger until the top and bottom of the can touched. Eric started. He hadn't even used his entire hand, and the can was suddenly crushed like he'd used a mechanical crusher.

Buck dropped the can into his own palm, his eye never leaving Eric's face. Eric couldn't pull his eyes from the can and the heavy hand it lay in.

"Sometimes," Buck continued, "The changes can be too much. Sometimes, you need help understanding them."

Buck casually closed his fist. The can groaned and crumpled. Buck's fingers curled around the metal. Then, Buck opened his fist and the remains of his soda can dropped to the ground with a quiet tinkle. It looked like a ball of Play-Doh squeezed in a child's fist. The imprints of Buck's fingers were as clear as if the aluminum were soft clay. Sharp edges jutted from the object where the metal had fit between Buck's fingers. Yet there was no blood. Eric looked down at Buck's hand, which lay limply open on his knee. There were no cuts. No scrapes. Nothing.

The blood in Eric's veins ran cold. Flattening an aluminum can was one thing. Crushing an already flattened can in one hand like it was nothing was something else entirely. Buck had to have skin like thick leather to not have been cut by the metal. The casual mangling of the can in such a way could only mean that Buck's strength was superhuman.

Buck was a Super-Powered Individual. A SPI. In the new world of the American Union, a SPI — pronounced "spy" in casual conversation — was the equivalent of a Communist from the old days, only much more dangerous.

"What do you want?" Eric asked once he'd swallowed the lump from his throat. He didn't dare move. Most SPIs had one or two enhancements. Some had three. If Buck had enhancements to speed, there was nowhere Eric could run.

"Your discretion, for one," Buck said. "I won't hurt you, Eric." He picked up the ball of aluminum and rolled it between his hands. With no effort, the jagged can was smoothed against the unnaturally thick skin of Buck's palms. Buck tossed the former can at the ground, and it wedged itself into the concrete to half its length. The ease with which he'd found and stuck a weakness in the concrete, a crack Eric hadn't even noticed before, spoke of superhuman hand-eye coordination on top of the strength and endurance.

Three enhancements. How powerful was this man? Only the rarest of SPIs had three physical enhancements.

"What..." Eric began, but his voice froze in his throat.

"I recognized something in you, Eric. I need the truth from you. Are you like me?"

Eric blinked. He thought back to the punch that had laid out the star running back of Marshall High School. No. That was just a normal punch. He'd just slipped free of one of the strongest athletes in school and broke the face of the fastest kid in school.

That's all.

Right?

To stall, he drained the rest of the cola. The fizz and cold soothed his throat, which had become constricted. Then, he held the can in his hand. His hand wasn't as large as Buck's. It didn't fit around the can with the ease the old man displayed.

He squeezed his fist around the can, and it crumpled. The thin metal of the can's sides crushed inward. The top canted to one side. Eric took the can in both hands and finished the job, flattening it so that the top and bottom touched.

He shook his head.

"Doesn't look like it," he said in a trembling voice. The trembling was matched by a rumbling in his chest, the same feeling that had plagued him the last few days, especially when he was confronted. It was nerves. He felt like he was fighting for his life now, even more than he had been just a few minutes ago in the park.

Buck hummed a deep baritone, his eyes on the can Eric had crushed with perfectly human strength.

"Why are you doing this?" Eric asked, his voice feeling thin.

"I don't mean to scare you, Eric. I won't hurt you. I just needed to know." Buck rose and took one awkward step away from Eric. His hip hitched as he took the step as if putting weight on it pained him. A SPI with enhanced endurance wouldn't ever have something as simple as joint pain. The whole thing with the limp had to be a ruse. "I trust," Buck said as he prepared to leave, "That you will continue your discretion. I promised not to hurt you, but I can't do the same for others. I won't become this week's prime time entertainment."

Buck moved slowly away as Eric wondered what it would be like if the AU police were forced to try and arrest Buck. How many would die in the attempt?

Buck's confidence put doubt in Eric's mind that anything they could do would be enough to easily stop him. Something told Eric that Buck's ability to reduce a soda can to the size of a cigarette was just scratching the surface of his abilities.

Two years ago, a man with speed and strength enhancements had slaughtered an entire baseball stadium full of players, officials, and baseball executives, leaving the fans untouched. Over two hundred people had been killed in a matter of minutes, athletes, trainers, doctors, scouts – some of them in the stands scouting for other teams – and stadium employees. Buck had at least three enhancements. How many more could he kill if he tried?

Eric didn't want to risk it.

He wondered if he would regret it.

AUPrimeMovies - In Theaters Now

ZERO-G

Ripped from the headlines!
When the world faces destruction, only the best need apply.
Seven deadly SPIs, two fearless officers of the law.
George Clooney and Rooney Mara star in this year's best
action thriller!

In theaters now!

September 11, 2017

Eric woke on his birthday unsure, as always, if he wanted to get up. This day of all days he half hoped he wouldn't wake up at all. Patriot's Day, they called it. But it was the saddest day of the year, not a celebration of American patriotism. It was a memorial for the millions of Americans who gave their lives so the United States could crumble to its death.

He'd shut himself in his room after the conversation with Old Buck, the SPI. He hadn't left it all Sunday, though his stomach grumbled to protest the unexpected fast. There was no news about the result of his encounter with Leonard and Ken on Saturday. Leonard could be dead for all he knew. But no police had shown up at his door to arrest him, so he supposed that was a good sign.

At about three in the afternoon on Sunday, he'd realized he was afraid to go out, even to ride his bike. All he could see was the gray-haired old man who could pound him to dust with barely more effort than it took to sneeze. Was Buck watching him now, waiting for Eric to talk? Would he be standing on every street corner now? Would he emerge from the shadows to bash his head in when he least expected it?

Buck thought Eric was a SPI. Maybe the old man saw a modicum of safety in the idea. Surely Eric-the-SPI wouldn't snitch on Buck-the-SPI. They were practically family, right?

The thought just made his chest shudder uncontrollably. He laid his hand on his bare chest and felt the muscles there quivering.

He looked down at himself. His heart skipped when he saw his fingers blurring where he touched his bare chest. There was a spot the radius of a teacup in the center of his chest that was similarly blurred. Eric laid his palm over it, and his entire hand blurred.

His heart skipped.

What was happening?

He leapt from the bed and rushed to the mirror that was mounted on the back of his dresser. The reflection confirmed what he'd seen with his own eyes. He lifted his hand away and saw the spot on his chest that had been bothering him for days now. It was quivering so fast the smooth skin just above his solar plexus looked as if it were swirling or oscillating.

Then, he looked at his hand and saw that it was still blurred as if whatever was happening to his chest had been spread to his right hand like a disease. He slapped the hand onto the dresser, trying to steady it against the wood.

But upon contact with the simulated woodgrain of his cheap self-assembled furniture, his hand fell through. Eric stumbled and fell, his legs giving way beneath him. He landed on the floor, his back against the boxspring of his bed.

The quivering stopped. It didn't fade or stutter as it left. It just stopped. Eric looked down at himself and at his hand. Both were as solid as they'd been before.

"What the fuh?" he whispered. He sat there, just breathing for a moment. He looked up at his dresser. It was still whole. It hadn't fallen apart. It hadn't broken. It stood there as if this were an ordinary morning. As if Eric's world wasn't falling apart in front of him.

He pulled himself to his feet and touched his fingers to the top of the dresser. It was dusty. Clean lines appeared as he ran his fingers over the top. In a patch to one side, where his blurred hand had gone through it just moments before, the dust was… disturbed. Eric looked in awe at the pattern of dust there. He'd seen something similar before.

Last year in physics class, they'd been studying vibration and sound waves. Mr. Turner had brought in a large box-like contraption. In the box was a layer of sand. When sound was passed through the box at certain frequencies, the sand moved into unique patterns. Eric had thought it all fascinating. As the frequency rose beyond the human ear, the patterns became very complex.

This pattern of dust was one of those patterns. It had settled in a fractal swirl confined to a space roughly the shape of a human hand. Eric laid his own hand atop it, confirming that the hand print was his own.

What the hell was happening to him?

Eric sank back to his bed, sitting on the edge and staring into the mirror. Buck was right. Eric was a SPI. There was no other explanation.

But what kind of SPI was he?

The powers of SPIs were all enhancements to human abilities that had been around since man had learned to walk. Even telepathy and telekinetic abilities had been documented long before the first SPIs appeared, though they were often dismissed as hoaxes.

But what Eric had done, passing his hand through the perfectly solid dresser as if it didn't exist, was something different. Such a thing had maybe been imagined in a science fiction story, but never reported in real life, right?

The key, Eric thought, lay in the pattern in the dust. It had to have been caused by a high-frequency vibration. Eric tried to think of some physics principle that would allow for such a thing. He wanted to classify this in some sort of scientific way. Anything else would threaten his sanity.

The door rattled as someone knocked on it. Eric jumped. For an instant, he thought he'd done it.

"Eric, are you up?" Gillian asked through the door. "I'm making breakfast. Come out and eat."

For the first time, Eric noticed the smell of someone cooking bacon. He'd been too shocked by this strange turn of events to realize before that it was coming from inside the house.

"I'm up," Eric said, trying to keep his voice steady. "I'll be right out."

He stood and tapped his chest. It was solid now. He didn't feel the strange grumbling that he'd felt the last few days. Had he been triggering this new ability for days and not realizing it?

As he was pulling on a shirt, he froze, the cloth covering his face.

The park.

He'd felt the strange vibration in his chest at the moment he escaped from Ken's grip and laid into Leonard. Was that his power?

Had they noticed it?

Eric thought back to the faces of the three who had seen what he'd done. Kristin, Leonard, and Ken had all worn looks of shock as if they couldn't believe what he'd done. But had they recognized it as the powers of a SPI?

Oh Lord, had he been found out already?

He pulled the shirt down. His chest shuddered again. Quickly, Eric looked in the mirror. He couldn't see the blurring through the shirt. Whatever it was that caused the blurring wasn't visible through his clothes. Maybe he'd stayed hidden after all.

He finished dressing and stood in front of his closed door for a while, eyes closed and breathing in deep, slow breaths. The vibrations were caused by his nervousness, he guessed. He needed to calm down, and hopefully, the power wouldn't trigger where someone, even his own mother, could see it.

Before leaving his room, he brushed his hand across the fractal of dust on the dresser, obliterating it.

The kitchen was warmer than usual. The stove was on, and a pan of bacon was sizzling on a burner. A paper towel-covered plate was already loaded with bacon. In another pan, Gillian was finishing up the scrambled eggs. As Eric walked in, the toaster popped.

Eric stood in the doorway for a moment. The table was set

with two places. Cups of orange juice were set by the clean plates, napkins, and utensils.

It looked like something out of a family sitcom.

"Happy Birthday," Gillian said, glancing away from the eggs to give him a smile. She was dressed. She wore a red linen blouse and a pair of stonewashed bluejeans. She'd done her make-up, subtle but enough to cover up the unnatural redness in her cheeks caused by her constant drinking.

She looked great. She looked sober.

Eric could only stare and blink.

"Sit down and eat. We need to be on the road by ten."

Eric did as he was told.

"On the road?" he asked.

"We," Gillian declared, "are going to celebrate your 16th birthday the right way." She brought the pan of eggs to the table and spooned a generous helping of them onto Eric's plate, then a smaller portion onto her own. She brought the plate of bacon over and put it on a pad on the table. Eric helped himself. Another plate of toast followed the bacon. Only then did Gillian sit down.

"Meaning?" Eric asked, unsure. He still couldn't wrap his head around his mother, cleaned up and sober on Patriot's Day.

"We are going to McAlester. An early movie at the Legend followed by steaks at Gilbertsons, then whatever else you want to do."

Eric cocked his head. He'd been to Gilbertsons twice in his life, both times had been the best meals of his life. He loved the place but had never outright said so. Still, something triggered the trembling in his chest. He clenched his teeth and concentrated on his breathing to try and settle it before his mother noticed.

"Something wrong?" Gillian asked. "You don't like the idea?" Her face fell, and a hint of the red-faced drunk returned to her pretty face.

"No," Eric said. "It sounds fine. I just..." he couldn't explain it.

"I know," Gillian said, "It's okay. I promise no drinking today. I'll stick to iced tea."

Eric swallowed. He hadn't much thought of that. It was a gift, he knew. For the first time in years, Gillian Sumner was sober on the one day of the year she was never sober, and she was promising to stay that way. Even if it was only for today, it was a gift.

He nodded, then he dug into his food. The eggs were good, the bacon was crisp, and the toast was perfect slathered with butter and strawberry jelly. She must have done grocery shopping sometime in the last two days, as she'd promised the day before. None of this had been in the refrigerator on Saturday morning.

He tried to avoid thinking that if she'd gone grocery shopping, then he'd need to go mine sweeping tonight. Even if she promised not to drink today, she'd go right back to it when they got home or when he was at school tomorrow. Maybe he could nip it in the bud this week, and she wouldn't have any alcohol to turn to at all.

That would be nice.

Gillian made a one sided conversation as they ate. She asked him how school was going and how his weekend had been so far. He answered with non-commital grunts. He didn't know what to do. It was like he was having breakfast with a stranger.

Still, Gillian seemed happy enough with that. She finished up her food, then stood, picking up her plate. She shook her head at him with a small smile on her lips and just said, "Teenagers," before starting the cleanup. Eric was still munching on his toast when she ruffled his dark hair. "Finish up. We gotta get going if we're going to catch the movie."

The drive to McAlester was about forty-five minutes. Eric spent the time staring out the window at the empty fields surrounded by ancient barbed wire fences as they passed.

"You okay, kiddo?" Gillian asked about half-way into the trip. Eric looked at her and tried a smile.

"Yeah," he said. "It's just weird."

Gillian's returned smile fell a little. She knew what he meant.

"It's been hard, I know," she said, "I'm trying, kiddo, I swear."

Eric nodded. "I know."

"Just try and enjoy the day. It's your day."

Eric huffed a laugh. His day: Patriot's Day.

"Isn't it ironic," he said.

"Dontcha think?" Gillian finished the song lyric. They both laughed.

They chose an action movie. George Clooney played an aging cop on the trail of a team of SPI assassins. His partner, played by Rooney Mara was the young rookie cop. She was the real protagonist, as Clooney's character was killed about a third of the way through the movie. The rest of the movie was about the young cop outsmarting the powerful SPIs to get revenge for the death of her partner while saving the world from destruction.

Eric sat through the movie in the darkness, his heart pounding during the action scenes. As Rooney Mara singlehandedly offed the SPIs one by one until the final confrontation with the SPI leader, Eric found himself sympathizing with the SPIs. It wasn't like they were being hunted for no reason. In fact, it was clear these SPIs were psychos bent on global destruction – not even domination. Still, Eric couldn't help but cut-and-paste his own face on each of the SPIs as Mara found inventive ways to use their powers against them.

Was this his fate? Was he destined to be twisted by his power, whatever it was, and become like these psychotic murderers? Would he be hunted for the rest of his life until he was caught and executed?

By the time the credits rolled, Eric was trembling. He felt a cold sweat on his face. He wiped at it with his hands as the lights brightened in the auditorium.

"You okay, kiddo?" Gillian asked as they gathered their things.

"Yeah," he answered. "Just not feeling good. Maybe something I ate."

"Oh, didn't I cook the eggs right?"

"No, no, they were fine," he said hurriedly. "I'll be fine. Don't worry. Maybe I'm just hungry."

Gillian put his hand between both of hers, pressing her hands together for a long moment. Eric stared at her thoughtful face. Then, as if she'd done nothing strange, she dropped his hand and smiled.

They filed out of the theater with the rest of the audience.

"That was a pretty good movie, wasn't it?" Gillian asked. Eric avoided her gaze.

"Yeah, it was all right," he said.

"Well," Gillian said, hesitation in her voice. "Let's get something in your stomach. Maybe a good steak will cancel out my nasty eggs and bacon." Her voice was teasing. She was trying to cheer him up.

It worked. Eric couldn't help but smile, though the images of the SPIs in the movie being killed off one by one still haunted him.

How does something change so quickly? Yesterday, he was a normal kid. Today, he identified with the most horrible of movie villains. It was frustrating and depressing.

When they got to the restaurant, Gillian vanished for a while, heading to the restroom, she said. It wasn't until after the meal that Eric realized what she'd really been doing. Five servers came to their table singing "happy birthday," their own server carrying a small chocolate cake with ice cream. Eric smiled, his face flushing in embarrassment to be the center of attention for the entire restaurant.

To his surprise, he was still smiling when everything returned to normal. He shared the cake and ice cream with his mom. Gillian teased him for the flush on his face, claiming playfully he had a crush on their thirty-year-old server. Of course, Eric had to deny it, though she was pretty.

Even after they left and began the drive home, Gillian teased Eric about his "cougar." Eric spent the trip again staring out the window, but more to look at the reflection of his mother in it. He couldn't keep the smile off his face. He'd had a better time than he'd expected at the restaurant, especially after his sickened reaction to the movie.

"We should do this more often," Eric said as they reached the Ender town limit. "Not the whole birthday thing, but just spending some time together every so often."

Gillian nodded, not saying anything. Eric wondered if she'd go back to drinking tonight or tomorrow. Had this been a one time thing? There wasn't much hope she'd be able to suddenly be the sober, happy mom she'd been today. She was sick. It was too much to expect that she'd get better in one day.

When they got out of the car at the house, Eric went to Gillian and hugged her.

"Thanks, Mom," he said. "I love you."

She hugged him back

"I love you too, kiddo," she said. She pulled him away and held him at arm's length, suddenly earnest and sincere. "I hope you remember that. Every day, not just today."

Eric nodded and smiled.

Later that night, Eric lay in his bed staring at the ceiling. Through the day, at least since the movie, he'd nearly forgotten his power. He hadn't felt the vibration in his chest at the steakhouse or after.

But thinking about it now, it came out to remind him it was still there. Just a soft hum in his chest. He pressed his hand there and felt the power rumble into his fingers.

His brow furrowed in worry. What was happening to him? Was he safe? Would this strange change in his body end up killing him? Who could he trust to help him? Surely not the homeless SPI. He was just as dangerous as any of the terrorists in that movie.

Anyone else would turn him into the authorities. Anyone.

He had to hide it. He had to learn to control this thing in his chest, to keep it from going off at the strangest times. One day, it would be noticed, and it would all be over. He'd be the next guy up in front of a firing squad on AUPrimeNews.

Sure, easy. It was his body after all right? He could control a simple thing like a superpower. A superpower of which he had no idea what it was. What was this mutation within him? How could he learn to control something he didn't understand?

His life was looking bleaker and bleaker. He closed his eyes and took deep breaths. That seemed to help a little. The vibration calmed. But that wasn't something he could do every time the power threatened. He'd look like an idiot.

He shook his head on his pillow. He'd get it. He'd figure something out to avoid suspicion and hide his power from students, teachers, and anyone else at the school.

It was another hour at least before he finally found sleep.

September 12, 2017

Buck stood on the curb in front of the middle school. He held up his cardboard sign, stooping into his voluminous coat to hide his true physique. When people asked, he said he had a deformation of his spine. It was a good way to garner sympathy and get a few more dollars in his pocket. Besides, what would they think of the 7'4" homeless man with a bodybuilder's form? Would they wonder where he hid his gym? More likely, they'd mark him for what he was.

He pulled a Coke can from his pocket and sipped it.

Buck hadn't been watching Eric Sumner for three years to have the boy slip through his fingers. Eric was the key to everything Buck needed. But at the same time, Buck couldn't just grab the boy and go. If Eric was to be of any use, he had to be a willing participant. Buck couldn't go to Eric, that was made clear this past weekend. The kid would deny it until it became undeniable. Buck feared that would only happen when the AU Security Service came to take him away. No, Eric would have to come to him. For now, all Buck could do was make himself available while he tried to figure out a way to get the boy to change his mind.

On schedule, Eric slid around the corner toward the school. He coasted his bike through the turn and up the drive toward the bike racks. He appeared to be in no hurry this morning.

Eric's eyes glanced in Buck's direction, but he showed no signs of changing course. In fact, he showed no sign of recognition at all.

So that was how it was going to be? Eric was apparently determined to ignore his budding abilities, and Buck in the process.

Buck shook his head and stood. The old pain in his hip that had been there as long as he could remember flared as he put weight on it. His power ate the pain almost as soon as it appeared. It would return with every step he took, though. Something in his heightened endurance had broken inside of him. Though his skin was as impenetrable as stone, some of his internal injuries had not healed properly. The flashes of pain were just there to aggravate him.

Like the kid.

The kid was being stupid. If he continued like this, he'd get caught. The next time he was bullied, maybe this time in a more public setting like the middle of the school hallway, his powers would trigger. His body would do what it knew to do to avoid pain. His animal brain would try to get him to react and fight back. Then, it would become obvious what he was.

Eric Sumner would be taken out of Buck's reach forever. He'd become the latest prime-time entertainment on AUPrime TV.

And Buck would never discover what he'd forgotten.

Eric locked the bike to the rack and adjusted his backpack on his back. He glanced around nervously for Ken or Leonard. He expected trouble with them today, retribution for Saturday's events at the park.

At least now, they weren't waiting for him. Maybe he'd be able to avoid them today.

Two steps up the stairs to the front door of the school, an arm grabbed him, accompanied by a soft voice.

"My hero," Kristin said close to his ear. Her breath triggered a pulse of vibration in his chest. He took a deep breath and tried to will it away. Now was most definitely not the time.

Eric pulled away from her before the vibration could be felt in his arm.

"What are you talking about?" he asked.

She stopped between him and the door and crossed her arms.

"Did you already forget? You laid out Biff!"

Eric blinked.

"Biff?"

Kristin rolled her eyes, "Back to the Future?" Eric shook his head. He hadn't seen that one. He'd heard the lead actor, Eric Roberts, had ruined the whole movie.

"You ran off before the best part," she said as she took his hand and led him through the open doors to join the other kids filtering into the school. He pulled his hand away but stayed beside her. She didn't protest. The rumbling in his chest was going strong now. Eric didn't want Kristin noticing it if it vibrated through to his hand.

"Best part?" Eric prompted. He had to admit he was eager to find out what had happened after he left. Did anyone suspect him as a SPI for what had happened?

"The blood stain is probably still in the grass. They had to bring an ambulance for Leonard. I think you broke his jaw."

"I did?" Oh god, that was the worst that could have happened. Could someone break a jaw with just a punch? Someone normal that is? How much power did it take to do that?

"Ken was stupefied," Kristin said as if she hadn't heard him. "He kept saying he had you. The idiot. I saw him push at you. If he hadn't, you might have just left a bruise. Instead, Leonard's best friend is the one that helped you break his face." She laughed and twirled in glee.

The shuddering in his chest suddenly calmed. Kristin was convinced that whatever had happened was entirely normal. That was good news.

"I'm so glad someone put that asshole down," Kristin said.

"Really?" Eric asked, uncertain.

"Yeah. He's been a dick since I started cheer, thinking he's God's gift. At least you waited until after the game to wail on him. I think the season is a lock now, with or without him."

Eric found himself suddenly in the cafeteria, a place he never went. It was crowded for the breakfast rush. Kristin led him to the front of the line, where she hugged another girl, probably one of the other cheerleaders, and took a place behind her in line. The other girl, a blond with a tiny, pointed nose and thin lips, glanced at Eric and narrowed her eyes. At the look, Kristin shrugged her shoulders and deftly ignored her friend's disapproval.

"This is the guy that put Leonard in the hospital," Kristin said proudly. "Eric, this is Stacy. She's JV cheer captain." Stacy gave Eric a down-up look, doubt in her features.

"So you're the guy who destroyed our season?" Stacy said. She turned to Kristin. "What are you doing with him?"

"Chill, Stace. We don't need Len. He's overrated. We've got this. Ken and Bryan could take the rest of the division by themselves. Besides, Eric was watching out for me. I owe him."

Eric's lips twisted. He wasn't really looking out for Kristin. She was the one who tried to stand up for him.

But Kristin repaid him anyway, buying him a thick brick of soft, cinnamon-y coffee cake, one of the best school foods on the planet. The cake was soft and moist, while the crumbled crust on top was sweet and spicy. Every bite was a little bit of heaven.

They sat at a table. Kristin's smile never left as she watched him enjoy the cake. She picked daintily on her own.

"You like, huh?" she said when his was gone, and hers was only half eaten. Eric laughed

"I don't usually get to eat these. I wish I could get one every day."

"Done," she said with a grin. "As long as you eat with me, it's on the house."

Eric's smile turned into a grimace of suspicion.

"Why? You don't know me. I got lucky the other day. We both know that. I could just as easily be the one in the hospital."

"You can never have enough friends."

Eric looked away from her. "Yeah, you can."

She raised one eyebrow.

"Then maybe I want someone to do my chem homework for me. Is that more believable for you?"

He cocked his head. He didn't get it. He could understand her wanting to treat him to a cake after what she thought he did for her, but wanting him as a friend? She was a cheerleader. He was at least three social tiers below her, which had been made clear by the way the cheer captain had looked at him.

At the same time, he couldn't just say no. It felt rude and mean to reject her after she'd just gifted him with one of his favorite things.

"Okay, then. I'll help you with chem, but I'm not going to do your homework."

"Even if I bat my lashes at you like this?" she blinked her eyes at him rapidly. He laughed in spite of himself, but he shook his head.

"I decided a long time ago I wouldn't do anyone else's work, no matter how much they bully me."

Her eyes widened in mock shock.

"Bully?!" she gasped.

"Yeah," he said, leaning forward over the table a little. "Guys do it with loud words and muscles…"

"Being idiots," Kristin suggested, as she rested her elbows on the table. Her lashes rising and falling purposefully.

"…Girls do it with pretty smiles and lash batting."

"Oh, so you think I have a pretty smile."

Eric's chest nearly roared beneath his shirt. He pushed himself away from the table, leaning back in his chair. The hard plastic chair-back seemed soft to him. It felt as though he was sinking into it.

His mind flashed him an image of his hand passing through the hard wood of his dresser.

He was saved by the early bell. He shot out of the chair and snatched up his bag.

"Sorry, I wanted to get to homeroom early. I have some English work to finish up."

Without waiting for her reaction, he bolted from the cafeteria. His heart was beating hard, and his chest sent pulses of vibration through his body. Would he have really passed through the chair? Would he have fallen through it onto his ass? Was that what this power was?

He didn't understand the physics behind it. The power manifested as an uncontrollable shaking in his body. Wouldn't something like that just rattle whatever he touched? How come nothing he touched vibrated in sympathy to his body like a cell phone on a table?

Whatever it was, it was telekinetic. It had to be. He was somehow manipulating things with his mind, yet he didn't have control of it. He was affecting his own body. Something like that could kill him. Would he spontaneously combust? That was something that had a record in the past. There were photos of people from the 19th century who had just burst into flame for no apparent reason. Was this what that was? The friction from these vibrations might start him on fire one day, and he'd just burst into flame and die.

By the time he reached homeroom, his hands were shaking, and a scary chill flowed up and down his spine. It wasn't his power. It was stark fear. He was a SPI, and his power would one day kill him.

By lunch, he calmed. He immersed himself in his classes to get his mind off the terror that had overcome him that morning. As an extension of that, he found solace in his lunchtime routine. He took his bagged lunch to the flagpole and sat on the cold concrete. For a moment, he laid his palm flat on the stone, feeling the cool solidity of it. His power had calmed along with his nerves. It was good to feel the inert material on his skin.

He was just starting in on his PB&J sandwich when someone came out of the school and headed toward him. It was Jason Williams, a kid in his grade. Eric didn't know much about him except that he was always wearing black rock and roll t-shirts and ripped blue jeans. When the weather was cool, like now, he added a jean jacket festooned with heavy metal logo patches.

His blond hair was long and straight, hanging to the middle of his back. While the hair might have made him look like a girl from the back, a look at his face would dispel that notion. He had a chiseled, masculine face and dark blond fuzz that might one day graduate into a goatee.

"Eric Sumner, right?" Jason asked as he approached.

"Yeah?" Eric asked his sandwich halfway to his mouth.

"I'm Jason Williams, The Marshall."

The Marshall was the school newspaper. So Jason was a journalism student.

"What do you want?" Eric asked.

"Chill, dude," Jason said, "I wanted to talk to you about Leonard. I heard you effed him up pretty good."

"It was self defense. You writing an article about it?"

"No," Jason said. "I was just curious. There weren't a lot of eye witnesses. All I heard was a rumor that filtered down from on high."

"'On high'?"

Jason shrugged, but Eric could imagine. The cheerleaders seemed to know everything about what happened this morning. They probably spread the news around to anyone who would listen, meaning Kristin was the source of the rumors.

"I heard you broke his jaw with a single punch," Jason said, pantomiming a vicious uppercut like a shadowboxer. Eric shook his head. It was just that sort of thing that would out him as a SPI sooner or later.

"Exaggeration," Eric said. He decided to go with what Kristin had told him this morning. "Ken Hunter pushed me into Leonard at just the right time. Momentum and all, you know. I probably got him at just the right angle, too. It hurt like a bitch." Eric rubbed the knuckles of his hand to press the point. That was all true, he guessed. His power didn't give him super strength. He'd already demonstrated that with Buck's soda can. However it was that he'd broken Leonard's jaw, it was probably pure luck.

Jason nodded, though he looked disappointed. Did this kid want Eric to be a SPI? Was he hunting for someone to turn into the cops? Eric had heard of just that sort of bounty hunter before. There was money in turning in someone who tested positive on a DNA screen. But the cost of being wrong – thereby wasting AU time and resources – was heavy, so only professionals really spent the time and effort to actually go looking for SPIs.

"Whatever it was, dude," Jason said, "Just getting Leonard out of here for a few weeks was a gift."

"Tell that to the football team," Eric said.

Jason laughed.

"I'm speaking for those of us who don't give a crap about football." His gesture encompassed both of them. "Leonard was a pain in the butt for all of us." Jason didn't use the word "losers, " but Eric was sure that was what he meant. "You're the only one who stands up to him. You should be more popular than you are, you know."

"Whoever said standing up to bullies works never met Leonard," Eric said. "He hates me because I don't cave to him."

"It worked this time," Jason said.

"He'll be back," Eric said, "Even if his jaw is wired shut. He'll come back, and I'll have it worse than anyone."

Jason didn't respond to that.

Eric ate some of his sandwich. He glanced across the street. Sure enough, Buck was there sitting on the curb, looking at him. If Jason was looking for a SPI, Eric could point him in the right direction. Maybe they could split the reward.

No, that wouldn't be a good idea. Eric was shackled as far as Buck was concerned. If what Eric surmised by what he'd seen the other day, Buck could turn Ender into a war zone. Not only would Eric be responsible for who-knew-how-many deaths, but it would also bring AU Security Services to Ender looking for more SPIs.

"Listen," Jason said, turning Eric's attention away from Buck. "I do have an article to write. I wasn't going to ask you, but I think putting you into it would be a big help, to more than just me."

Eric shook his head.

"I don't want to be the center of attention," he started. Jason threw up both hands, palms out to forestall Eric's concern.

"You won't, I promise. I can even make you anonymous if you want. I was supposed to write a story about those of us on the fringe, you know? The unpopular kids. But I think I could turn that into an exposé on bullying. We could give the other kids who have a hard time a way to see themselves getting out of it."

"By telling them about how I broke a kid's jaw?"

"Sure, why not? They need to know that they can fight back. If the school won't do anything about buttholes like Leonard, we need to."

Eric thought about it. He didn't want to do it. He knew that any publicity for him was bad publicity. He couldn't draw attention to himself, especially by telling his story in the newspaper. His words could be picked apart and used to clue in anyone who wanted to know that he was hiding something.

But, just like with Kristin, he couldn't just outright say no. Jason was trying to do good here. Eric couldn't bring himself to resist that.

"Okay, but nothing comes back to me, okay?"

"Of course," Jason said, smiling. Something in the metalhead's eyes made Eric instantly regret saying yes.

Eric rode home reluctantly. Despite what had happened over the weekend, the first day back at school had gone surprisingly well. He hadn't given himself up in a blazing explosion of stupidity, though he'd been close that morning with Kristin. Probably because of that, he'd been able to keep himself from falling through his chairs during classes. Keeping his mind off the power had been a big help. Maybe if he could convince himself it didn't exist, he could be rid of it entirely.

All he had to do was try not to think of a pink elephant.

Sure.

He didn't know yet what to make of the thing with Kristin. Was she going to take up all his mornings now? She'd sat at the desk next to him in chem class, though she hadn't said any-thing to him. What was it she wanted from him?

Jason was easier to classify. He definitely wanted something from Eric. They'd made plans to meet tomorrow at lunch to continue the interview and work on Jason's article together. It was dangerously close to Eric's rule about not doing other peo-ple's homework, but in this case, Eric was Jason's homework. Hopefully, once the article was done, Eric could return to eat-ing lunch on his own.

He coasted into his cul de sac. The red sedan wasn't in the driveway. Gillian was out, which could be a good thing. If she was driving, chances were she wasn't drunk. His mother was at least that responsible.

He locked up his bike and went inside. There was no mail. The house was locked up, forcing Eric to use his key for the first time in ages. Even when she wasn't home, Gillian forgot to lock the door four times out of five. Good thing the chances of burglary was slim in a small town like Ender.

When Eric opened the door, the scent of pine cleaner assailed his nose. He widened his eyes as he made his way through the house. Gillian had spent the day cleaning. The carpet was vac-uumed, the furniture was dusted, and the kitchen was spotless. There wasn't a single sign of bottle or flask. Only a half-empty glass of water sat near the kitchen sink.

Eric moved from the spotless kitchen to the dustless living room, then to the back hall to his room. When he opened his own door, he found that Gillian had been here, too. His bed was made, and the carpet was clean. Eric's head swiveled slowly to the dresser. The mirror had been wiped down, as had the pre-viously dusty surface of the dresser.

He took a deep breath and touched the place where his hand had passed through the wood, producing the fractal in the dust. He'd dodged another bullet today, by wiping off the handprint he'd made on the dresser. If Gillian had seen it…

Just as he thought of her, the front door opened.

"Eric?" Gillian's voice called. "Come help with groceries,"

Groceries, again?

Eric went out to the living room and found a pair of paper grocery bags on the floor there. He picked them up and took them into the kitchen, where he looked inside curiously. They were filled with just about every food you could imagine, mostly vegetables in one bag and fresh meat in the other.

"I thought of things that I could make for dinners this week, so I went back out and finished up the shopping," Gillian said as she came in with another pair of bags. "Are you in the mood for chicken or fish tonight?"

Eric stared at his mother. She was again dressed and made up as she had been yesterday for his birthday. There wasn't a sign of alcohol on her breath or in her features. She was sober for the second day in a row.

When she saw him staring, his face frozen in confused wonder, she came to him and kissed his forehead, gripping his hand between both of hers as she had outside the movie theater.

"I'm trying, kiddo," she said. "Just go with me on this." He nodded, smiling cautiously.

"I was thinking mac and cheese tonight," he said. "But if you're gonna go all out, chicken sounds good."

"Mac casserole with chicken it is, then. As long as you eat the vegetables, too."

He shrugged. What the hell? Was he living in the twilight zone all of a sudden?

"I am your mother," she said in response to his expression.

"I guess you are," he said. "I've got homework to do."

"Okay, I'll call you when it's ready."

Eric returned to his room where life was a little less surreal. He'd spoken to two people today who were not teachers. He'd agreed to be a friend to one of them, one of the most popular girls in school. Now, his mother was sober and actually acting like some mother off a TV program.

He touched the gently vibrating spot on his chest through his shirt. His fingers passed through the fabric to touch skin. The skin felt normal, save for the hum that passed through to the bones of his hand. When he drew his hand away, it was blurred softly. There was a little pain, like a dull joint ache. He held it up before him in the mirror, seeing that the glass reflected the blur exactly as he saw it with his eyes. Then he pressed the hand down on the wood dresser. It passed through just as it had before, though now he expected it and didn't overbalance and fall. He waved it through the wood left and right. He could feel what was inside. His hand passed through clothing, feeling like a whisper of wind on his fingertips.

He pulled his hand from the dresser, and it became solid again as if his hand knew it was okay to do so. The ache of the transformation faded instantly, and his hand tingled like it had fallen asleep. He shook his arm and eventually the tingling passed. All his fingers worked. No harm had come to him. Even the rumbling in his chest had stilled. He'd have to be very careful at school and when he was out. The blurring was obvious. Good thing it was hidden well enough by his shirt that the circle of blurring skin on his chest wouldn't be visible, as long as he didn't pass it off to his hand like he just had.

It was a bonus that would help him stay safe.

As long as he was careful.

He thought of when he'd nearly passed through the cafeteria chair. What would happen to him if his entire body went through something? Would he land on the ground or would he go through the floor too? Could he get stuck? Could he become solid inside something?

Great. Not only was it possible he could spontaneously combust, now he could fuse himself in plastic or concrete or wood.

He took a deep breath and flopped onto his bed. It was too much. He needed to keep himself from using this power at all. He needed to stay hidden, most of all. But he also needed to stay alive.

"Eric!" Gillian called, "Dinner's ready."

Eric snapped out of his reverie and glanced at his clock. It had been nearly an hour. He hoped he'd just been dozing and time travel wasn't part of this new power.

Alec Gunn

AUPrimeHistory: True Conspiracies

(Airdate: 9/11/2008)

PROJECT BROOKLYN

<Archive footage of the Pentagon and mysterious wood paneled hallways>

According to classified records recovered after Marshall's Coup in April of 2005, the United States government participated in illegal human experimentation on American soldiers in World War II. That experimentation resulted in the genetic enhancement of an unknown number of individuals. While the drug cocktail enhanced a soldier's strength, endurance, and agility, it also warped their minds.

But when the war was over, the government continued to capture, train and use these monsters in covert operations around the world. While the world enjoyed an unprecedented age of peace in the aftermath of World War II, the United States of America used these "super-soldiers" in violent military operations to unilaterally interfere with foreign sovereignty in places like Vietnam, Grenada, Panama, and Iraq. The goals of theses operations were not known, but they were successfully kept secret for decades.

<Slideshow: Archive photos of the ruins of Wichita Falls, 1997>

Then, in 1997, the government used these operatives, by now codenamed "FORCE (Field Operations and Reconnaissance Corps - Enhanced)," to put down a political protest in Wichita Falls, Texas. The entire town was destroyed in the battle against normal, peaceful civilians. No witnesses survived. However, we have photographic evidence of the massacre thanks to the heroic sacrifice of press photographer, Susan Harris.

<Slideshow: "FORCE in Texas" ©New York Times, Inc.>

The United States government denied the events, even after the photographic proof was revealed by the New York Times. Only when the photos were verified as undoctored and under great popular pressure, did the government publicly reveal the existence of FORCE. But they spun the reveal as the unveiling of a great "super-hero" team formed to protect the United States from foreign aggression. The Texas Massacre was spun as a botched attempt to repel Mexican invaders, who were using their own enhanced-human team.

<Slow-motion: Footage of the FORCE presentation>

But the people didn't buy it. Investigations continued by news agencies and corporations. Unfortunately, it was too late. Just four years after the Texas Massacre, the villains of FORCE struck again. This time, in the most populous city in America.

Alec Gunn

\<Fade to Red\>

More when True Conspiracies returns.

\<Commercial Announcement\>

September 15, 2017

The first week back to school after the holiday went quickly. Eric participated reluctantly in Jason's article and made time in the morning for Kristin and the coffee cake she provided. Each was the counterpoint of the other. While Jason demanded Eric talk about the park and what had led up to Eric punching out Leonard Strange, Kristin didn't really expect much out of him. She was the one who did the talking. Eric just listened as he ate his cake.

He learned a lot about the upper tiers of high school society from Kristin. She loved cheer. She loved her friends. She spoke of even the faults of each as if they were lovable foibles. She spoke fondly of the challenges of putting a cheer together and laughed at the relationship drama.

"Why do you put up with all that?" he asked her. Her laugh trailed off. She regarded him with interest.

"They're my friends," she said.

"It seems like they're more trouble than they're worth," Eric said.

"They're worth a lot more trouble," she said. "Everything they do is part of who they are, and I love them for who they are."

"What about when they hurt you?"

"They've never hurt me. They never will. I'm their friend." She smiled sympathetically at him. "You do know what a friend is, right?"

He looked away from her, watching the kids in line to get breakfast.

"You have had friends, right?" she asked.

"One," Eric said, unable to believe he said it. "He was supposed to my friend. Or at least he wasn't supposed to leave."

"What happened?" Kristin's voice was quiet and intense.

"What always happens," Eric said. "He left."

Feeling pressure at the corner of his eyes, he fought off tears as he rose from his seat and left before he embarrassed himself.

When Jason came for the interview at lunch time, Eric found himself tiptoeing through the events of the previous weekend, careful not to mention anything that might tip the journalist off to Eric's emerging powers. He underplayed the moment he'd struck Leonard.

"I seriously thought he was getting up to come after me," Eric told Jason during their interview. "So I got out of there as fast as I could. I didn't find out what had happened until yesterday."

"What made you do it, though?" Jason asked. "What pushed you over the edge? You've stood up to him before, but you've never actually fought back, right? What was different this time?"

Eric thought back to that moment. He hadn't really thought about it. What should he say that wouldn't raise Jason's suspicions?

"I was just trying to get away from Ken. Kristin—"

"Kristin Matthews? The cheerleader?"

"Yeah, I guess. She was trying to stop Leonard. To get him to stop hitting me."

"Really?" Jason asked, distrust on his face.

"Yeah, he knocked her down, and I think that distracted

Ken. I was able to tear myself away from him. Ken pushed me, and I sort of ran into Leonard."

"With your fist…" Jason's eyes narrowed. Eric felt his power thrum in his chest. He'd said something wrong. He'd tipped Jason's suspicions.

"So," Jason said slowly. "Leonard hits a pretty girl, and you go berserk and break his jaw." His eyebrows rose. His lips curled up on one side. His voice rose to a soprano, "My hero!" He clasped his hands together at his chest.

Eric couldn't help but laugh, partly in relief. "I guess?"

Jason smacked Eric on the shoulder, "You dog! Are you getting some of that now?" The gesture was so alien to Eric that he jumped a little, but he resisted the impulse to move away.

"No!" Eric said his face flushing. Jason laughed.

"It's the dream of every nerd, you know," Jason said. "Save the cheerleader and get a little bit of that action."

Eric shook his head, but he couldn't help smiling. He thought of Kristin and how nice she'd been to him since the weekend. Still, those kinds of things didn't happen in real life. It was absurd to think a cheerleader would be interested in him like that. She just liked to make friends with everyone, she'd pretty much said so herself. He wasn't anything special to her.

"Would you have done it differently?" Eric asked Jason.

"Hell no, dude!" Jason said. Then he shrugged. "Really, I probably would have let him wail on me for a bit, then pretend to faint or something." He scowled. "That's the point of this article, dude. I couldn't ever fight back like you did, but I want to help make it so we don't have to. We need to send a warning to guys like Leonard. Don't eff with us."

"Writing the article is how you fight back," Eric said. Jason spread his arms wide.

"The power of the pen, dude."

"You say 'dude' a lot."

"Suck it… dude."

They both laughed.

Jason joined Eric for lunch every day after that. At first, Eric was annoyed. He depended on his lunch time for the solitude he craved during the crazy school day. Soon, however, he realized he enjoyed Jason's company. They began to talk less and less about Leonard Strange, and more about things that interested them, like music.

"Metallica," Jason started one conversation. "Most underrated band ever. They never made it big, but when they rocked, they rocked."

"Maybe that's why they never made it big," Eric said. He'd never heard of them himself.

"Dude, you need an education. Imagine guitars making sounds you can never imagine."

"Sounds like a hard thing to do."

"Like someone tearing a sheet of music in half so the melody grinds, flowing from one note to the next like a musical white water rapid."

"Ouch."

"Drums like machine guns thumping through your chest."

Eric winced. He knew what that one was like.

"Heaven," Jason finished dreamily. Eric huffed a laugh.

"I'll take your word for it."

Jason sat up straight on the concrete slab at the base of the flagpole and turned to face Eric.

"No you won't. I'll bring you a tape."

"A tape?"

"Cassette tape. All the best music is on tape."

Eric shook his head.

"If you actually want me to listen to it, you'll have to rip it and give me a disk or USB."

Jason sighed.

"I guess."

"Jessie just walked up to him and slapped him across the face!" Kristin said gleefully. "I swear, she got a finger in his eye while she was at it. He started bawling! Like real-life bawling."

her voice rose to a teasing squeak, "The big jock can't handle the sting!"

She burst out laughing. Eric took a bit of his coffee cake and smiled as he chewed. "Sounds like he got what he deserved."

"You bet your ass he did," Kristin said fiercely.

She fell silent for a while, eating her cake. She glanced up at him from time to time, as if expecting him to say something.

"Are you coming to the game tonight?" she asked him. Something in her eyes glittered, making it seem like she was asking him more than the obvious question.

His chest thrummed in response. He scowled and took a deep breath to calm it.

"No," he said. "I've got chem homework to do."

"So do I, remember? You were gonna help me."

He shrugged.

"It's Friday, Sumner. We have plenty of time to do homework over the weekend."

"I have to do it first if I'm going to help you on Monday."

Her head jerked back as if he'd tried to punch her in the face. She stared at him in silence, her eyes flat, her lips tight.

What did he say?

"Okay," she said. She rose from the table, leaving her coffee cake half-eaten. "I'll see you on Monday, then."

She walked away just as the early bell rung. Eric put the last of his cake in his mouth and considered the remains of hers.

It had happened, at last. She'd lost interest in him. That would probably be the last bit of coffee cake he'd have for a while.

He snagged her half and took it with him.

Kristin glided through the hallway toward homeroom. Her arms swung angrily, giving her a haughty, rich-girl look, she was sure.

That was okay. She didn't want to look like she wanted to talk to anyone right now.

What was wrong with that guy? She asked herself. Did he

really think she wanted — or needed — help with her homework? He wanted to keep to himself? Fine. She could let him do that all he wanted. She didn't need to spend so much energy trying to get to know him, did she? It was a waste of time if he really didn't want anything to do with her.

She jerked in surprise as an arm grabbed hers, pulling down hard. The next instant, Stacy was skipping along behind her, dragging at her arm like a shark on a fisherman's line.

"Krissie," Stacy said, using the nickname Kristin hated. Stacy knew better, really. "We need to talk." Stacy's smile and buoyant energy belied her words. She was putting on a show of friendship, Kristin knew, when she really wanted to talk about something serious.

When Kristin nodded, Stacy steered them both toward the girl's room. When they were safely ensconced in relative privacy, Stacy released Kristin, and her facade vanished. She stood before Kristin, her look screaming white-blonde-cheer-captain. Her uniform's blue seemed more intense than Kristin's, the gold trim seemed to glitter, even though it was only a dark yellow velvet — not really gold at all.

It was times like these that Kristin felt a little dirty. Her mulatto skin seemed permanently dirty instead of the creamy latte color her grandmother liked to call it. Her face itched as if her freckles were little bugs eating at her skin. Her father had been a straight up pale-skinned ginger, her mother had had skin like her grandparents, dark chocolate. Kristin had never met either of her parents, she only had pictures of them. They'd seemed happy, but then, pictures always made people seem happy, especially the pictures of the old days before New York.

"What?" Kristin asked when Stacy didn't speak immediately.

"Are you still hanging with that loser?" Stacy asked. Kristin blinked. What did that have anything to do with anything.

"I can hang with whoever I want," Kristin said. Stacy nodded, but her infectious smile was gone, her exuberant energy was muted.

"Sure, sure. But it feels awkward, you know? You're not

hanging with us as much. When you hang out with him, you're cutting out your real friends."

"We can all chill together sometime," Kristin offered. Stacy laughed, her hands coming up as if to stop Kristin from continuing.

"That would be the top of awkward, Krissie. He's not one of us."

"He's a nice guy."

"Nice guys finish last, you know that." Stacy jumped forward and gave Kristin a quick hug. "I just wanted to let you know how we feel about it." She let go and started for the door. "I'm glad we had this talk."

Then she was gone.

Kristin stood in the middle of the bathroom floor, stunned. Did Stacy speak for the entire squad? It had felt like that kind of talk, almost a disciplinary discussion.

She tugged at the skirt of her uniform. Would it come to that? Would she need to choose between her sisters in cheer and a guy?

A freaking guy?!

She liked Eric, despite his frustrating obliviousness. He was quiet, sure. But he was intelligent, and — yes — nice. He was brave and could stand up when he needed to. It couldn't have been easy, doing what he'd done for her.

She'd always done the comfortable thing. Her friendly, outgoing personality had led her right up the social ladder to the top, as far as anyone could get in high school. But she'd been ensconced in that clic since middle school. She'd just ridden the wave to JV cheer. Next year, if she continued riding it, she'd be Varsity, the very tippy-top of the ladder.

Still, every fiber of her being told her that Eric was worth having around. He needed her, she could tell. She thought maybe she kind of needed him as well. He was everything that cheer was not. It was uncomfortable in a way Kristin knew was good for her.

Kristin went to the sinks and checked her makeup. It was fine, but that really wasn't what she was checking. She found herself looking into her own brown eyes.

She didn't have to make a decision now, she told herself. She'd be fine. They were her friends. They'd come around to her way of seeing it. Eventually, they'd see Eric as she did. They could all hang out together. That would be awesome.

She needed to stay by Eric for now. At least until she could really measure his interest. He had hang-ups, but she guessed that he liked her. She remembered how he'd looked at her at the park before everything went south. He'd tried to hide his interest, a sure sign that there was interest. As shy as he was, it must take a lot for him to hang out with her even as much as he did. He just needed to take a step forward. She could help him do that, right?

Besides, she thought as she headed back toward the hallway and homeroom, who else would help him stay out of trouble, given what he was?

October 9-13, 2017

L eonard returned to school the second week of October. Eric was lucky enough to spot him from the street as he rode his bike around the corner to the school. He didn't turn into the school parking lot right away. Instead, he rode around the block, to give Leonard a chance to go inside the school and engage himself with his friends and whatnot.

As he came around the corner again, Eric spotted Buck chatting with one of the parents of a middle schooler just outside the school. As Eric turned in to the High School, he saw Buck look up at him from his crouched position next to the car.

A flash of anger ripped through Eric. From the moment he'd punched Leonard across the face, Buck had known. How? Was there some sort of "SPI sense" that let SPIs know each other? That was stupid. Eric didn't have any idea about Buck before the old man had shown him what he could do.

Why couldn't Buck just leave him alone? He was constantly outside the school, watching him. Eric had begun to notice him on weekends, too, if he went to the park or into town. Buck was always around, limping along on the street as if he weren't following Eric, just there in the background of almost everything Eric did.

Eric dropped his full weight back on his pedals with a violent jerk, skidding to a halt next to the bike rack. As he began to run the cable through the rack, his hands fumbled with the lock. The bike started rolling away. Furious, Eric grabbed the frame and pushed the bike back into position. The frame scraped against the metal rack, causing a screech that grated Eric's ears.

Eric froze, staring at the gash he'd created in his bike's blue and silver paint. His throat constricted, and tears came to his eyes. He'd worked for years to keep the bike pristine. It was the only object he owned that he truly cared about.

He clicked the lock into place and ran his thumb against the scratch, hoping it might be superficial, something he could just wipe away. But the rack had scored deep into the paint and even a little into the metal, causing a scratch along the top bar of the frame as thick as his finger and almost as long.

Eric stood and looked up at the facade of his school, wiping his eyes dry. He took a deep breath and clenched his fists. He didn't want to go in there.

He looked down at his damaged bike. He should just go home, see if he could somehow buff out the scratch. Maybe he could find something in the garage to cover it, something that would look cool and hide his stupid mistake. He could maybe wrap it in duct tape and use a marker to add a cool design to it.

Of all the stupid ideas...

The door to the school opened, and Eric was surprised to see Kristin coming out. She saw him and made a beeline to him.

She'd shown him a strange combination of affection and aloofness in the last few weeks. Despite his belief that he'd somehow gotten on her bad side, she stuck to him, greeting him every morning and occasionally still inviting him to breakfast. He'd begun to feel like he was some project she was working on, like a biologist trying to socialize an orphan monkey.

"Leonard is here," she said in a warning tone.

"Yeah, I saw him," Eric said.

"That why you're still out here?" she softened her words with a sympathetic smile.

"Something like that," he said, glancing at his bike.

"You'll be fine. He's not in any of your classes, and he'll be too busy trying to catch up to go looking for you. Just avoid him between class, and you'll be fine."

"You don't want me to knock him out again?"

She laughed and surprised him with a quick hug that was over before he could respond to it.

"Don't get me wrong," she said. "I know you could wipe the floor with him, but you don't need the hassle." She flashed a quick smile. "You'd get expelled, then I'd never see you again."

"His dad would arrest my ass," Eric said, quirking his lips into a forced half-smile. Leonard's father was the County Sheriff. Not just a deputy, but the real, no-kidding, elected Sheriff.

"Exactly," she said with a smirk that, for some reason, didn't seem to reach her eyes. "The last thing you want." She joined him as he headed toward the doors, walking beside him, but not touching him. It felt strange.

He felt for sure that they should be holding hands.

The first day, Eric was either lucky, or Kristin was right. He was able to make it from class to class without encountering Leonard. He moved his lunch time from the flagpole to the baseball field bleachers and determined that he should move his lunch to a different place every day to avoid being found.

The following day, he showed up to the school just before the late bell and went straight to homeroom without stopping to see Kristin or get breakfast with her. He avoided talking to anyone, even Kristin or Jason. He pretended he was a ghost, just going about his after-life in silent repetition from day to day, his primary goal was to avoid football players, especially those with broken jaws.

It worked for four days. Then, Eric got complacent.

He was heading to English class, walking swiftly through the hall, when Leonard Strange came around the corner. He was walking alone, his eyes roaming, scanning every possible place.

Their eyes locked and Leonard's hand came up slowly, finger pointing firmly at Eric like some zombie from a bad horror movie. He didn't say anything. His jaw was still wired shut. His lips pursed and he shook his finger at Eric.

Eric looked frantically for an escape. For some stupid reason, he decided to duck into the boy's restroom. Too late he realized that he'd just thrown himself into a dead-end.

He jumped into a stall and shut the door, locking it behind him. He climbed up onto the toilet. He'd seen it in a movie once. Leonard wouldn't be able to see his legs from beneath the door.

He shook his head, frustrated with himself. It wouldn't matter if Leonard couldn't see his legs. His stall was the only one with a locked door!

He climbed down, trying to be as quiet as possible. He'd just reached his hand out to unlock the door when he heard footsteps at the entrance.

"Get out here, Shumner," Leonard growled between clenched teeth. The footsteps continued almost immediately. Leonard wasn't going to wait for him.

The door to the only other stall in the bathroom slammed open, rattling Eric, who now leaned against the metal dividing wall, as close to the tiled back wall as he could get.

The power in his chest thrummed like a lawn mower starting up. He tried to calm it, afraid that Leonard would hear it in the powerful acoustics of a public bathroom.

The door to his stall shuddered, but it was still locked.

"E'm not gonna to wet for you, Shumner," Leonard said. He pounded a fist against the locked door. Eric stiffened. There was no way Leonard could get through that door. If he tried crawling under it, Eric could kick him in the face, probably re-breaking his jaw.

He prepared to do just that when the shadow of Leonard's legs shifted. But instead of ducking down to crawl under the door, Leonard reared back and struck the door with the flat of his booted foot. The entire stall shook. The metal door flexed, but the lock miraculously held.

The power in Eric's chest flared. The vibration spread down

his arms and legs, feeling like the uncontrollable shiver of a sudden chill without the cold feeling. Eric felt himself falling backward, toward the stall's dividing wall. He stumbled back…

… through the wall!

When he blinked again, he was in the adjoining stall, his nose nearly touching the dividing wall and his butt against the half-open door of the stall.

His eyes widened.

What the hell had just happened?!

The stalls shook again as Leonard kicked the locked door again. The lock gave, and the door slammed hard enough to shake the stalls again. Eric felt the metal wall press up against his nose for just a moment.

"What the F–?" came Leonard's voice. Eric stepped back into the other stall, stepping around the toilet. To move, he had to push against the door to this stall. The motion alerted Leonard, who stepped quickly back into the bathroom proper. In seconds, Eric would be caught. He had nowhere else to go.

Except that, apparently, he could walk through walls.

For the first time that he could remember, Eric consciously called up the power in his chest in full force. He remembered the feeling of his entire body shivering, and the power spread down his limbs again.

Then, hoping beyond hope that he wasn't just about to kill himself, he stepped toward the tiled back wall.

For a moment, he could see nothing. He had to take a second step for his vision to clear again.

He found himself in a mirror image bathroom, standing in an open stall nearly identical to the one he'd just left. Only the color of the stall's walls told him he was in the girl's room, the light pink a stark contrast to the dark brown paint on the stalls of the boy's room.

Shuffling feet from outside the stall alerted Eric that maybe Leonard had somehow deduced his escape and come to investigate this room as well. He jumped up onto the toilet seat and slowly inched the door closed just enough to hide him.

"I don't think she gets it," said a girl's voice that echoed through the room as voices usually do in bathrooms but seemed very loud to Eric. "I told her how we felt about her running around with that loser. But she's still doing it."

"Not so much," another girl's voice said. "I think she heard what you said and she's toning it down."

"She needs to break up with him," Girl 1 said. "That's all there is to it. It's embarrassing."

"Oh, come on, Stace," Girl 2 said. "It's only embarrassing to her. If you don't like it, why don't you just cut her?"

Eric blinked at that. Were they actually talking about cutting a girl because of who she was dating? A bit extreme, wasn't it?

"No," Stace said — Cheerleader Stacy? "We need her. She's good. We might even make it to regionals with her this year."

Eric nearly slapped himself in his face. Not like knife cutting. They were talking about cutting a girl from the cheerleading squad. Eric's eyes narrowed. They weren't talking about Kristin, were they?

Suddenly, a masculine cry of rage erupted from the hallway outside.

"Oh my God," Girl 2 said, "I gotta see this."

Footsteps trampled out the door. Eric took that as a sign that the bathroom had emptied out. He crept out of the stall and cracked the door to the hallway. Stacy and another cheerleader were buzzing around Leonard, who was chomping at the bit, growling at them through clenched teeth. Girl 2 was Jessica Harrington, a girl Kristin talked about often. Her straight brown hair framed South-Asian features.

Just as the trio was about to spread out to look for Eric, the bell rang for class. Jessica shrugged and made her apologies as she raced down the hallway. Stacy looked at Leonard and shook her head before she, too, headed for class.

Eric kept the door to the girl's room cracked just enough to see Leonard until Leonard, scowling, moved away.

"Are you going to let me get to class now?" said a soft voice behind him. Eric turned, his face burning. A girl who must have been in the other stall was standing behind him, her books clutched to her side and gigantic nerd-glasses on her face. Her stance was more impatience than anger.

"Yeah, um, sorry," he said, moving away from the door.

"I get it," she said as she slipped out the door, "If I were hiding from a bully, I'd pick the boy's room." Eric peered back into the bathroom, hoping no one else was in there staring at him.

Satisfied he was otherwise unobserved, he followed the girl out. At least the only one to see him was one of Jason's "losers" and not another cheerleader.

Alec Gunn

AUPrimeNews Archive

(Posted: 3/24/2009)

EUP INVADES NEVADA

In the latest show of aggression against the American Union (AU), forces from the Estados Unidos del Pacífico (EUP), raided a military watch post on the Nevada border. Super-Powered Individuals associated with the EUP government and modeled after the original United States government sponsored team, FORCE, attacked the base, laying waste to billions of dollars of equipment and killing several dozen soldiers who attempted to defend the installation.

The SPIs associated with the attack were led by none other than the number 1 most wanted SPI terrorist, the telepathic mind-controller, Mental Block, who participated in FORCE's attack on New York on September 11th, 2001. He led a team of enhanced persons consisting of the agility/strength duo Fight and Flight, as well as speed-enhanced SPI, Freeway. The true identities of these terrorists have been a closely held secret of the EUP since its break from the AU in 2008.

President Marshall in Chicago decried the attack as an act of war and promised reprisals. He stated that new technology would soon become available that would level the field against the SPI aggressors. He condemned the so-called government of the EUP for ordering the strike.

The response from the EUP was a simple statement that the "raid" was undertaken as an act of self-defense following an "assassination attempt" by a covert AU special forces squad sourced at the targeted facility. No evidence of any "assassination attempt" could be found.

Stay tuned to AUPrimeNews for further developments on this story.

October 13, 2017

Dude."

Eric sat in the bleachers that rimmed the football field. He'd taken one bite of his sandwich. A pair of girls ran long-legged sprints around the brown, dirt track. Those two were on the track team. He'd seen them running with the team around the neighborhood after school. How did they have the energy to run after school and at lunch? Just the idea wore him out.

"Dude."

A thump on his shoulder made Eric look up. Jason stared at him.

"Are you alive, dude?" He glanced out to the track, "They're not that cute. You know runners don't shave their armpits, right?"

"What?" Eric asked. The idea was ridiculous. And why would he care? "What the hell are you talking about?"

"Friction. Having hair there is like ball bearings in a— nevermind. You can't just stare at girls, you know. You have to ask them out."

Eric looked from Jason to the running girls who were just now passing in front of them at a full sprint, then back to Jason. He opened his mouth to speak, and realized he couldn't think of anything to say to that.

"I wasn't looking at them," he finally said. A lie, but enough of a truth to counter Jason's meaning.

"Well," Jason said doubtfully, "If you weren't looking at them, then you were staring out into space. What gives?"

"I can't have private thoughts?"

Jason looked back to the track.

"So you were looking at them," he said with a mischievous smile.

Eric growled and looked away from him just in time to see Kristin climbing the bleachers up to them. He'd never seen her at lunch. He assumed she spent the time hanging out with her cheerleader cadre. Since the bathroom incident this morning, Eric had been moving through the halls like a special forces operative sneaking into an enemy base, making sure Leonard was no where in sight before moving from class to class. He wondered if Stacy really had been talking about Kristin. Who was she dating that they had a problem with? A rush of jealousy ran like a pulse from his power through his bones.

"There you are," Kristin said by way of greeting when there were only a couple rows between them. "I've missed you."

Jason gaped in shock, his head swiveling from Kristin to Eric to Kristin.

"Duuuuude!" he said in a breathy whisper, "You guys hooked up?"

Kristin glared at Jason.

"No," Eric said at the same time he realized that Stacy might have been talking about him, "We did not hook up."

Kristin turned the glare on Eric. What had he said to deserve that?

"He's helping me with my chem homework," Kristin said, her scowl turning to a grin.

"Oh," Jason said, "Is that what the kids are calling it these days." He laughed.

"We've been hanging out at breakfast," Eric explained, "That's all."

"But he's been skipping since Leonard came back," Kristin

finished, her smile souring. She took a seat next to Eric and looked out at the track and the running girls. "So this is what brings you out here," she said elbowing him in the ribs. He squirmed away from the blow, his power thrumming lightly in his chest.

Eric glared at Jason. Why did everyone think that? "No, it's not." Jason suppressed giggles by pretending to wipe the sleeve of his jean jacket over his mouth.

"Busted," Jason mouthed to Eric. "I keep telling him," he said to Kristin, "They're not that cute."

Eric wanted to throw a backhand into Jason's face at that moment, but he suppressed the urge.

"It's okay," Kristin said. "Not like we're dating or anything." If that was true, why did Stacy and Jessica think they were?

Why were these two hanging with him in the first place? What did they want from him? What did he have to offer them?

"So, how's the chase?" Kristin asked into the uncomfortable silence. "Leonard find you yet?"

"I'm still in one piece, aren't I?" Eric said. "He almost got me this morning, but I got away. I think he's too busy to really come looking."

"What did I tell you?" Kristin said.

"You should just take him at school," Jason said. "Do what you did at the park with about a dozen people watching and he'll stop coming for you. Hell, you probably only have to slap him in the face at this point. His jaw probably hurts like a sonofagun."

"I'm not gonna get suspended just to put Leonard in the hospital again," Eric said as if he was confident he could take Leonard out again.

"It would totally be worth it, dude."

"It's really not a good idea," Kristin interjected.

"I actually like school," Eric said. That was true, bullies notwithstanding.

Jason clutched at his heart as if having a heart attack. He gasped in mock pain.

"Take it back! Take it back!" he moaned. Kristin laughed. Eric smiled.

The after-lunch bell rang. Eric rose and looked at his "friends." A chill of uncertainty ran up his spine, triggering a purr from his power. He puffed out his shirt to be sure the blur in his chest wasn't visible to them.

"I'll see you guys later. I've gotta get to class."

"There's a game tonight," Kristin reminded him.

Of course, he thought. Friday.

"Are you coming?" she asked.

"No, sorry," he said. "Homework."

He didn't wait for her disapproving look before he leaped down the bleachers. The running girls were gone. There wasn't a sign of anyone here. They'd all be retreating back into the school to return to the day's drudgery.

Suddenly, Jason was at his side.

"Dude," he said by way of getting his attention, "That girl is pissed."

"What do you mean?"

"You were supposed to say something like, 'sure, I'll be there to see your little dance and twirl show.' Instead, you blow her off. For homework? A girl like that? What are you gay? Wait, you're not gay, are you? I mean, just to let you know, I don't swing that way."

"I'm not gay, Jason," Eric said, exasperated.

"But that girl is into you. A freakin' cheerleader, dude. Is into you." Jason punctuated that with a poke on Eric's arm.

Eric stared at Jason for a while. He didn't know what he was supposed to say. Was he supposed to go back and apologize to Kristin? Tell her he would be at the game tonight? At the thought, his power thrummed in his bones.

No. He couldn't. It was too much of a risk.

He shook his head and picked up his pace. He needed to get to class.

Jason didn't follow.

October 14, 2017

Eric woke on Saturday morning with a new plan. Since his discovery that his power allowed him to walk through walls, he decided he would find a nice, secluded place outside of town and practice what he was coming to call in his mind "ghosting." All he'd need was a place where no one was watching and a few things to walk through: rocks, trees, whatever.

Gillian had breakfast ready for him. He was starting to become less and less surprised by her sudden mothering. For the last few weeks, she'd been staying sober, at least when he was around. The house was cleaner than it had ever been, and she'd been cooking dinner for them both. On weekends, she did breakfast and dinner, leaving only lunch for him if he wanted it. Eric guessed she was trying to give him some teenage autonomy by leaving him responsibility for his own lunches. He was okay with that. After so long not having a real mother, it was sort of stifling to suddenly have someone expect him to be home at a certain time and to sit at a table eating real food instead of taking a bowl of mac and cheese into his bedroom as he used to do.

"Sleep well?" Gillian asked.

"Yeah," Eric said as he took a seat across from his mother at the table. "You?"

She nodded, her shoulders coming up in a slight shrug.

"I slept better when I was drinking, I think. But I'm okay." She took a bite of her food, seemingly just so she couldn't continue talking.

Eric grimaced uncomfortably.

"I've got a meeting this afternoon in McAlester. You gonna be okay for dinner?"

"Yeah, mom. I think I'll manage."

The refrigerator had more food in it than Eric was used to. To keep herself from drinking, Gillian had become something of an uber-homemaker. She went grocery shopping regularly, she cooked and cleaned, and she even did yard-work. Eric never saw her sitting in front of the TV anymore. The television, especially AUPrimeNews, had always been a trigger for her drinking.

She'd been going to alcoholic meetings in McAlester on a weekly basis. There just weren't any in Ender. Drunks in Ender usually preferred to stay that way. Since his birthday, she'd made it a point to stay sober. Eric wasn't sure what the impetus for her new determination to get healthy, but he was glad it was happening.

Eric finished his breakfast and went to get dressed for his day out. He put on a pair of black jeans and a black t-shirt with a silver eagle printed on it. He found a loose, light jacket in his closet and put that on as well. The weather had turned cool in the last few weeks, and the sun outside his window was battling the clouds for dominance of the sky.

As he readied himself, he felt his power hum in his chest, as if in anticipation of what he was about to do.

When he was as prepared as he was going to get, he went out to his bike and let it carry him down the driveway before pedaling it down the street away from where he usually went. He rode in the opposite direction from town, away from the school, the park, and everywhere else he was used to going.

After ten minutes of riding, he escaped the clusters of houses and yards and found himself on the road to the middle of nowhere. There were copses of trees on either side of the road in little clumps. A short barbed wire fence ran the length of the road on the right side, indicating that the land was privately owned there. On the left, a long hill rose from the road, obscuring the land from his sight.

He'd never come out this way or this far on his bike before. He wasn't familiar with the land out here. It was almost as if he was escaping Ender and traveling to a new town. The road was empty this early on a Saturday morning. Only one car passed him, going the opposite direction, for as far as he rode.

At last, he spotted a dilapidated shack not far from the road. It looked unused. One of the doors hung open on one hinge, canted at an almost diagonal angle. The windows were broken, and any paint that had once tinted the wood was worn away by time and weather.

This was perfect!

He turned his bike from the road and across the packed earth and long grass to the shack. Weeds and vines had worked their way between the planks of wood that made up its outer walls. It seemed to be an old tool shed. Probably a place to store equipment for a farmer that had long ago had his farm sold to Monsanto or something.

Eric leaned his bike against the wall opposite the road. He didn't want anyone seeing the shiny bike by the ruined old shack and investigate what was going on.

The front door of the shack tilted across the opening, its remaining hinge barely holding it in place. Eric glanced around at the emptiness around him. Seeing no one watching, he concentrated on his power and felt it spread through his body as it had in the bathroom yesterday. He stepped into the door and passed through it into the shack.

He felt the wood pass through his body like a shiver. His vision blackened for the length of a slow blink as his face passed through the door. When he emerged on the other side, the ache of his transformation faded as he phased back to normal.

It really was like he was a ghost passing through a wall.

Sun streaked through slits in the wooden planks of the walls and through the broken eastern window. Within the golden shafts of light, dust floated in thick clouds. Eric's every movement stirred up little tornadoes of dust. Shelves lined the walls, once home to tools or devices for farming. Now, all that remained were a few glass jars and a rusty hand trowel with a dust-caked wooden handle. It seemed this place had been a catch-all for all sorts of junk near the end of its life. A rusted-out push-style lawn mower sat in one corner, its blades nearly rotted completely and its rubber tires completely gone save for shreds clinging to the edge of the metal wheels.

A ladder led up to a tiny loft at the top of the shack, more of a wide shelf under the roof eaves. Up there, a forgotten toolbox sat, a padlock holding in whatever contents still remained.

Intrigued, Eric pulled the toolbox down and set it upon a narrow workbench next to the ancient mower. He examined the lock and found the hasp frozen, perhaps fused shut by rust. No matter that, there was no key anywhere in the shack, though a row of little hooks were screwed into the wall near the broken front door. All the hooks were bare.

An idea for a simple beginning to his training sparked in his head. He concentrated and felt his power trigger in his chest. Then, he touched his hand to that vibration, causing the power to spread to it.

Next, he reached out with his blurred hand toward the toolbox. He pushed his hand through the metal. It felt different than passing through wood. He couldn't quantify it, but there was a slight change in the tactile sensation in his fingers as they passed through the metal.

To confirm this, he moved his hand from the toolbox to the wooden workbench. As his hand passed from metal to wood, there was a strange shifting feel of the vibration in his hand. It was the density of the material. His power had to adapt to different densities in order to phase through the atoms. It probably also had to do with the organization of those atoms. He'd learned in chemistry that metal atoms bond differently than carbon atoms, which made up much of organic matter. Metallic bonds were tighter and more organized. There was less physical space between them.

Eric guessed it would take more effort to pass through metal than other materials. He hadn't thought of it when he ghosted through the bathroom walls. He'd been too desperate to think much about what he was doing. Now, he was ghosting relatively easily through the panels of the toolbox. The metal was thin. It would probably be harder to pass through a thicker sheet of metal or a steel girder if he even could. Would he be able to pass through something as dense as lead?

As he ghosted through the wooden table, he felt a slight change near his fingers. He looked down at what he was doing and noticed that he'd just touched a nail within the wood. He'd been able to feel the difference!

A thought struck him.

With his hand still vibrating within the wood, he reached with his fingers and tried to grip the nail that had been hammered into the wood decades ago. He felt the metal between his fingers and made a conscious effort not to change his phase. Even though his fingers were inside the wood, he felt the cool touch of the metal nail on his fingertips.

He pulled his hand out and laughed. What an amazing thing!

He glanced at the toolbox and grinned.

Reaching into the toolbox, he focused on the sensations in his fingers. He poked about inside the toolbox. There was a plastic, divided shelf inside, probably the kind that is attached to the lid and rises up on special hinges when the box was opened. Eric was able to grip it and feel it as if he was searching for something in the dark. Yet, at a thought, he was able to phase through that, too and feel around the box itself. There were still tools inside: Some sort of heavy adjustable wrench, a ball-peen hammer with a wooden handle, and what felt like a blade... no, a pair of shears, also with a wooden handle.

He picked up the wrench and rattled it around inside the box. He nearly startled himself with the sound of it. Part of him had been thinking he'd only imagined being able to touch it.

Somehow, he was able to pass through the metal sides of the toolbox, yet at the same time touch and lift the metal wrench.

The action of the atoms in his hand and arm must be in some sort of mentally controlled flux. Some of them adapting to the density of the box while others returning to their normal phase in order to pick up the tool.

He pulled his hand back, still gripping the wrench. The metal wrench slapped up against the side of the toolbox, and Eric's hand came out of the box empty. He couldn't bring the tool out of the box. It must be something about the difference in density.

He stood in front of the box for a while, trying to think of a way he could get the items out of the box without needing to crack open the lock. It was a puzzle for him, full of mathematics and theoretical calculations.

He tried to work it out through trial and error. First, he grabbed the wrench, willing himself to bring it out of the box, then pulled.

His hand came out empty.

Maybe if he tried it with one of the wooden tools?

He took the handle of the ball-peen hammer and tried to pull that out of the box.

The result was the same.

He took a deep breath and stepped back from the box, his arms crossed and his lips twisted in concentration. What was it that was not working here? Was he unable to pass his power to objects in the box, even if he was holding them? Shouldn't his very touch cause the objects to vibrate in sync with his own body?

Maybe not. This might be a limitation of his power. If it was telekinetic in nature, maybe he was limited to only being able to manipulate his own atoms. But that was stupid. Why only his own atoms? If he could mentally manipulate any atoms at all in the way he'd been doing, he should be able to control anything in the same way.

It was like if Jitterbug could have lifted cars with her mind, but not cardboard boxes.

Just ludicrous.

He tried again and again, convinced that he must be doing something wrong. But each time, he got the same result. His hand came out of the box empty.

After a dozen failures, Eric screamed in frustrated rage. He brought his hand up over the box in a fist. Just as he brought it down to pound on the metal toolbox in a frustrated tantrum, he felt a spike of pain in his hand, as if someone had dropped a twelve pound sledgehammer onto his hand.

Then, his fist struck the toolbox. He might as well have been wearing a lead glove. He didn't feel the impact. His fist hammered into the top of the tool box. The red metal near the handle crumpled under the blow, denting the box. The plastic handle cracked.

Eric stepped away from the box in shock, lifting both hands as if a cop had aimed a gun at him. He looked at his right hand, which now felt normal. There was no pain, nor indication that he'd just hit a sturdy metal toolbox hard enough to nearly break it. The bottom edge of his hand felt fine, with no bruising or abrasions, even though he'd broken the plastic handle.

Had his power given him super strength after all? He summoned his ability again, feeling the buzzing in his chest. Then, willing himself to be as strong as he'd just been, he hammer-fisted the workbench, intent on breaking straight through it and shattering it to pieces.

His hand indeed went straight through it, but only ghosting through the wood as he'd already known he could. He tried again, forcing himself to ferocity. He growled and punched the workbench again. Again, his hand merely passed through.

He tried the same on the toolbox. Maybe he could only do such a thing to metal. But the result was the same. He felt the changes as his hand passed through the different metals and woods, but when he raised his hand again, there was no change to the box or the workbench.

"Okay, okay," he said to himself, trying to soothe his frustration. "It's the first day. You're not going to figure everything out on day one."

Already, he'd learned how he could control his power better than he'd known before coming here. That was progress. He should be happy.

But what was that strange ability? He knew now how he had been able to break Leonard's jaw. It hadn't been because Ken had pushed him. It hadn't been because he'd been falling forward. Sure momentum might have been part of it, but this other ability he had was part of it as well. It hurt in the instant before contact, but not because of the contact or any damage he was doing to his body. Was it another aspect of the manipulation of his atoms?

He clenched his right fist, staring at it. He could move his atoms in such a way that he could safely pass through just about any material. But this thing had been something different.

Maybe the opposite?

If the atoms in his hand had suddenly become super-dense, frozen, or arranged like those of the metal atoms in the box, it might explain what had happened. His hand would have become incredibly hard, preventing impact damage.

What affect would doing that do to his body? The act hurt. It hurt badly. If he was somehow rearranging the atoms in his hand, he'd probably stopped all activity in his flesh. It had stopped blood flow, had frozen his nerves and every other biological function in his hand.

And the action had been accidental. He didn't know how to control it. He didn't know how to bring it about, and he didn't know what he did to return his hand to normal.

Eric swallowed through a lump in his throat. If he made a mistake and forced his whole body to do something like that, even for a moment, it was very possible he could kill himself with his own power, stopping his heart, stopping electrical activity to his brain, freezing his lungs and blood. Would he be able to recover from that, or would it be like he had turned to stone forever?

It was one more thing to add to the list of dangers: spontaneous combustion, solidifying within something, now turning to stone. How was he going to live with this?

Eric stared into space for a long time, mulling over the possibilities. His euphoria at discovering new aspects of his power chilled with this realization.

He resigned himself to wondering about it. He decided that maybe he should just take a step back and work through this later. He ghosted through the wall and stepped out into the empty field.

Except it wasn't empty. A lone figure stood not ten feet from the shack, big arms crossed over the chest of a blue and gold letterman jacket.

"I knew it," Leonard Strange said through his clenched jaw, "I knew you had to be one."

AUPrimeHistory: True Conspiracies

(Airdate: 9/11/2008)

CITADEL

<Archive Footage (Aerial): Ground Zero, New York City, September 20th, 2001>

But what really happened that day? Government records claim that FORCE was sent to New York City to prevent a terrorist attack on the World Trade Center. But, thanks to secret communications between Washington, D.C. and the sole survivor of the attack, FORCE operative codenamed "Mental Block," we are now able to surmise what truly happened that fateful day.

Mental Block

"He did it. The bastard actually did it..."

Spec Ops Control, Washington D.C.

"Block! What happened? We lost comms. What the hell happened?!"

The "bastard" is this man: the first and most powerful of the Super-Powered Individuals, or SPIs as they have come to be called.

<Image: Freeze-frame close-up of Citadel from FORCE presentation, 1999>

Codenamed "Citadel" due to his extreme endurance capable of resisting nearly any man-made weapon or injury, classified documents have redacted any mention of his real name. In addition to impervious flesh, Citadel boasted immeasurable strength. He is reported to have been able to throw a multi-ton military vehicle over a hundred yards. Even depleted-uranium rounds could not penetrate his armored flesh. Only being in the immediate vicinity of a nuclear explosion ended the reign of one of the most deplorable villains in history. Citadel, through his direct command of FORCE over a thirty-year period, is responsible for thousands of deaths.

Review of archived film over the years has revealed that Citadel had a front-line role in the US government.

<Archive Footage: Kennedy attack - November 22, 1963 - Dallas, Texas>

The earliest known record of Citadel is this photo of him leaping to the defense of President John F. Kennedy in a November 1963 assassination attempt just weeks before Kennedy ordered FORCE to Hanoi, a military raid in the Vietnamese country that resulted in the wholesale slaughter of much of Vietnam's existing government. Shortly thereafter, American advisers left the country, ending American involvement in the insurrection there. That top secret raid was just the first of a series of actions that FORCE is recorded to have taken to unilaterally shape the world's political landscape.

<Archive footage: FORCE presentation (edited) - Team member close-ups>

But FORCE was more than just a one man army

in the form of Citadel. On the day that sounded the death knell of the United States of America, three others were present to cause the utter obliteration of millions.

More when we return.

<Commercial Announcement>

September 14, 2017

"You're a SPI," Leonard said. A triumphant grin spread his clenched jaw like some sickening clown.

"What are you talking about?" Eric asked. He tried his best to keep a tremor of fear from his voice. All his best efforts and he'd just shown his powers off to this idiot. The one guy in all of Ender guaranteed to turn him in and laugh while he was executed on national TV.

"'What are you talking about,'" Leonard imitated. "E'm talking about you walking through that wall, Shumner."

"I used the door, asshole," Eric said. Maybe he could still salvage something from this. "You can't prove anything. Walking through walls? What kind of science fiction crap is that?"

Instead of any kind of uncertainty, which was Eric's hope, Leonard's grin only widened.

"Who shehs I want to prove anything, Shumner. Maybe I jusht want to kick your ash where no one ish here to shtop me, not even your shlut."

A burning sensation rose from Eric's stomach and joined the vibration in his chest. His lips twisted into a grimace of hate.

"Oh, I knew that would get you. It got you going the last time. You're just so shweet on that bitch. Rather pathetic, really. Do you think about her at night while you lay in bed touching yourself, cause I know you didn't get any of that."

With the power roaring in his chest, Eric took a step toward Leonard. In response, Leonard set himself as if to charge. Then, in an instant, the runningback was gone. Eric felt something pass through him, something soft and fluid unlike anything he'd felt before.

Then, behind him, Leonard cried out in pain as he crashed up against the wall of the shack. Eric whirled around to find Leonard crumpled in a ball on the ground at the foot of the tool shed.

Eric's mind raced, but not as fast as Leonard had moved. Leonard had charged him, that was clear. Leonard had moved at a speed that should have been impossible but obviously was not.

Leonard Strange was a SPI, too!

But it was clear that Leonard was of the more conventional sort. A speedster, with enhancements to reflexes and sheer muscle speed. Most speedsters also had enhancements to agility, the two enhancements pretty much went hand in hand. It would be pretty embarrassing to be able to move at the speed of Corvette but not be able to control yourself enough to stay on your feet.

It seemed, from the current situation, that Leonard's agility enhancements were pretty limited. He hadn't been able to stop himself in time to keep from hitting the shed. Now, it seemed he'd been knocked unconscious by his own mistake.

Eric had to move quickly, pun not intended. He had no chance of stopping Leonard once the kid was up and running after him. Eric had to find what speed he could muster and get back to town. He had to find a public place where Leonard couldn't use his abilities against him without being marked a SPI. They both needed to stay hidden or suffer the consequences. Out here, Leonard could do whatever he wanted.

Eric rushed to his bike, mounting it on the run. He pedaled it up to the street then pushed as hard and as fast as he could on the pedals, heading up the road toward Ender. The wind whipped at his hair, flipping it occasionally across his face. For a moment, Eric regretted not going to the barber that often.

The next time his flapping hair, now wet with sweat, fell in front of his face, he jerked his head to move it away. When it fell away, Eric saw something that made him crush the brakes.

Leonard Strange stood in the road ahead of him.

Eric's heart hammered in his chest. If the organ hadn't been a part of him, Eric was sure his power would have let it escape through his chest and jump down the road ahead of him.

He turned the bike into his skid, jamming on the front brake and pivoting the bike around the front wheel in a stunt that would have made a professional BMX rider proud.

When he was turned completely around, he began pedaling as furiously as he could.

Now facing back toward the shed, Eric had to think about what lay in that direction. The next town, Antlers, was ten miles away. The only thing that lay between here and there were ten miles of woods and empty fields. Eric didn't have ten miles to run.

To confirm his fear, Eric blinked his eyes and found Leonard once more in front of him. This time, Leonard was closer, Eric couldn't stop or turn in time. Leonard reached out an arm to clothesline Eric. Eric's power thrummed within him, and the arm passed harmlessly through him.

So did his bike.

Eric tumbled to the ground, his power padding him from any injury while not letting him fall through the asphalt completely. His once-pristine blue-silver bike, suddenly riderless, rolled a few more feet before dumping to the road. The sound of metal scraping across the pavement was like a scream of pain to Eric's ears.

All at once, Leonard was there. He tried a punter's kick through Eric's mid-section, but like in Peanuts, Eric pulled the football away. Leonard's foot passed through Eric like a gust of wind in his hair. Leonard stumbled and almost fell, his enhanced agility barely keeping him on his feet.

Eric rose to his own feet. He watched as Leonard stared him down, chest heaving with effort. No enhancements to endurance then, Eric's analytical mind called out.

"What are you?" Leonard panted through his clenched teeth, the air whistling through them like jets of steam. Eric was disappointed that Leonard's impact with the shed hadn't re-broken the jaw enough to keep the kid from talking at all.

Eric straightened and faced his enemy.

"I'm untouchable," he said. Leonard shook his head.

"No, you're not. I'll find a way. Thish ishn't over, Shumner."

"You out me, Lenny, I out you," Eric said in a voice too confident to be his own. "Make sure you remember that. Maybe we'll share the same firing squad. Wait, no, they hang speedsters with blocks tied to their ankles so they can't escape."

Leonard growled.

In one last futile effort, Leonard charged Eric again. Again, he passed through as Eric's power hummed within him unconsciously. Leonard didn't stop. Instead of turning to try again, he continued down the road back to Ender, vanishing quickly to Eric's eyes.

Strangely calm, Eric went to retrieve his damaged bike, a smile of satisfaction warming his face. It had been the uncertainty of what Leonard would do that had made him most nervous. Now he was sure there was nothing that could be done to hurt him.

He truly was untouchable.

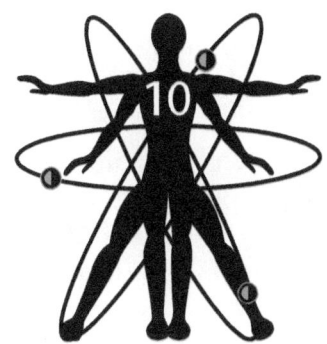

October 16, 2017

He rode slowly to school on Monday morning. He was nervous. His power bubbled in his chest, eager for action. His body was taut with a strange sort of confidence mixed with fear. As he locked his bike up and the power still hummed. He felt good. He was untouchable. He'd shown a speedster the door. He should just let himself go. Nothing could stop him.

As he opened the door to the school, he stopped.

That kind of thinking was dangerous. He had to remember that if he was caught, he was dead. Even if he thought that he couldn't be caught, he had to be cautious. The AU was resourceful and powerful. They'd been dealing with SPIs for ten years, and they had the knowledge of the US government, who'd been dealing with them a lot longer. He couldn't be stupid.

He took the reins of his power and held them tight. He couldn't risk coming out now, especially with a speedster literally running around. Leonard was still dangerous.

No sooner had he done so, than a heavy hand fell on his shoulder. His power thrummed to life, but he pushed it down.

"Hey buddy," Leonard said at his side. Eric's heart skipped a beat, and he almost lost his hold on the power. The kid must have been waiting near the door for Eric to come in. "I've been thinking about this whole thing we talked about on Saturday."

Leonard's voice was sounding normal, though his jaw was still wired closed. He kept his voice down so only Eric could hear him.

"I told you," Eric replied in the same discrete tone, "you do it, I do it." Leonard laughed.

"We'll see," the big football player said, "We're going to play a game." He patted Eric's shoulder to feel the solidity. "Whoever cracks first loses, get it?"

Eric shook his head. "No," he said. Leonard chuckled again, punching Eric playfully on the arm.

"You will." Then he moved away. Eric watched him go, not daring to move. What was happening?

It wasn't long before Eric found out what Leonard meant. Throughout the day, Leonard appeared, seemingly out of nowhere. He passed Eric in the hall, came up from behind Eric, and even stood outside Eric's classes waiting for him. Each time, as soon as Eric was within reach, Leonard reached out and slapped him on the arm, shoulder or back. To anyone watching who didn't know better, it might seem like Leonard was gifting Eric with a fond greeting. But Eric – or more importantly, his power – knew better. Each time Leonard's hand reached out, Eric's power flared in his chest. He had to physically restrain it every time.

It was an insidious plan, one Eric was surprised Leonard had thought of. It was as if all Eric's early attempts at evading Leonard had been a joke. Nothing Eric tried could keep him away from Leonard, who seemed to be everywhere. He wondered if Leonard was somehow using his speed to catch Eric unaware. That should have been impossible. Someone would see him.

Leonard only left him alone at lunch and after school. In those brief periods of respite, Eric struggled with his power, which insisted he was still in danger. He couldn't eat. His stomach rejected anything he tried to put in his mouth. After the third straight day of this, Eric could only sit quietly and breathe. These meditations were the only thing he could think to do to let his fight or flight response reset itself.

"What the hell are you doing, dude?" Jason asked him. "This is worse than staring at track girls."

Eric had anticipated the question and had thought of what he would say.

"Just trying to relax," he said, "If I don't calm down, I'm going to hit Leonard back one of these times, and I'll get suspended."

"I keep telling you," Jason said, "laying that d-bag out again would be so worth a few days sitting at home."

Eric shook his head.

By Thursday morning, even Kristin noticed the toll Leonard's torture was taking on him.

"You sleeping at all?" she asked him before popping a piece of coffee cake into her mouth.

"Yeah," Eric said. "Why?"

"Um, you look like you're not sleeping."

"Just been a bad week," he said. He smiled at her reassuringly. "I'm good."

She didn't buy it.

"You need to tell someone what's going on," she said. "This is getting out of hand."

"I've tried that before," Eric said. "It didn't end well. Leonard is protected. Between the school and his father he's… heh, untouchable." He shook his head at the irony. "I'll figure something out."

She left it at that. Perhaps she sensed she couldn't convince him to do anything. Eric just hoped she wouldn't go to the principal herself. That might cause problems for her.

On Thursday afternoon, just before the final class of the day, Eric finally broke. Leonard passed by him, surrounded by a gaggle of Varsity cheerleaders. They flowed around Eric, effectively trapping him within Leonard's reach. Leonard's hand whipped out, just barely too fast to be normal and slapped him across the face. The force of it spun Eric's head around, and the crack of the contact triggered laughter from the girls.

Eric held it together until they'd passed. Then, his power broke free. His body shook uncontrollably, the vibration in his chest spread through his whole body in a way he'd never felt before.

He felt like he was falling apart.

Terrified that someone might see it all happen, he ducked into the first boy's bathroom he saw.

He checked that the stalls were empty, then he locked himself in one, he thought about how much he was getting to know all the bathrooms in the school. He was going to be spending a lot of time in here if he didn't get this thing under control.

His entire body shook. It wasn't like the kind of shaking you get in your hands when you eat too much sugar. No, this was a rapid vibration in his skin, his muscles, even his bones. What parts of his body he could see were now blurred, making his skin indistinct.

He reached out to the metal walls of the bathroom stall. His fingers sunk in smoothly. He looked down at his feet and noticed they were sinking into the tiles. The white soles of his sneakers were nearly buried in porcelin tile.

No, no, no! This can't be happening now.

He closed his eyes and concentrated on settling the shaking in his body. He felt his arms settle. He stepped high with his feet and felt himself step up onto the tile a few inches.

When he opened his eyes again, he was mostly solid.

He dropped down onto the toilet seat.

What was he thinking? How the hell could he hide this forever? He was a SPI. There was no getting around that. He couldn't hide it forever. He was doomed to be standing against a wall in front of a firing squad. He'd die as a terrorist and a traitor to the AU, that was what everyone would think of him whether it was true or not.

A flash of anger carried with it the idea he should just not hide who he was. He should just walk out there, and be who he was. If he needed to walk through a wall, he should damn well do it, whether he was seen or not. If his power went crazy when he was around Kristin, he should just admit to her what he was. What was the worst that could happen? He had no illusions she would stay his friend. Eventually, she would see what he truly was and avoid him. It was inevitable. That was how it worked.

As for Jason, the "dude" would write about him in the school paper. "My friend, the SPI." It would be a scathing exposé worthy of the old United States conspiracy articles about aliens and secret government torture rooms.

He almost started crying right there. To forestall it, he sat on the toilet for another few moments, breathing heavily and evenly, consciously working to tamp down the power. Eventually, it passed.

Except for the heaviness of depression in his heart, he felt okay. He could work through this. He could persevere. He didn't want to die either killed by his power or whatever brilliant method the AU would concoct to kill the Untouchable Boy. That was the bottom line. He needed to survive, and to do that, he needed to get the power under control. Once he was able to do that, he could ignore it and once more live a normal life, free of fear.

He'd learn how to not think of the pink elephant if it killed him.

Of any chance he'd have to encounter Leonard at school, he felt most vulnerable at lunch, even though Leonard had left him alone at lunch all week. No matter where he sat – he tried to make it a different place every day – he felt as if Leonard would pop out of a shadow and take him by surprise again.

By Friday, he'd given up trying to run. He was too exhausted to try, so he went back to the flagpole. Jason found him after ten minutes, disturbing his meditation exercise.

"You need to start telling me where you're going to be," Jason said. "I didn't think you'd come back here. First obvious place and all."

"Sorry," Eric said without conviction. He looked across the street, where of course Buck was sitting on the curb, watching. He felt bookended by evil SPIs right now. At least Buck hadn't made his move yet.

"I want to show you something," Jason said. Eric glanced at

him and saw that the kid was nervous, glancing left and right. "Promise you won't tell anyone about this, especially Kristin."

"What is it?"

"Promise."

"Fine," Eric sighed. Jason reached into his backpack and retrieved a thin black binder. It looked more like something from an office, not the brightly colored and designed binders most often seen at school.

Jason opened it, revealing several sheets of segmented plastic. They were the type of plastic used for storing collectible cards. In each of the pockets was exactly that. The cards were cardboard, like baseball cards. But they didn't have photos of sports figures on them.

Instead, they had photos of SPIs.

Eric's eyes widened. Something like this was illegal. It was the sort of thing you might see in the EUP, where SPIs were accepted and even worshiped. But anyone caught in the AU with something like this would be arrested as a SPI sympathizer.

"Where did you get those?" Eric asked in a harsh whisper.

"I have a cousin in California. He owns a collectible shop. He had these smuggled out to me, one at a time."

He paged slowly through the binder, letting Eric see the cards in detail. Eric wasn't familiar with any of the SPIs on the first few pages. The photos were new and modern. The models posed in a way to display their enhancements. Little icons in the corner of each card indicated the enhancements each possessed. None of them had more than two icons.

It was insane looking at SPIs like this. The Estados Unidos del Pacificos celebrated it's SPI population, calling them "Superheroes." In the EUP, they were celebrities, hunted only by photographers and persecuted just for their fashion sense. They were figures of awe and respect, thanks to a multi-million dollar government propaganda machine.

Eric had once seen an AUPrimeNews documentary on the phenomena. While the people of the EUP fawned over these icons of power, this only served as a reminder of who was in charge there. The strength and power were always visible; the

SPIs feared like gods. The documentary had referred to the EUP as a theocracy, with the religion of the SPI at its core.

Given that, the idea that these cards were collected and traded, like these people were mere sports figures, seemed very strange. These cards treated "gods" in an oddly mundane way.

On the next to last page, the cards were trimmed in silver foil. At the top of each was the tagline:

FORCE Legacy

At the bottom was the name of the SPI in the photo. There was a card for each of the major EUP SPIs, the members of the EUP's core defense force. These were the elite of the elite, the pinnacle of the EUP pantheon. Each card had at least two icons, if not three.

Fight, a strength, endurance, and agility SPI, was depicted as a woman in sleek black body armor. She was shown breaking through a concrete wall with a roundhouse kick.

Flight flew into his frame on a compact jetpack wearing a uniform exactly like Fight's. His enhanced agility would enable him to control his flying as if born to it. His enhanced coordination made him a marksman with his automatic pistols, which he wielded in the picture as if aiming for the photographer. He also had icons for strength and endurance but wasn't displaying them in the photo.

Freeway was a speedster, the only one with just two icons on their card, speed and agility. The background in the photo of him – or maybe her? – was blurred as if the camera had been swishing left to right in order to catch the subject. Freeway was the only EUP SPI that wore a facemask. The mask had a shiny metal faceplate with a tinted eyeslit. Rumor had it that Freeway was extremely disfigured, the result of his/her first experiments with his/her power. After seeing Leonard smack himself into the shed wall, Eric could understand. Of course, Freeway had both speed and agility enhancements in the extreme range, making it unlikely he/she might make the same mistake twice.

There were a few other top EUP SPIs Eric had heard of on AUPrimeNews, but their cards were missing here, and Eric couldn't remember their names.

On the last page, there were four cards trimmed in gold foil. These were obviously the most valuable cards in the collection. At the top of each read:

FORCE Prime

The photos on these cards were different than any of the others. They were high quality black and white images, taken with a professional camera but not in a studio.

"Are those photos from Texas?" Eric asked. The destruction of the Texas town of Wichita Falls by FORCE was the first time SPIs had exposed themselves to the public.

"Yeah," Jason replied. "Those are the original photos published by the New York Times in 1997."

Each was an image of one of the members of FORCE in action on that fateful day.

In the first, a small woman in a black military uniform stood with her hand raised. A large bank truck, one of the armored kinds, seemed to float in the air. On the opposite side of the image, three figures stood under the bank truck, which seemed to be toppling onto them.

The large-lettered caption at the bottom of the card proclaimed this to be "JITTERBUG," the powerful telekinetic. She had three icons, Intelligence, Telepathy, and Telekinesis.

The second card merely showed a blurry image of a large black form. It was crouched at the knees, wearing the same uniform as Jitterbug. The big man's arms were stretched to either side, as if for balance. It seemed a benign picture until you noticed that the man's feet were buried in the asphalt road he was crouched on, and bits of asphalt were flying up to either side. The man had leaped from a great height, his landing captured on film at the moment of impact.

The caption on this card read, "CITADEL." It had four icons: strength, endurance, agility, and speed. Citadel had borne all of the physical enhancements to one degree or another, it seemed.

The third card was remarkably clear, almost a staged portrait. A youthful, middle-eastern man leaned against a brick doorway, his face pensive. He might have merely been a bystander but for his black uniform, identical to the others.

The bottom of this card read, "MENTAL BLOCK." This was the member of FORCE who had survived New York and even now led the insurrectionist SPIs in the EUP. He could read and control minds on a massive scale. His icons showed intelligence and telepathy.

At the bottom of the last card, the title read, "RUMBLE." The image was of a man standing next to a building, his legs braced and his palms planted on the wall as if he were performing runner stretches. But the brick of the wall, identical to the brick in Mental Block's portrait, was cracking around Rumble's hands. Was he pushing the building with immense strength, or was it something else?

Eric remembered the short mention of Rumble given in the TV show "True Conspiracies." Rumble had been able to shatter steel with his touch. Here, he must have been trying to collapse the building he was touching. What sort of power could do that?

Eric noticed that Rumble had no icons on his card, a strange omission.

These were the terrorists of FORCE, the villains that had destroyed both Wichita Falls and New York City. Eric stared at their pictures, eyes wide. He took them in, memorizing them knowing this might be the only time he might see them.

"This is amazing!" Eric breathed. At the obvious awe in Eric's voice, Jason relaxed.

"I wasn't sure if this would be cool with you. I heard your dad was killed by a SPI."

Eric frowned. Is that what people were saying about him? Eric guessed that was better than the truth. He considered telling Jason what had really happened.

"Something like that," he said instead. Steven Sumner had been a casualty of the chaos years. After the US fell and before

Marshall's Coup that would lead to the founding of the AU, there had been little to no law west of Virgina. Eric's dad had been hard pressed to support his family in such an environment. Unable to stand the pressure, Steven had taken himself to Kansas City where, in a cheap motel, he had taken his own life, leaving his mother and four year-old son alone. Gillian must have spread the rumor that he was killed by a SPI, or at least let the rumor be spread. It was better than admitting your husband was weak and a coward.

"Must have been tough," Jason said.

"It's all good," Eric said, swallowing hard past the lie in his throat. "It was a long time ago. I don't even remember him."

"But don't you hate SPIs?"

Eric glanced to where Buck stood with his cardboard sign. "Some of them, I guess."

"Dude, they're monsters. They can crush you with barely any effort. Some of them can even do it with their minds!"

Eric looked at Jason, confused. He risked himself by carrying this binder, yet he feared the people these cards idolized.

"Do you think it's the power that makes them bad?" Eric asked. "Or are they bad people with power?"

"What's the difference?"

Eric shrugged. He'd had his power for weeks now. He didn't feel any different. He didn't feel like he wanted to take over the school, or Ender, or even to do bad things to Leonard — well, no more than anyone else in his situation would.

Leonard was twisted, out of control. But then, Leonard probably had a couple years on him. How long had he been able to run as fast as he could? Had his power driven him insane? That was what the TV has been saying since he was a little kid. The human mind couldn't handle the great power that SPIs were cursed with. The stress fractured their psyche, it was inevitable. There was no treatment for them. They could only be put down when they became rabid.

The stress was real. He'd already cracked under it once, nearly falling apart — literally — in a school bathroom. How much worse would it get? How long until Eric became like

Leonard?

Eric looked across the street at Buck, wondering who he'd become.

Ken Hunter punched Leonard hard in the arm.

"Come on, man," Ken said. "You need to get over this shit. Let it go."

Leonard Strange nearly hit his friend in the face. His arm smarted, but he wouldn't give Ken the pleasure of rubbing his throbbing bicep.

"Screw you," Leonard said. "I'll stop when I'm ready to stop." He rubbed his aching jaw. It was pretty much healed, but it still bothered him when he talked after a long silence.

"It's getting boring, Lenny."

"Fine, go find something else to do and someone else to do it with."

Huffing angrily, Ken walked. Leonard watched him go, shaking his head. He wouldn't understand. This had to be done. It was his patriotic duty.

He sat at a picnic table at Saints Drive Park trying to figure out what more he could do. The kid had become hardened to his surprise attacks and nothing Leonard could do triggered a response like he'd gotten at that farmer's shack weeks ago.

Maybe if he held Sumner down and choked him out. He'd have to change to get out of that, wouldn't he? Was that too extreme to do in public though? Leonard had to think about his legacy. He'd subtly broken nearly every record at Marshall High and even some of the state records. He had the best time in the 400m, the longest touchdown run, and had led the team to two championships in his Freshman and Sophomore years. He'd thrown the championship game last year to discourage scrutiny. Then, this year, he hadn't even been a part of the team for half the season, and they barely made the playoffs before losing the first game.

If the school or anyone found out that Leonard was a SPI, all those records and championships would go away like smoke in a windstorm.

He had to do this with just as much subtlety as he'd won those games.

A heavy weight dropped onto the bench next to him. Leonard started, cursing himself for getting lost in his thoughts and getting surprised.

"Kid," the big man said. "You make a decision yet?"

The dark man had the physique of an obsessed body-builder. He wore a Gold's Gym muscle shirt that couldn't contain his huge arms and traps. More dark skin was evident below the legs of his workout shorts, revealing hard muscle at thigh and calf.

The man, who called himself Rockhide to conceal his real name, had come to him even before the September incident with Eric Sumner. At first, he'd told Leonard that he was a scout for Illinois University. He wanted to recruit Leonard for the football team in Chicago. But then, when Leonard had broken his jaw, and he'd had to explain to the recruiter why he'd been taken out of his senior season by a scrawny nerd, Rockhide had revealed his true affiliation with the AU government. He'd also revealed another truth.

Rockhide was a SPI.

He knew Leonard was one, too.

What he was really being recruited for was a special, secret task-force within the AU Security Service. A cadre of SPIs with the mandate to hunt down and capture rogue SPIs like Eric Sumner. Rockhide wanted Leonard to out Eric Sumner. The AUSS couldn't move in until the SPI was revealed to the American people. The government needed proof of SPI activity.

It had been Rockhide's idea to put Eric through the wringer in an attempt to get him to reveal himself. An idea that hadn't born fruit.

"No," Leonard said in answer to Rockhide's question. "I need more time. I know I can break him." There must be something else he could do to out Eric without outing himself. His legacy needed to survive his graduation.

"Don't take too much time," Rockhide said. Leonard

couldn't tell if the man was angry or not. "You're golden after you graduate, no matter what happens, but this SPI needs to be outed. His family, his friends, the town — everyone — needs to know what he is. Then we can move in and take him."

"Why not take him now?"

"It's just how this all works. We'll explain everything when you start your training. Okay?"

Leonard nodded.

"I'll get it done," he told Rockhide.

Rockhide smiled and laid a powerful hand on Leonard's shoulder. Leonard could feel the weight of it, heavier than even his father's angry grip. But instead of squeezing, Rockhide just used Leonard to lift himself to his feet.

"I know you will."

AUPrimeMovies - Saturday at 3pm

FROM MANHATTAN TO BROOKLYN: A GENETIC TALE

Note: This program fulfills the weekly Education Programing
Requirement (EPR).

For the first time in ten years, the secrets of the Brooklyn
Project are cracked open.

Let eminent filmmaker Michael Moore take you on a genetic
journey that explains how the Super-Powered Individual was
created, and why this incurable disease will one day erase civilization as we know it.

Geneticist, Dr. William Nye joins Michael in the first in-
depth documentary into the secret science behind the worst ep-
idemic since the Bubonic Plague.

October 20, 2017

Saturday morning, Eric was out just as the sun was peeking over the horizon. He needed to shed all the stress from the previous week. Riding to the abandoned shack, he spent hours letting his power free. It felt good to let it roar through him, unconcerned if the vibration was heard or if he was seen blurred. He took to the toolbox again, trying again to extricate the tools from the locked box. But no matter what he tried, he couldn't pull them through the painted metal case.

When he finally gave up, he didn't feel frustrated. He decided that this was just a limitation of his power. He couldn't bring anything through with him.

The exercise felt good, though. The pulses of his power running through him seemed to soothe his tight muscles like a good massage. When he decided he was done for the day, he felt refreshed and relaxed.

Eric returned home to find his mother returning from her grocery shopping. Though she'd been sober for the last month, Eric was still surprised when he saw her out and about, fully dressed, especially before noon.

He rushed to park his bike and helped her bring the groceries in.

"What are you doing running around this early on a Saturday?" Gillian asked as they both set bags on the kitchen table.

"Just riding around," Eric said, though the real reason was that he guessed Leonard wouldn't be up and about before 8 AM on a Saturday. He didn't play in the Friday night football games anymore, but he still went, and he probably still joined the others to celebrate their victories or lament their defeats until late at night. "All this grocery shopping," he continued, "You're making me eat more lately. I have to watch my girlish figure." He grinned. She glanced at him and chuckled. He noticed that the bags under her eyes had become wrinkles at the corners. Was it a sign that she was recovering, or that she was losing control?

"Well, you might have to go back to eating less," she said, "I've accepted a job at the grocery store. They needed a new cashier, and I interviewed for them yesterday."

"Great!" Eric exclaimed. He hugged his mom. "I'm happy for you."

"I'll be working afternoons," she said after breaking the hug, "so you'll have to fend for yourself for dinner."

"Argh," he groaned playfully, "I guess that means it's back to boxed mac and cheese."

She slapped his arm and motioned to the bags.

"Get that put away," she said. Then she went to the back of the house.

Eric grinned as he began unpacking the groceries. It had been a long time since Gillian had had a job. His father's life insurance checks kept them alive and with shelter, but didn't provide for much else. Having some extra money come in would let them do more. Maybe more trips up to McAlester like they'd done for his birthday.

Things were starting to look up.

He was just putting a tub of ice cream in the freezer, the last of the groceries, when the doorbell rang. Eric's brow furrowed. Who would be coming over to their house?

Leonard?

No, stupid, Leonard wouldn't ring the doorbell.

He leaned over from the fridge, looking around the corner to the front of the house. He saw a familiar figure on the other side of the door. His eyes widened, and he ducked back into the kitchen.

Kristin!

How did Kristin find him here? What did she want with him? What was he going to do?

He couldn't avoid her. If he went around to the back hall-way to his room, he'd have to pass through the living room and right by the open door.

If he went through the wall to get to the back hallway, he could run into his mother.

He could flee the house all together, going out the back kitchen wall, but where would he go from there? His bike was in front.

He took a couple of deep breaths. His power was roaring in his chest. He put his hand there instinctively, accidentally passing the power to the hand. His hand blurred. He stared at it in horror. Any moment, his mother could walk in and…

He heard voices from the front. Gillian and Kristin were talking.

"Eric Sumner lives here, right?" Kristin was asking. "Is he home?"

Gillian said something, but Eric couldn't hear as she was facing out the door. Then, Eric heard footsteps approaching.

His hand was still blurred. He shook his arm, trying to settle the damned thing. He took quick deep breaths, trying to calm himself, but only succeeding in hyperventilating.

He whipped his arm behind his body just as Gillian came around the corner into the kitchen.

She stared at him for a moment. Eric was sure he was caught. She'd seen something, for sure.

"You know there is a girl out front looking for you?" Gillian said after taking him in. She spoke softly so her voice didn't carry to Kristin.

Eric nodded, afraid to say anything. He slapped his hand against his back, feeling the cloth of his jeans against the back of his hand. It had returned to normal.

"Well? Who is she?" Gillian's face was stern.

"Kristin," Eric said. "A girl from school."

"Well, I hope so. She's rather young. If she didn't go to school, I'd be very worried for her. And you." She looked at him longer, her eyes expectant.

"She's a cheerleader," Eric provided.

"Well, that's a plus," Gillian responded, "I guess. But the real question is why I had to answer the door when you're three steps away. Why aren't you rushing out there to say hi?"

Eric opened his mouth to answer, but nothing came out. He closed it again.

Gillian walked up to him and put a hand on each of his shoulders. Eric nearly tore himself away; his chest was still vibrating rather uncomfortably. However, her grip was strong, and he would have had to phase through her to get away. Her eyes narrowed shrewdly, and she sighed as if in resignation.

"Kiddo, I know it's been hard. But the world is not a place you can go through alone. Not this world. You are going to need all the friends you can get. Find the ones you can trust and hold onto them. This girl probably has a hundred friends out there, but she is here on a Saturday morning looking for you, not them. That's a good sign."

The power within him calmed slightly. He nodded to Gillian. He was still nervous, but she was right.

Gillian released him and grabbed his hand, the same one that had been blurred just moments before. She squeezed it between both of hers for a split second, then let it go. She nodded to him.

Eric went through the living room to the front door. He kept the screen door closed between himself and Kristin. She smiled at him, rocking back and forth on her toes.

"Hey," she said.

"Hi. Sorry about that, I was putting away the groceries. What's up?"

"Well," she said. Then she paused. Her smile vanished, and she dropped down onto her heels. "I'm sick of waiting for you to come to a damned football game, Sumner."

Eric rocked back at her sudden ferocity. He stammered for something to say, but the only thing he could think about was Jason saying, "Dude, that girl is pissed."

"So," Kristin continued, her voice returning to her normal, sweet voice, "I'm here to ask if you wanna hang out. We can go for coffee or lunch or something."

Eric's mouth opened and closed like a fish. He turned his head back toward the kitchen to find his mother glaring at him. She jerked her head furiously.

"I'll expect you back by dinner," Gillian called in a voice loud enough for Kristin to hear. Eric looked back at Kristin, who now wore a blazing smile that nearly took his breath away.

"Okay," he said. "Let me grab my stuff."

He checked his pockets and found that he had his wallet and house keys there already. He took his jacket off the hook on the wall by the door.

"Nevermind," he said. "Let's go."

He pulled open the screen door. As soon as his foot was across the threshold, the rumbling in his chest stilled.

Gillian breathed out as the door closed behind Eric. She took a few steps back into the kitchen and slumped into one of the dining chairs.

She hadn't imagined it.

She stared at the palms of her hands, still feeling the ghost of a tingle there. She'd felt it today for the first time in a month. She'd been so frightened, but it was okay.

On Eric's birthday, she'd been startled to notice the slight hum in her chair as she sat next to him watching that stupid action movie – propaganda for the damned AU war against SPIs. At first, she'd thought it had been the loud volume in the theater. But then, it had continued while the credits rolled. She'd noticed the source when Eric rose from his seat, and the humming stopped.

Something was happening to him.

Something she'd seen before.

The power had destroyed Steven. Something more than a mere SPI enhancement, it had taken a good man and ripped him apart inside to the point where he had taken his own life.

And then there'd been Russell.

She hoped Eric would turn out like Russell. Though ultimately it had killed Russell as well, that hadn't been his fault. He'd been learning to control it, letting others help him, where Steven had taken it upon himself to wrangle it alone. She hoped Eric would let others help him. She'd hoped he would ask for help from her before now, but the Sumner men had always been stubborn. She couldn't make him accept her help. He had to decide on his own to trust her.

She'd done so little to make herself trustworthy.

She'd tried to change things. Since that day in the theater, she'd tried to make up for everything she'd done wrong for the last decade and more. To make herself his mother again. But did she really deserve his trust? Could she do anything to help him when she didn't even fully understand what was happening to him?

All she knew was that, in Russell, the power had manifested in his hands. She hadn't felt it there in Eric. Today, she'd felt it in his shoulders. The power came from deep within him, so powerful, it had shuddered up into his shoulders.

Like it had with Steven.

Also, like Steven, he was trying to hide it from her, trying to hide it from everyone. Steven had eventually told his wife, of course, but not until they were married. And even she never knew his full power. He'd pushed it down, frightened or embarrassed by its potential. In the end, Steven had withdrawn from everything and everyone. He'd become a ghost of his former self. His brother's death had been the blow that had led to giving up on himself.

And his family.

There was also the danger that Eric would become exposed, something Steven hadn't faced. Unlike ten years ago, the AU was strong now. It was always watching for exactly this sort of thing. It was clear that many of the "SPIs" they captured and executed on TV were fake. There just weren't that many real SPIs in the world. But that didn't mean that they'd leave Eric alone if he were caught. Maybe they'd wait until he'd done something stupid and they could publicize his powers. But eventually, they would close in and take him.

If nothing else, Gillian had to be there to prevent that. She couldn't let anything happen to her son. She had to protect him until he learned to protect himself. She could watch out for him, make sure the AU didn't find him, but she didn't know how she could guide him in developing his powers. She only knew the slightest bit about how the Sumner brothers' powers had worked.

She did know that Eric needed help from someone he trusted. Someone he could talk to, tell everything to. It had become clear over the last month that person was not Gillian.

So, she put both her hope and fear into this Kristin girl. She had a good feeling about the young lady, an intuition she'd come to trust during the chaos years told her that Kristin was… good. But the AU was relentless in its propaganda. How many of the young people in America believed everything the government claimed about SPIs? Was it worth the risk to let Eric get close to a girl who could expose him? Would she be his lifeline, or the rope used to hang him?

Gillian went to her room and opened the bottom drawer of her chest of drawers. Among her panties and bras, she found the last of her bottles. Eric had found them all but this one. She hadn't given him reason to look for weeks, and it had stayed safely hidden.

She stared at the bottle, a flask-sized glass bottle of rum. She stared from it to the mirror on the wall behind the chest of drawers. It wasn't the first time she'd done this. The bottle hadn't always been in that drawer. It had moved all around her room as she circled it, forcing herself to look at it and put it back.

Whatever the outcome of Eric's friendship with the girl, Gillian had made her decision. Based on intuition alone, she'd thrust Eric's fate into the hands of a stranger. Someone who could make him great or get him killed.

What kind of mother was she?

She put her hand on the screw top. In the mirror, she saw the look in her own eyes as her fingers tightened around the cap. The moment the smell of the alcohol hit her nose, it would be over. Then it would really all be in this girl Kristin's hands.

She didn't like the hungry look in her eyes. She thought of Eric. He needed her, even if he didn't know it now. There must be more she could do for him. At the very least, she could make sure Kristin didn't do anything to hurt him. She couldn't abandon him like his father had.

"Steve, you bastard," she hissed. Almost of its own volition, her hand twisted the top off the bottle.

Eric rode shotgun in Kristin's car, a little green hatchback the size of a pill bottle with the extremely appropriate name, "Mini." It looked brand-new, the smell of new plastic and upholstery permeated the interior.

"Remember," Kristin said, as she took the corner out from the cul de sac about ten miles per hour too fast. "If we get stopped by the cops, you are my twenty-five year old cousin."

"You don't have your license?" Eric asked, gripping the handle above the window, so he didn't fall over the center console into her lap.

"Permit. But I'm a good driver."

"You're insane," he said.

She gunned the little engine in response and ripped down the street, exceeding the speed limit by a fair amount. Eric held on for his life. His eyes scanned the blurring sidewalks, looking for anything that would indicate Leonard had found him or was chasing after them.

After a few minutes, he relaxed. It was unlikely he'd come after Eric when he wasn't alone. Kristin was just the buffer he needed. To attack Eric now, Leonard would need to out himself to Kristin, who would definitely not stay quiet.

She grinned at him when he let his hand drop from the overhead handle.

"You look better than you did yesterday," she said. "A little more relaxed."

"It's Saturday," Eric said. "He's probably giving me a break over the weekend so he can work me up again on Monday." The car slowed, Kristin taking her foot off the gas. She turned to look at him as if the car had its own eyes.

"Rule number one for dates with Kristin," she said, "No negativity. You don't get to be sad, afraid, or stressed when you're with me. Got it?" She glanced forward for just long enough to ensure she was still in the right lane, then returned her gaze to him, waiting for confirmation.

Eric smiled sheepishly. She'd said "date." Was this what this was?

"Got it," he said, "But we need a rule number two."

"Which is?" she asked, her smile dazzling.

"Watch the road. I'd like this to not be my only date." She laughed but turned back to the road.

"I think you're getting ahead of yourself," she replied, pressing her foot hard on the gas pedal. The car leaped forward, tearing down the nearly empty rural road that connected Ender with McAlester at freeway speeds. Eric rolled down his window, letting the wind blow into his face.

"Where did you get this car?" Eric asked.

"I gave it to myself for my birthday in January. Sweet sixteen, you know?"

"You gave it to yourself?"

At the question, Kristin's smile vanished.

"Yeah, well, my parents couldn't give it to me. They're dead."

Eric's good mood evaporated. He rolled up the window.

"What happened?" he asked soberly.

"New York happened," she replied. "My dad owned a financial strategy company in Chicago. He was on a business trip that day to New York. He'd taken mom with him so they could go see a Broadway play together." She shrugged. That was all she had to say really. Everyone knew what had happened. "I was a baby. They left me with my nanny in Chicago. When the chaos settled, I was brought here to live with my grandparents."

"Wow, I'm sorry. That sucks."

She smiled at him gratefully.

"That's okay," she said, "I never knew them. My grandparents are the best I could ask for. My real parents left me money and a company to run when I grow up. 'Poor little rich girl.'"

Eric leaned back in his seat and stared at the road ahead. Kristin wasn't just popular at school. She was rich. She had everything she could ever want. She'd paid for it with dead parents, but like she said, she'd never really known them. She had her grandparents for parents. What more could a girl like that want? Why would a girl like that want a social reject like him when she could have anyone.

"Does it bug you?" she asked after a long period of silence. She'd slowed the car to the speed limit. Was she having second thoughts about this?

"Do you want the truth?" he asked, a small smirk on his lips.

"Tell me what you think I want to hear," she said, the playfulness returning to her eyes.

"It doesn't bug me. It makes me wonder, but it doesn't bug me." He realized that the words were the truth. What was going on? Where was his power? Why wasn't it rumbling inside of him like a lawn mower? How could he be so relaxed right now?

She laughed and gunned the engine again. The little car leaped forward, the yellow dashes running down the center of the road zipped by like bees.

"Why you?" she asked. Her lips were parted, showing teeth and a little bit of her top gums. Eric found that strangely cute.

"I mean, come on," he said, "I'm about as much a loser as you can get. I have no friends. I study science stuff all day. I even read science books for fun."

"Really?" she asked, chuckling a little. "How is that fun?" Eric shrugged.

"I like it."

"What about Jason? He's your friend, right?"

Eric paused, thinking about that.

"I met him the same day I met you. I don't know if he's a friend."

She nodded.

"It's a little sad," she said. Eric glanced at her. She was watching the road intently. "Not that you're 'sad,'" she corrected herself. "I just can't imagine spending all my time alone. Friends and family make life… life. You can never have enough."

Now Eric felt something in his chest. At first, he thought it was a hint of his power, a slight hum. But no, it wasn't a hum, it was an opening of the deep pit he often felt when he lay in bed at night staring at the ceiling. When he thought of his dad.

"That's not my experience," he said quietly.

Kristin glanced at him.

"Damn it, Eric!" she said suddenly, "Rule number one."

"You started it," he said with a wry grin. She slapped his leg.

"Open that damned window and enjoy the wind, Sumner." She pressed the accelerator to the floor. "Let me try and ruffle that beautiful hair of yours."

Blushing, he did as he was told. He lowered the window and stuck his head out. Before he knew it, he was laughing as the rushing wind fluttered his hair. The wind pressed against his lungs through his nose and mouth. It felt strange, but it also felt good.

They arrived in McAlester in what Eric suspected was record time. Kristin moderated her driving a bit when they reached the remains of the Chaos Wall, which marked the city limits. The Wall was a hastily constructed barrier built during the Chaos Years. It was meant to repel the gangs that rose up to take advantage of the anarchy when American police and military forces dissolved. The desperate attempt to protect themselves had failed, and the city had been under gang rule for two years before Marshall's Coup liberated it. Between the gangs and Marshall's army, not much of the wall remained standing.

She took them to a small café in a what might be considered a hipster part of town. Many of the businesses here had signs bragging about being established pre-Chaos Years, a feat few here could boast. When they got out of the car, Kristin ran around it quickly and threw herself at Eric. She hugged him tightly.

Surprised, it was a moment before Eric returned the hug. Just the act seemed to fill up that hole in his chest, the lonely part of him. He found himself holding her just as tight as she was holding him.

They loosened their holds on each other at about the same time. She looked up at him, and for probably the first time, he got a long look at her deep brown eyes and chocolate freckles. Even under her steady gaze, he didn't feel like looking away. He wondered what it would be like to kiss her. He reached up to touch her curly hair, and maybe her face if she'd let him. But she spoke.

"You hungry?" she said softly. His hand froze before it could rise even as high as her shoulders. "Your stomach is growling." She smiled, suppressing a giggle.

He pulled away from her and took a breath. "Starving," he lied. When his arms weren't around her anymore, the rumbling in his chest faded.

They headed into the café, Kristin gripping Eric's hand. He held it back, comfortable with her touch. His power didn't come back.

They ate sandwiches and drank fancy coffee-milk concoctions. Their conversation didn't again veer into the depths that their talk on the road did. Kristin gave Eric the latest gossip about the cheerleading squad and the football team. They'd won the game the night before, despite Leonard Strange sitting on the bench. It was yet another stain on Leonard's ego.

"If anyone has ever had a worse senior year, I can't think of them," Kristin said gleefully. "He deserves every second."

Eric nodded in agreement, though his mind fell for a moment to his last week of torture. Every setback Leonard encountered would make things worse for Eric come Monday.

"He'll get over it," Eric said, careful of violating Rule One. "Maybe the whole experience will make him a better person."

Kristin jerked her head back in mock surprise.

"Eric Sumner! Is that faith in the human race I sense?" She giggled.

"I'm not a monster," Eric said, giving her a self-conscious grin. His mind flashed suddenly to the fact that he was indeed a monster.

"You most definitely are not," Kristin said. She reached across the table and squeezed his hand her eyes touched his again, and he again felt the urge to get closer to her.

After lunch, they took a walk through the streets of suburban McAlester. Fall colors were on display in the trees. And some of the yards were littered with fallen leaves of red and yellow. The air was chilly, but they both wore appropriate jackets. As if she didn't, Kristin leaned against Eric as they walked, her arm coiled around his.

The whole thing felt right.

"I keep forgetting I'm still mad at you," Kristin said after a while.

"What do you mean?" Eric said, suddenly worried.

"You kept blowing me off. You were such an idiot at school. You're not gonna be like that when we go back on Monday, are you?"

"Like…" he was confused until he remembered Jason's advice: Dude, she's pissed at you. "Oh, that."

"Yeah, 'that,'" she said, pushing playfully against him with her shoulder.

"I don't like football," he said.

"You mean you don't like people."

He shrugged, unable to argue with that. It wasn't really that he didn't like people. Just that he felt extremely uncomfortable in crowds. He felt like he was always being judged by what he did, how he stood, or just by his mere presence. Now, it was even worse. Now, for all he knew, he could be judged not by who he was, but by what he was.

"I'm not asking you to join the cheer squad," she said. "Just come and hang out."

He hesitated. He couldn't bring himself to agree just now.

"We'll see," he said. She tightened her grip on his arm momentarily and let the subject pass. She probably didn't want to violate her own rule either.

She drove him home. They sat in the car silently. Eric's fingers fiddled with the latch on his door, but he didn't open it.

"Damn it, Sumner," Kristin said. "You're hopeless."

With that, she hooked her hand behind his head and pulled him toward her. She pressed her lips against his. He returned the kiss as best he knew how which wasn't all that well.

When she let him go, she smiled.

"Not bad," she whispered.

"Liar," he told her. "That's my first time."

"Then you just need practice."

She kissed him again.

His lips still buzzed when he opened the door to the Sumner home. The feeling had nothing to do with his power, but it seemed like all the blood had rushed to his face, especially around his mouth. It felt good. He'd never imagined anything like that, no matter how many descriptions he'd read in books or how many times he'd seen it in the movies or on TV.

Stepping through the door, he was greeted by a depressingly familiar sight. Gillian lay on the couch in her night robe. The TV was on, and a bottle lay in her limp hand.

All the good feelings he'd felt just an instant before vanished as if they'd never happened. He scanned the room out of habit. The bottle in her hand was a tall, rectangular bottle of some dark liquid, probably whiskey. On the coffee table, an empty flask-shaped bottle of rum stood, drained of any liquid. Not even a drop remained at the bottom.

The muscles in his jaw trembled as he took it in. He'd thought this part of his life was over. He now saw that his hope had always been in vain. This had always been an inevitability, just like everything good in his life.

Muscle memory took over.

Eric turned off the TV and carefully worked the bottle from

Gillian's hand. She stirred as he lifted it away. Her eyes opened and worked to focus on him.

"I'm sorry, kiddo," she said, slurring. "I just… Don't hate me, kiddo. Don't hate me. I'm sorry."

She reached out weakly for the bottle, but Eric moved it beyond her reach.

"I don't hate you, Mom," he said.

"Yeah you do," she mumbled. She was already dropping back off to sleep.

Eric put the bottle on the coffee table next to the other and pulled at Gillian's arms.

"Come on, lets get you to bed. You shouldn't be sleeping on the couch."

He pulled her up. Beneath the robe, she was dressed in her blouse and jeans, the same clothing she'd worn while urging him to take the date with Kristin. The sight jarred him from the routine.

He helped her to her room. As they moved down the hall, she clutched at him.

"I'm sorry, kiddo," she said again. "I tried. I'm sorry."

"It's okay," he told her, hoping she'd stop if he reassured her.

"You hate me," she accused. He opened the door to her room and led her in.

"I don't hate you, Mom."

"Yes, you do." Her slurred voice was insistent

He wanted out. He wanted to get away from this. He never wanted to run away from this place more in his life. He pressed his lips together and stuck it out.

He helped Gillian into the bed, not bothering that she was fully dressed. She wouldn't care.

She settled into her pillow as he pulled the blankets over her. Her eyes closed slowly as she sunk into the bed.

"I love you, Mom," he told her as she fell asleep, "I do."

He returned to his room and slumped onto his bed. He stared at the ceiling, trying not to cry. He took a deep breath and released it. He wanted to sleep, too, though it was barely five o'clock. He wanted to escape. Maybe he'd dream of Kristin. It would be nice if his subconscious would be kind and let him forget this for a little while.

But no, he couldn't do that. He pulled himself from the bed and removed his jacket. Dropping it on the bed where he'd rather be, he sighed.

He had mine sweeping to do.

October 21, 2017

On Sunday, Eric kept himself to his room, telling himself he had to prepare for more of the same from Leonard. He found a plan of the school on the internet, studying the paths he normally took between classes. He memorized routes he could take by "ghosting" through walls, emerging into nearby janitor's closets or restrooms. If he needed to, he could cross the entire length of the school without being seen. He could detour into a bathroom or janitor's closet and vanish like Houdini. If he was careful, he could emerge into main hallways just steps from his classes without being noticed.

He told himself he could only use this as an escape plan if the worst happened. This was just the kind of thing Leonard was trying to do to him, force him to use his power. The risk of discovery was high. For now, it seemed Leonard just wanted to test him. Leonard wasn't ready to out himself with a full confrontation, yet. But Eric couldn't be sure how desperate or crazy Leonard would get in the future.

With that in mind, he committed the entire blueprint to memory right down to the machinery rooms in the basement and on the roof.

The next few weeks went by in a blur. Mornings were becoming routine with Kristin and lunch was normally a quiet affair with Jason, but sometimes Kristin joined them. She always sat close to him, making sure some part of her was touching some part of him, even if it was just his hand. Jason tried his best not to comment, but Eric could tell that was a strain. The metalhead wore a mischievous smile every time the three of them were together.

Thankfully, Leonard was out of school another week as he went through his last surgery to free up his jaw and get him back to normal. The week without him was an exercise in dread while at the same time a needed respite. Once Leonard was healed, how much worse would things get?

Eric spent his Saturday mornings at the abandoned tool shed practicing with his powers. He'd given up on trying to phase the tools out of the box. It was impossible. He couldn't get the things he touched to join him in passing through the metal of the box. Instead, he practiced walking through objects. He developed the habit of pushing his head through a wall first so he could check if there was anyone observing from the far side, especially to make sure Leonard wasn't waiting for him again when he came out of the shed. Then he'd walk the rest of the way through. He imagined what it would look like if someone saw a teenage boy's head sticking out of the wall. But what else was he supposed to do?

Since the date with Kristin, he was more confident around her. Somehow, when she was around, the normal buzz of his power was gone. It still came up in classes or at home. But when he was with Kristin, he was calm, even when they stole kisses before school or after chem class.

He didn't want it to end, but he knew that one day it would. One day, he'd lose control and be outed. Even if it was just Kristin that found out, that would be enough. Her parents had been killed by the four SPIs of FORCE. She wouldn't accept Eric for what he was. She'd hate him and turn him in. It was a painful thing to think about, even as he considered it as inevitable as his mother returning to her bottles.

At least there was Jason. Eric began to consider telling his friend what he was. Jason had become more confident about talking about SPIs around Eric. Soon, it became apparent that Jason was obsessed. He loved the idea of super powers. One time the topic came up on a very personal level.

"If you could have one enhancement," Jason asked him one day in early November, "what would it be?" Eric nearly laughed out loud. For a split second, he nearly told Jason everything then. But his common sense overruled him. Instead, he decided this would be a good time to test the waters.

"I'd love to be able to walk through walls," Eric said. Jason glared at him as if the joke was beneath the gravity of the topic.

"No," Jason said, "a real enhancement. Physical or Mental. You can't fly or turn invisible or walk through walls. That's just stupid."

"Couldn't a telekinetic manage it?" Eric asked. "I mean, a person is just a collection of atoms, just like any other matter. Couldn't a telekinetic manipulate those atoms to pass through the spaces between the atoms of a wall or something?"

"Oh, now you're going all nerd on me?" Jason said with a grin. "Okay, I'll play. No. It can't be done. Telekinetics have only ever been able to move whole objects. They've never been able to work on the molecular level. The force they exert is too broad."

"Sure, but…"

"On top of that," Jason broke in, "telekinetics can't target their power inward. The force a telekinetic exerts is the same as if they were acting physically. You can't lift yourself off the ground with your arms. They can't do it with their power. If they could, don't you think they'd be able to fly? But no one has ever been able to fly. Ever."

Eric nodded. Jason's tone was becoming a bit heated. Eric didn't want to argue about it. Technically, the kid was right. No one had ever been able to manipulate matter at an atomic or molecular level before. At least – as far as Eric knew – until Eric himself.

"Even Rumble had to physically shake entire objects," Jason added. Eric frowned.

"Rumble?"

"Yeah," Jason said. "Duh, dude. You know, Rumble? The FORCE guy who they say could shatter steel? He did that by shaking it so fast, it stressed the material to its breaking point. He was just a telekinetic who didn't have the power to lift anything."

"I'd think it would take a lot of power to shake something until it broke," Jason argued.

"Maybe, but he still couldn't lift a penny."

"How do you know?"

"It's in the records, dude," Jason said. "I've read all the FORCE records that were released ten years ago. Most of it is covered in black marker, but the readable parts are pretty clear on that fact."

Eric considered that. All he knew about FORCE was what had been said on "True Conspiracies," which wasn't much.

"Do you still have those documents?" Eric asked.

"Sure, they're in my collection."

Eric was afraid of what Jason meant by collection. He imagined the metalhead had a stash somewhere that would get him arrested three times over.

"I want to see them," Eric said. "Can you bring them to school?"

Jason brought them the next day. It was in another black binder, each page needlessly displayed in a plastic sleeve. Jason explained that he hadn't wanted to hole-punch them, even though they were just print-outs from the internet, not even remotely originals.

Jason even let Eric borrow them, as long as he promised not to remove them from the plastic. Eric agreed readily enough. He hoped that if he was able to study SPIs in more depth, he might be able to crack some secret to controlling his power better.

Jason had been right about the pages. Most of the text was redacted. Entire paragraphs were lost in thick black lines. Sometimes, when referring to one of the members of FORCE, a single word was redacted. That would be the SPIs true name. The document had been thoroughly scrubbed of names, except for codenames. Even the names of other personnel: doctors, scientists, even clerks, had been redacted to protect anyone involved in the program that was codenamed "Project Brooklyn." Brooklyn, Eric remembered, had been a neighborhood in New York City. There had been another famous US project named after a part of New York City: the Manhattan Project, the program that had developed the first atomic bomb.

According to Jason's documents, Project Brooklyn had originally been a program set up during World War II to create enhanced soldiers. Everything else about the program was redacted. Presumably, as "True Conspiracies" had mentioned, the project had worked. It had created the first SPIs.

Somewhere down the line, Brooklyn had become the name under which FORCE had first been assembled, proving that the WWII project had resulted in those SPIs.

Eric finally found the pages where the members of FORCE were initially described. Again, their real names were redacted, as were their other personal information. Even their ages were blacked out. But the description of their powers and their codenames were not redacted.

CITADEL:
Enhancements: Strength (superior), Agility (minor), Endurance (superior), Speed (average)

Eric paused. "True Conspiracies" only ever mentioned Citadel's Strength and Endurance. But according to this, Citadel also had enhancements to Agility and Speed, though at lower levels.

Eric moved onto the next entry, which followed a completely redacted paragraph.

JITTERBUG:
Enhancements: Intelligence (Average), Telekinesis (Superior), Telepathy (Minor)

Eric was surprised to see that Jitterbug was also a telepath, even if a minor one. After another redacted paragraph, there was another entry

MENTAL BLOCK
Enhancements: Intelligence (Major), Telepathy (Superior)

Another redacted paragraph and finally Rumble's entry.

RUMBLE
Enhancements: Unknown

Eric cocked his head at that. Rumble didn't have physical or mental enhancements listed as the others did. But Rumble's accompanying paragraph was not completely redacted.

"[REDACTED] shows a possibly telekinetic gift for breaking down solid material. [REDACTED] vibration until the material breaks. Steel shatters, rock and concrete crumble. Also has the ability to [REDACTED]."

One word in the paragraph stopped Eric cold.
"Vibration"
Jason had obviously fixated on the words "possibly telekinetic," though admittedly, that was what Eric believed his own powers to be. But Rumble hadn't had the requisite enhancements to intelligence that mentally enhanced SPIs nearly always had to some degree or another. If he had, it would have been listed as it was with Jitterbug and Mental Block.
Eric looked to see if there was any other description. The previous paragraph had come at the end of a page. He turned the page and was surprised to see a page completely redacted. However, the pattern of lines matched the pattern of a new personnel entry.
Had there been a fifth member of FORCE?

Eric scanned the rest of the document, but couldn't find any other reference to a fifth SPI in the FORCE or Brooklyn program.

He did find the entry that described the mission FORCE undertook to New York City on September 11, 2001. A lot of it was redacted.

It described an infiltration by helicopter and the disembarking of Citadel, Jitterbug, and Rumble onto the roof of the South Tower of the World Trade Center. Mental Block remained on the helicopter. His powers could be used at a distance, so it was deemed safer to remain on the aircraft.

The next few paragraphs were completely redacted. The next was a transcript of Mental Block's last communication to headquarters, the one played on "True Conspiracies." But even that had spots of redaction. Eric guessed that in a panic, the principles in the conversation had used the real names of the team.

Based on what was printed, though, it was clear that Mental Block blamed someone on the team, either Citadel or Rumble, for the detonation of the nuclear explosion. "He did it," the transcript said, which obviously ruled out Jitterbug, the only female member of the team.

But from what Eric read, he felt that Mental Block believed the explosion was an accident, or at least that it wasn't part of the original plan. Had Citadel betrayed his own team? Or had it been Rumble, the one with the uncertain abilities?

Either way, New York City had been annihilated. Those parts that hadn't been destroyed had been rendered uninhabitable. No matter how it was meant, millions had died in an instant.

Eric closed the binder and put it on the table near his bed. He took a deep breath to soothe the vibration in his chest.

Vibration.

Had there already been a SPI like him? Had Rumble been able to control the atoms of the objects he touched? Was that really telekinesis or something else? The writer of the document hadn't listed telekinesis as an enhancement. They'd said "possibly telekinetic gift."

Eric slumped back against his pillow and spent the next hour staring at the ceiling, considering the possibilities.

December 12, 2017

By December, the pressure Leonard applied on Eric became the new normal. There were no more episodes of lost control. Eric was always ready for something, so when Leonard appeared from nowhere, Eric was able to suppress his power's response pretty easily. In fact, it was Leonard who began to appear more and more frustrated with Eric's resistance. Eric took comfort in that, though it didn't help him sleep any better at night.

The stress of keeping a lid on his abilities under constant threat took its toll. Eric was hardly ever hungry. He ate only because it was time to eat. He picked at any coffee cake Kristin got for him in the mornings. Ate only half his sandwich at lunch and didn't even bother with dinner if Gillian wasn't sober enough to cook. He knew by the looks Jason and Kristin directed his way that they could see the physical changes it was bringing on him.

Only private time with Kristin gave him a break from the turmoil. He credited it with probably saving his life.

They went on more dates to McAlester. Kristin always chose the place, mostly quiet, private places where they could generally be alone: the cafe, the movie theater, or even just a stroll through the slush-covered streets of the city as if prepared for

143

Christmas in unseasonably warm weather. In McAlester, a pop-ulated city with a police presence, Eric could be confident that Leonard would not appear to torment him. It was also a great place for them to just be with each other away from people they knew.

Eric quickly learned to be a competent kisser.

He also bought himself a phone, a little pay-as-you-go thing, the bare minimum. He only had one person who would be calling him. He didn't even give Gillian the number. He even learned how to text on it so he wouldn't use up all his minutes.

As the school-year progressed, Eric focused less on his homework than he had in the past. He found less of a desire to test for next year's AP physics and chemistry classes. He spent more and more time away from home. When he wasn't with Kristin, he spent time at the shack, often just to sit in the silent darkness, hidden from the world.

Rockhide only visited Leonard when he was alone. This time, the SPI strolled up to Leonard from behind as the young man passed Ender Lanes. They walked together silently for a few steps before Rockhide spoke.

"It's time, you need to decide. My boss is not happy with the delay." Rockhide shrugged helplessly.

Leonard scowled. He had moments now to decide which was more important, his legacy, or his future.

"You can protect me?" Leonard asked.

"If the kid is outed, yeah. We'll be so 'busy' taking him down that you'll be forgotten. You can come work for us. You'll dis-appear."

"I want to do it," Leonard said. "I want to be the one to bring him down."

"Leave that to the professionals," Rockhide said.

"But—"

"You've never done this before, kid." Rockhide broke in. "After you're trained and on the payroll, you'll get plenty of chances to be the hero."

Leonard let out a frustrated sigh.

"We'll give you a front-row seat to his execution. On site, not on a TV screen. I know this is personal for you."

Leonard scowled. That sounded like the best deal he was going to get. "Fine."

"Remember, if this goes south, we'll have to take you in. Publicly. It won't be fun for you. So get the job done."

Leonard stopped walking. Rockhide didn't.

What had he gotten himself into?

Alec Gunn

AUPrimeHistory: True Conspiracies

(Airdate: 9/11/2008)

FORCE

\<Archive photos: World War II era comic books>

In the Final War, as World War II has been called, the USA spent millions producing propaganda in the form of illustrated books for children depicting heroic "Super-Heroes" battling the nation's enemies.

But when the reality of Super-Powered Individuals struck the United States, the truth was more terrible than any "funny-book" writer could imagine.

\<Archive Footage: FORCE presentation - slow pan of FORCE>

Their names have been redacted out of existence, leaving only strange and wild code names. The only surviving images of their faces is this footage from their first and only public appearance in 1999. Their covert actions have indelibly shaped the world as the despotic United States government once saw fit. We know very little about them.

\<Archive Footage: FORCE presentation - Close-up Jitterbug>

Citadel's closest companion and his second in command was the strange telekinetic called by the silly codename "Jitterbug." Her mind was her weapon, a cannon more powerful than a howitzer that needed no ammunition to wreck havoc.

<Archive Footage: FORCE presentation - Close-up Mental Block>

Next, was the formerly mentioned "Mental Block," a telepath who can control minds, creating illusions and convincing ordinary people to perform horrendous acts. Somehow he escaped the nuclear explosion when the helicopter transporting him crashed into the sea.

<Surveillance Photo: March 23, 2007>

He is now one of the primary targets of the AU, and this photo, blurry though it is, shows Mental Block in command of a terrorist action in Las Vegas Nevada that cost the lives of twenty-four security personnel.

<Archive Footage: FORCE presentation - Close-up Rumble>

A mysterious, unique SPI, "Rumble" reportedly had abilities never before documented by the government agency that oversaw FORCE. His sole power was the ability to shatter any material he touched, whether it be stone or steel. He reportedly had scant control of his abilities, which has caused some to speculate that his powers triggered something within the World Trade Center building that reacted on a nuclear level.

But was this on purpose, perhaps at the command of Citadel himself? Or was it an accident? When we return, we'll explore the class-action

legal case against the United States of America
and the constitutional crisis that necessitated
the Marshall Coup and the New Constitution.

\<Commercial Announcement\>

December 13, 2017

"Eric," Mr. Turner called from his classroom door. Mr. Turner didn't have a homeroom class. He was purely a science teacher. One of the only teachers not to do double duty for study hall or homeroom. "Can I talk to you for a sec?"

Eric veered off his path and approached the teacher.

"I need to get to homeroom. I've already been late once this week."

"That's okay," Mr. Turner said. "I'll explain it to Mrs. Happ." Eric's brow rose that Mr. Turner knew who his homeroom teacher was. Mr. Turner jerked his head to indicate Eric should come into the empty classroom.

"What's up?" Eric asked, though he was already sure he knew what this was about.

"Is everything okay?" Mr. Turner asked. "You've been falling off the last few weeks. If I didn't know better, I'd expect you were a standard A-minus student." He grinned, his large front teeth showing.

"I'm fine," Eric said. "I guess I've just… I don't know."

"If you need to talk about anything, I'm here for you. You're one of the brightest student's I've ever had."

That comment sent a chill through Eric. He was a SPI. If his powers were based on telekinesis, he would have enhancements to intelligence as well. He'd have to be careful how "bright" he truly seemed to people.

He shrugged. "Maybe I've just hit a wall." Mr. Turner nodded.

"If you need help with anything, I can work with you. We can ease through any walls you have, together. I don't want you leaving Marshall without a scholarship to an excellent science program. I know you have it in you to be one of the brightest minds ever."

Eric's brow furrowed at that. Mr. Turner's comment about "easing" through walls was a little too close to home for him. Shouldn't he have said "breaking" through walls? Did Mr. Turner know something? Had Eric let something slip in class that tipped Mr. Turner off to his abilities?

"I'll let you know," Eric said. "I might just have a case of burnout, ya know?" He didn't want to blame his lack of performance on the fact he had a girlfriend, a super power, and was being tormented by a super-fast SPI bully.

Mr. Turner nodded. Eric left the room just as the late bell rang. He picked up his pace, considering if he should cut through the walls at the back of the library in order to shave off a few seconds. He turned a corner, only glancing up from his feet when another foot tangled with his own.

Too late, he realized he'd let his guard down. He went sprawling to the floor. The shock of impact brought forth the thrum of his power igniting in his chest. He concentrated on his palms, making sure they stayed planted on the tile. The last thing he wanted to do was phase into the floor in front of – he looked up and back to see who had tripped him.

Of course, it was Leonard Strange.

Leonard stepped around Eric slowly. His stance and glare threatened him, daring him to rise and make a stand. His jaw worked in circles as if he were working through the memory of the pain Eric had inflicted on him two months ago.

"I think we've reached the end of our road, Sumner," Leonard said. "I think it's time we lay it all out there, don't you?"

Eric's blood ran cold. This wasn't happening. He'd been sure Leonard wouldn't risk outing himself in public. What had changed?

Leonard crouched down next to Eric who remained frozen on his hands and knees.

"Me," Leonard said, "I can be pretty obvious when I want." Suddenly, without seeming to move, Leonard was on Eric's opposite side in the exact same crouch. Only a breath of air stirring Eric's long hair betrayed the motion. "But I think you need a little bit of persuasion."

Leonard stood and grinned at Eric, who stared up at him in horrified silence.

"How about it, Sumner? I'm ready to go public if you are. You're not the only one who has been trying out new things."

Eric cried out and rolled over. Landing on his back. The blow to his ribs had come without a sign that Leonard had moved. Even the speed of thought hadn't given Eric time to ghost through Leonard's kick.

"See that?" Leonard said, pointing to a camera placed in the corner to monitor the hallway. It was pointed right at them. Leonard had planned this entire thing right down to location. "You're going to show the world what you are. I'm gonna kick the crap out of you in real time. I figure if I hurt you enough, you'll crack and show everyone what you're really made of." He bent over close to Eric's ear and whispered, "I told you, you aren't untouchable."

Eric's chest rumbled as Leonard kicked him again, slower this time. He felt the blow hit him, but only softly. It seemed as if his power softened the impact, letting the kick pass through partly. To hide it from the camera, Eric curled up around the kick.

"You getting fat, Sumner?" Leonard taunted. "You feel a little softer than the last time." He chuckled, perhaps feeling his impending victory.

Eric fought to suppress his power. This was different than all the other times Leonard had come at him. This wasn't going to be a one-touch guerrilla attack. Leonard was out to hurt him, perhaps even kill him. How close to death would he have to be before his power kicked in to save his life whether he wanted it to or not?

Leonard bent down and gripped Eric's coat at the front, hauling him to his feet. The analytical part of Eric's brain noted again that Leonard had no apparent enhancements to strength. Leonard was just a speedster.

Eric turned his mind back to his task. Logical thought was a distraction Eric didn't need right now. His chest roared with his power, scaring him more than anything Leonard had done up to this point. All that needed to happen for Leonard to win was just one instance of Eric ghosting through a blow or being pushed through a wall.

That push came first thing. Leonard heaved with his normal-person strength, throwing Eric toward a bank of lockers.

Time seemed to slow as Eric fell backward. His power thrummed, and Eric could feel it spreading throughout his body, readying him to pass through the lockers to whatever safety was on the other side. Desperately, Eric focused all his strength on pulling back the power. All these last weeks had been a training ground of sorts. He had learned how to hold back the power when he needed to, even when the attacks came out of nowhere. In that moment of time between when Leonard pushed him and his intersection with the locker doors, his power reacted to his will.

He struck the doors of the lockers, causing a crash of metal on metal. One of the latches dug into his back painfully, and he cried out in agony.

Time flashed into full motion again. As Eric rebounded off the locker, Leonard grabbed him again and spun him around, throwing him across the hall to the other wall, which was just painted cinder block. His momentum and Leonard's swift aid hurtled Eric toward that wall even faster than the first.

The power obeyed one more time. Eric's breath exploded from his lungs. He crumpled to his knees. Leonard followed up with a savage kick to Eric's groin.

The pain was unbearable, and his power once more tried to save him from it. As Eric curled up in a ball on the floor, his chest virtually roared, the sound of it even catching in his ears. But before the next blow came, he pushed it down, forcing it deep within him as he was lambasted with repeated kicks to the hard parts of his body.

The blows came fast.

He barely had time to register the pain of one blow before another came. In seconds, his whole body burned in agony.

He covered his head with his hands, trying to at least protect that from Leonard's fury.

"Do it!" Leonard screamed. "Do it!"

Through the pain, Eric heard the hallway begin to fill with students and teachers.

"Stop it, Leonard!" came an adult voice. Eric couldn't tell who. His blood was rushing in his ears. Pain wracked his muscles, his bones, and especially the pit of his stomach, where that first, devastating kick to the groin still resounded.

"Eric!" screamed a feminine voice. Kristin. He couldn't respond, though.

Leonard pushed Eric over with his foot and jumped onto him. If his foot wasn't going to trigger Eric's power, maybe his fists would. Leonard got in two hard punches to Eric's head before someone grabbed him and pulled at him.

"He's a SPI!" Leonard screamed. "I can prove it! I can prove it! SPIiiii!"

The third punch missed his face and struck the side of his neck. Somehow that was worse. Pain exploded through his face and down his shoulder, like Eric's very blood had been bruised.

Eric's entire focus was concentrated on holding back his power in front of all these people and the camera above. He was only peripherally aware of what was going on around him.

Then, someone screamed, and the doors at the end of the hallway crashed open.

It was over.

Eric rolled onto his side and groaned. Kristin was there. She laid a hand lightly on his arm, but when he hissed, she lifted it away.

"Someone help him!" she screamed.

"We've called an ambulance," someone said. "They'll be here in a few minutes."

"Where did he go?" said a frightened voice, maybe a student? Had Leonard escaped?

"Eric," came a male adult voice. Mr. Turner. "You're going to be okay. Don't move."

Despite that, Eric struggled to his knees. He hurt all over. He looked around. It seemed as if the entire school surrounded him. There was no sign of Leonard.

"Take it easy," Kristin urged.

"Where is he?" Eric gasped. Mr. Turner looked around.

"Gone," Mr. Turner said. "Don't worry about it. The authorities will catch him."

"How can you be so calm?" the frightened student asked. Eric looked her way to see Stacy at the edge of the crowd, her face pale and hands shaking. "He could come back and kill us all! Oh my God, Leonard Strange is a SPI!"

"Which is why he's a long way from here," Mr. Turner said in a calm, sure voice. "The sheriff will be here soon, and the AU boys won't be far behind." Eric's head buzzed, and he brought his hand up to soothe it. Leonard's punches were kicking in past the numbness.

Mr. Turner's words and soft tone had a calming effect on Stacy and others who were beginning to get riled up by the cheerleader's terror. Stacy nodded, the flush on her face draining, and trembling hands stilling.

"First things first," Mr. Turner continued, turning back to Eric. "We'll get you medical attention."

Eric nodded in agreement, but inside, his thoughts were spinning. He had to stop them from getting him on an ambulance. Any kind of blood test would out him better than Leonard ever could.

"I'm okay," he said. "We don't need–"

"Let the paramedics decide that," Mr. Turner said. "Trust me." Eric winced at a further buzzing in his head. It wasn't a pain exactly, but a discomfort. Had Leonard broken something in there? Maybe he should have someone take a look.

"Eric, please," Kristin said. He looked up at her and saw hard eyes and a slight shaking of her head. She didn't want him to do anything that would get him hurt further. But he couldn't risk himself now, not after he'd gone through so much to hide what he was. He had to find a way to get out of here before doctors had a chance to look at him. An idea kindled as a wave of nausea passed through his stomach.

"Okay," he groaned. "But I think I'm going to be sick. Just let me get to the bathroom."

Mr. Turner nodded and helped Eric to his feet. He staggered down the hall a ways, Mr. Turner holding his elbow, one of the few places it didn't hurt. Eric looked at the floor and saw streaks of red. Was he bleeding that badly? Had he been dragged across the floor that much? He touched his face, and his hand came away bloody.

Once in the bathroom, Mr. Turner led him to a stall. Eric wretched into the bowl, spitting blood into it.

"Can I get some privacy?" he asked Mr. Turner, who was still standing next to the open stall door.

Mr. Turner hesitated for an instant, then nodded and closed the door.

"I'll be right outside," the science teacher said. "We'll come get you when the paramedics get here. It should only be a few minutes, so be quick."

Quick indeed. Eric didn't have to be reminded that he had to move fast. When it seemed that Mr. Turner had left, Eric latched the stall door locked and felt within him for his power. For a moment, he thought suppressing it like he had might have locked it away for good. But in a moment, his chest thrummed. With a sigh of relief, he ghosted through the tile wall into the girl's room, this time empty due to the distraction in the hallway. From there, he slipped through three more walls, following the map of the school he'd memorized. He knew just about everyone would be back at the site of the fight, so it was easy to make sure he wasn't seen. When he passed through the final wall, he was outside.

He didn't bother getting his bike. He just staggered home at a half-run, avoiding busy streets. He cut through Saints Drive Park, then one of the yards with an un-mown lawn. He circled around one of the rusted farming machines and climbed painfully over a battered wooden fence, eschewing his power in case someone happened to be looking.

The journey home felt so much longer than it did on his bike, even taking the shortcuts he did. Something about it made him think of being a small child with little legs. The blow to his groin still hurt, and he couldn't quite stretch his legs to their full length without a stab of pain there and in his right knee where it felt like someone had tightened a thick iron clamp to it.

Finally, he made it home. He groaned when he noticed the red car in the driveway. Gillian was home.

He circled around to the back of the house and tried to judge where his room was. Then, after looking around to make sure no one was watching, he ghosted through the wall. He came through inside his bed. When he was clear, he dropped himself down onto it, which squeaked as the springs bounced.

He winced at the sound, holding his breath in hopes that Gillian hadn't been alerted by the sound.

No such luck. In seconds, his bedroom door opened and Gillian stood there gaping at him.

"I thought you went–" Then her eyes really took him in. "Oh my God, Eric! What the hell happened?" She went to him and knelt by the bed. Eric couldn't do anything as she started examining his wounds. "Jesus Christ, you're bleeding."

She pulled at him, trying to lift him to a sitting position. His power thrummed, and this time he couldn't hold it back. He just didn't have the strength. He dropped back onto the bed, leaving his mother staring at her hands, which had just passed through his shoulders.

She slumped down, sitting on her heels. Her hands trembled as she touched Eric's arm tentatively.

"Did anyone see you?" she asked, her voice suddenly sober in a way that had nothing to do with a lack of alcohol. She wasn't shocked or surprised. She wasn't appalled at what he was. She ran her fingers along his arm, trying to be soothing without causing him pain.

"No," he croaked. He was still catching his breath from his run across town. "I don't think so. I was careful."

"Okay," she said, taking a deep breath and standing. "Get up off that bed. You're bleeding all over the sheets. Get undressed and let me see where you're bleeding from."

She stood over him until he did as she bid. He pulled off his shirt, already feeling stiffness and bruising on his back. He noticed in his mirror that a large patch of his back by his ribs was red and purple with new bruises. His face didn't look all that great either. Most of the blood was coming from there, minor cuts that bled heavily because they were head wounds. His bottom lip was split and bleeding, the source of a hot pulsing in his face. There was a gash on his left arm, probably where his body hit the metal locker.

He couldn't take a full stock of his injuries himself because he felt pain everywhere.

"God, kiddo," Gillian said. "You may be super, but you are not invincible. What did you do?"

"Got beat up by a kid at school so I wouldn't reveal myself."

"You did this on purpose?" Her worry turned to parental anger.

"No, no," Eric said, trying to make her understand. "He suspected me," he paused, considering telling her that his enemy was a SPI, too and that Leonard more than suspected Eric. He decided against it. She had enough to worry about. "He hates me. He wanted to prove that I'm a SPI, so he beat on me to try and get me to reveal my enhancements."

"Which are what, exactly," Gillian asked. Before he could answer, she fled the room and returned seconds later with the first aid kit from the bathroom.

"You aren't taking me to the hospital?" Eric asked.

"Hell no," Gillian replied as she opened the kit. "They'd do a DNA test on you, and you'd be dead by tomorrow night." She started first with a long compression bandage and tape, wrapping it around his bruised, possibly cracked, ribs. "So? Tell me." Eric sighed. Even though his mother was taking this a whole lot better than he expected, he still felt odd talking to her about it.

"I don't know exactly what it is," Eric said. "I don't have the normal enhancements. Nothing physical at least."

"I wish you'd gotten endurance at least," Gillian said, Finishing the chest wrap and pulling it tight before applying copious amounts of tape to keep it tight. He winced.

"Right now, so do I."

"So what is it?" Gillian said.

"I can pass through things. I think it's telekinetic. Not sure."

Gillian pulled away, looking at him. She lifted his hand putting it between both of hers. It was the same odd gesture she'd done to him after the movie theater on his birthday and a few times since.

He triggered his power and pulled his hand through hers, just to demonstrate to her how it was done. Passing through flesh felt a lot different than passing through wood or metal. It felt like his hand had become a fluid to pass through her fluids. He felt the bones of her hand on his fingertips. Their texture was so much different than her skin and muscle, it was like feeling the wooden handles of the tools in the toolbox.

"It's different," she said wonderingly. Eric's eyebrow rose. She moved away and sat on the edge of his bed, her hands in her lap.

"Different than what?" Eric asked. Gillian's eyes tightened as if she were feeling some internal pain that she was trying to suppress.

"It's not telekinesis," Gillian finally said. "At least that's how it was explained to me."

"Explained to you? Are you a SPI, too?"

Gillian shook her head quickly. "No. But your father was."

Eric's mouth dropped open. He pushed himself away, leaning his bruised back against the headboard of the bed. His father, Steven Sumner, had left them to commit suicide. Was this truly why he'd done it? Gillian had told him it was the pressures of trying to survive during the chaos years. He hadn't had the strength in him to hold out. Now, she looked at him, her eyes suddenly tired, the flesh beneath them sagging further than usual.

"Steven was a SPI. So was his brother, Russell. The government found Russell in '96. Steven hid his abilities from the agents who came for his brother.

"But Russell could barely control what he could do, and it was so different than what any SPI before him could do. The government took him away. To help they said. To make sure he didn't hurt himself or anyone else."

The pieces suddenly snapped into place for Eric. He remembered the dossier on FORCE that Jason had given him.

Possibly telekinetic.

Vibration.

"Rumble," Eric said. "He was Rumble."

Gillian just nodded.

"After 9/11, Steven and I fled the city. We came here. We knew something of what had happened. Russ's power... it was immense. There were earthquakes." She pierced Eric with her eyes nailing the point home. "Earthquakes, Eric. We knew Russ had to be part of what happened in New York.

"We tried to raise you as a normal kid. We knew that it was a good chance you would be like your father. Steven was younger than Russ. His power wasn't the same, nowhere near as powerful. But he was still frightened of it. Afraid of what what it might develop into."

"What was it?" Eric was surprised when Gillian laughed, bitter and sad.

"He could make sounds. Throw his voice, mimic other voices and animal calls perfectly." She smiled with the same wistful sadness. "He used to prank me with it. But he stopped using it at all after we came to Ender. When he vanished, I thought about that a lot. I think maybe it had become something dangerous. He was afraid of what it would do if he lost control of it around us. Six months after he went missing, someone came to tell me he'd been found in a hotel room in Kansas City. It took them almost a month to identify him, with records being what they were in those days. That was that. I was left alone to figure out how to deal with this moment."

She shook her head, tears coming to her eyes. "I don't know what to do, Eric."

Eric gaped at her, unbelieving. She'd had sixteen years to prepare. Sixteen years to tell him what was coming for him.

But, no. She'd checked out. She'd run away, abdicating responsibility for her own son, the SPI. She'd hidden in her bottles, letting him figure all this out on his own.

"I'm sorry, kiddo," she said, possibly reading something of his thoughts on his face. Her voice sounded like her drunk voice, even though at this moment, she was completely sober. Now he knew where that voice came from, shame and guilt.

Instead of screaming, instead of lashing out at her, Eric restrained himself. He closed his eyes and felt his breath. He felt the swirling thrum in his chest and turned it off. Just like that, he found the off switch. All it took was the worst beating of his life and a devastating truth.

"Don't worry," he told her, his voice cold and distant. "I'll be alright. I've been doing this for a while now without you."

He picked up the first aid kit and found a Band-Aid for a cut on his head. He got up just enough to look into the mirror to apply it, carefully avoiding her image in the mirror.

Gillian waited for him to acknowledge her again, even with a glance. When he didn't, she slowly left, giving him every chance to call her back. But he didn't.

He let her go, then tried not to cry as he finished bandaging his own wounds.

Try not to think of a pink elephant.

December 14, 2017

The next morning, Eric walked to school. He hadn't gone to retrieve his bike the day before. He'd just spent the rest of the day in bed feeling the pain in both his body and his heart. He'd heard Gillian on the phone to the school, assuring them that he was safe at home and getting medical care. So he was covered for sneaking out.

Still, he walked slowly, reluctant to be back among people who would stare at him or worse. There was also the threat of Leonard coming to finish the job. Would he come back so soon? He would be hunted now. He'd have to run from the police now. He wouldn't have the strength to run a lot, not without endurance enhancements. So Leonard could either run from the authorities or toward Eric, probably not both. Eric was certain Leonard would choose the former. Leonard would come back for him, but he'd wait for the attention to die down first.

At least, that was what Eric hoped.

He turned the corner on Wall Street to the school and stopped in his tracks. A huge black van, the giant kind with a roll-up door in the back, was parked in the middle of the road, blocking off the stretch of Wall that separated the middle school and the high school. The side of the van sported the shield of the AU Security Service, the branch of the military tasked with protecting citizens from SPIs.

Only then did Eric take a good look at his surroundings. He'd been so lost in his own thoughts that he'd been walking on auto-pilot along the familiar route. Dozens of men and women in black body armor patrolled the perimeter of the schools.

The armor was specially made of light materials and heavily padded on the inside. The plates were designed to absorb blows from strength enhanced SPIs or to cushion the impact of being hurled hundreds of yards by a strong telekinetic. Belts built into the armor carried the tools of the trade for the AUSS — or ASS as they were jokingly called behind their backs.

SPI deterrent technology was electricity based. Most SPIs, even some endurance enhanced SPIs, were susceptible to electric shock if the voltage was high enough. Long batons, cattle prods really, hung from the belts or were carried in the hands of the patrolling soldiers. Tasers were holstered in place of ballistic pistols on their legs.

Bullets were as much as useless for most SPIs. Telekinetics could deflect them, speed and agility SPIs could dodge them, and many endurance SPIs could just shrug them off. Only low-level SPIs or a distracted telepath were truly vulnerable to bullets, so the AU didn't bother wasting the money on handguns. You really only found handguns on local police anymore for normal criminals.

For the major SPIs, the AU deployed men in special, powered armor called S.E.A.S. — Strength and Endurance Armored Suit — impenetrable walking tanks armed with both ballistic and electrical weapons and enough plate metal to take a punch from a Citadel-level SPI or to resist the odd tanker truck being hurled by a Jitterbug-level telekinetic.

No power armor stomped along the street here. Leonard didn't seem to rate it. The camera would have shown the authorities that Leonard didn't have enhanced strength. His history of that broken jaw proved he had no special endurance. So he was just as fragile as a normal person. The AU here would employ speed traps to capture him, electronic devices that could shock a speedster so hard it would freeze their muscles.

Eric took in the set up quickly. He didn't want to be seen as hesitating too long at the sight of the AUSS. That would draw their attention. He also couldn't turn around and go home. He might be able to make an excuse to miss school for a couple days on account of his injuries, but it might seem suspicious if he stayed home the entire time the AUSS was here. Besides, it would be safest to be inside that perimeter if Leonard came looking for him.

He just had to make sure his power didn't even peek out in the remotest.

Having made his choice, he started toward the driveway up to the school. Almost as soon as he was even with the black van, one of the soldiers stepped out from behind it and stood in his path.

"Name," the woman said. Through the armor, it was hard to tell gender, but she had a voice pitched for a woman. Her full-faced helmet was as smooth as glass and darkly tinted. Eric thought he could see traces of lights at the edges of the visor. A heads-up-display? That would be cool.

After a moment of silence, Eric realized she was waiting.

"Oh, sorry. Eric Sumner. It's the first time I've seen one of you guys all dressed up."

"It's okay, kid," the soldier said, "We get that a lot. We're supposed to be intimidating, I guess."

The more she talked, the less intimidating she got. She really didn't sound like she could be a scary person if she wasn't encased in full-body armor.

"You're on the list," she said, "Our investigator wants to speak with you. Go to the library right away, we've set up a station there. Don't worry about your classes until you're done there. You must be the kid who got the treatment yesterday. You look like you've gone ten rounds."

"I'm okay," Eric said. "My mom's a good nurse." He gave her a fake smile and turned away. Now he wanted to get away. In fact, he wanted to go home. What was he thinking?!

Of course, they'd want to talk to him. What happened if he lost control right in front of an AU investigator?

He'd die, that's what would happen. They had to have something that could hold him. Could he pass through electrified steel? Could he phase through an electrified taser pin? There was just so much he didn't know.

And he'd called himself "untouchable." Leonard had been right. It was only a matter of time before someone found a way to take him out. Looking at everything they'd arrayed here to stop Leonard it was hard to believe they wouldn't be prepared for him, too.

Eric did as he was told and headed up toward the library. The library was at the center of the school building, adjoining the administrative offices. It was square with a large square area in the center flooded in sunlight from a sunroof. In the light, plants of all kinds grew. It was sort of indoor garden meant to give the library a soothing atmosphere. Eric sort of liked it, but not enough to make the library a hang-out place.

There were usually dozens of students here at any one time. Bookshelves lined the outer walls, and study desks peppered the floor. This was the place to hang out for a lot of the popular kids who liked to pretend they were studying. With a book open in front of them, they could carry on quiet conversation with friends instead of actually reading what was on the page.

Now, however, there were no students here at all. Some of the study tables had been moved around to make a general U shape. Two computer stations were set up and were managed by dark-suited AU agents. A third agent sat facing the door Eric came through. He was a big man, wider than he was tall. He wore a large, square suit, hiding what must have been a body-builder's physique. At first, Eric guessed he was a SPI, but he was employed by the AU. It was just as possible — more so given his employer — that he was a gym-junkie.

When Eric entered, the big agent sat up in the chair.

"Who are you, kid?" the man rumbled.

"Eric Sumner. I was told to come here."

The man scowled, sliding across the desk area and snatching up a computer printout. He scanned what was on it.

"Oh, you're that kid. Get over here."

The agent's manner was rough. Eric instantly had a feeling he wasn't liked, or even considered much, by this man, despite him being the victim of a SPI attack.

"Investigator Roger Hamilton," the big man said. "You can call me 'sir.'" His eyes came up to look at Eric for confirmation. They were a smooth, slate-gray peering from beneath thick reddish eyebrows a shade lighter than his short brown hair. "Sit down."

Eric saw a single chair set on the outside of the U of tables. He pulled it out and sat as he was told. As he had with his mother, he set the off switch on his power and concentrated on keeping it there. He didn't trust it any more than he trusted this AU government thug.

Agent Hamilton sat opposite Eric. "Give me the story, from the beginning." Eric was glad this man wasn't a doctor. He'd kill patients by his bedside manner alone.

"I'd just come out of a classroom and—" Eric started

"What were you doing in the classroom?" Hamilton cut in.

"Talking to a teacher about my grades. Mr. Turner." Hamilton nodded and made a mark on the paper in front of him, the same one he'd looked at to check Eric's name. "So, anyway, I was coming out of the classroom, and Leonard tripped me. Then he started wailing on me, screaming about how I was a SPI."

"Are you an S.P.I.?" the investigator asked. The other agents in the room all looked up at them from their computer screens. All eyes were on Eric.

"No," Eric said. A buzz of a headache washed over him, and he ran his hand back over his head to soothe it. He'd taken so many kicks and punches in the head yesterday. He wondered if the headaches would ever go away.

With that one word, the agents went back to their work. Hamilton nodded and made another mark on his paper. Finally, he looked up at Eric expectantly.

"That's it," Eric said with a shrug. "They pulled him off me. I don't know how he got away. I had my own problems. I wasn't paying attention."

"You didn't stay for the paramedics," Hamilton said. "Why did you leave?" His eyes were angry as if Eric were a drunk driver who'd fled the scene of an accident.

The headache roared back, forcing Eric to wince and lean his head into his hand.

"Can I get something to drink, and maybe a pain pill?" He circled his hand in front of his face to indicate his injuries. The Tylenol he'd taken earlier seemed to be wearing off, though it hadn't been that long ago.

"Answer the question."

"I don't know," Eric said through gritted teeth. "I'd just had my head kicked in a few times. I really wasn't thinking straight. I just wanted to go home."

Hamilton made a third mark on the paper. He wasn't taking notes. His marks were short and seemingly meaningless.

"Okay," the investigator said. He reached back around to one of the computer stations. "This ready?" he asked the agent there. He got a curt nod for an answer. It seemed no one in this room was a talker.

Hamilton took something from the desk and turned back to Eric. He placed it on the table in front of Eric. It was a small black plastic disk that looked a little like the flying saucers from the classic alien-invasion movies. On top of it was a red button covered under a clear-plastic dome.

"We want to keep an eye on you, in case Strange comes back for you. If you see him, even at a distance, you press the button." Hamilton's thick finger pointed to the obvious button on the disk. "All other times, you keep this in your pocket. Don't lose it. Understand?" Eric nodded. "Front jeans pocket. Not the back pocket. Don't sit on the damned thing." Eric nodded again. Hamilton's sleepy gray eyes rested on Eric for a little longer. "Don't try to take it apart. If it's broken when you need it, we won't be able to help you. Get it?"

"Got it," Eric said. Hamilton sighed.

"Good. Get out of here."

Eric got up and took the device. He made a show of putting it in his front jeans pocket, to which Hamilton nodded.

"At least you heard that much," the investigator growled.

Eric was glad to be able to leave that place.

Roger Hamilton watched silently until the boy was out of the room. Then he turned his chair around to face the others.

"I need to make a call," he said. They obeyed his unspoken command, rising from their seats and crossing to the other side of the library to take seats out of earshot. When they'd seated themselves, Roger took his cell phone from his pocket and placed it to his ear without dialing.

"That was Eric Sumner?" he asked out loud. Speaking was the only good way to focus his thoughts enough for his boss to hear him from several states away.

That was him, said the voice in his head.

"He was telling the truth?"

Of course not, the voice chided. Is your head as solid as your skin, Rockhide? I nearly revealed my own presence when I probed him. Those headaches of his were concealing his thoughts. But we know enough to know better.

"His ability?" Rockhide asked.

Possibly. Or his head trauma could be severe enough to cause interference. Make sure you're watching him. They're to monitor the device 24/7. If I ask where he is at any given time, I want an answer immediately, understand?

Rockhide nodded sharply. He was well aware of what happened when those who lacked faith in Edward disobeyed. Rockhide believed in Edward. The man had rebuilt a nation from the ground up after all.

"We'll get the answers you need, Edward."

Your first priority is to figure out Eric Sumner. But don't loose sight of the speedster either. You did well with your push. Now it's time to reel him in.

Rockhide nodded. He didn't need to acknowledge such

obvious orders. Not verbally.

He felt the presence in his head recede. When Edward was gone, Rockhide resumed his "Roger Hamilton" identity and motioned for his agent to come back to the tables. When they'd resumed their stations, he gave his orders.

"You take shifts. One of you is on this monitor at all times." He indicated the computer through which the tracker's signal was monitored. "All times," he stressed. "The other is working on the Leonard Strange issue. I want him found."

They both acknowledged the orders.

AUPrimeMovies - Monday at 7pm

THE SMURFS: A NEW HOME

Note: May be delayed for televised execution.

Join the Smurfs as they travel to new lands and battle the evil mad-scientist Gargamel (James Carrey) in their newest live-action adventure!

When Chicago falls under the dark cloud of Gargamel's SPI-machine, only Papa Smurf and his little blue family can save the world!

Fun, excitement and laughs abound in an adventure the whole family can enjoy!

December 14, 2017

When Eric stepped into homeroom, Mrs. Happ was nearly through the day's announcements. She paused as he entered. Eric felt every eye on him. He tried to ignore it and went to his seat. His power thrummed momentarily, but he shut it down with a thought. It still tried to have a mind of its own. He might have to spend full-time concentration on stilling it which would suck.

The teacher continued without a word to Eric. Apparently, getting your ass kicked by a SPI was excuse enough to be late the next day.

The kid sitting behind him poked him in the back, causing him to hiss in pain. He twisted in his chair to scowl at Andrew Stockton, a short fat kid with greasy blond hair.

"I heard you're a SPI," Andrew whispered. Apparently, he wasn't as quiet as he thought. Every eye in the adjoining desks turned toward them.

"If I were a fucking SPI," Eric hissed, using language he wouldn't have used if his body didn't hurt so much. "Do you think I'd let Leonard touch me without killing him? You're an idiot."

Andrew's eyes widened. "Well, he's a SPI, too..." Eric just scowled at him.

"Don't touch me," Eric added, "I hurt everywhere."

"Sorry, man," Andrew said. He really looked apologetic.

"Is there something you'd like to share?" Mrs. Happ said. Eric's head snapped to the front. At first, he was going to shake his head and be silent, but then he thought better of it.

"I was just telling Andrew not to kick my desk. I still hurt."

"Good advice," she said, "Everyone, Eric has been through a tough trauma. Please just give him a modicum of respect and peace."

Eric gave her a fake smile and nodded his thanks. A little over-dramatic, he thought, but it got his point across. He was a sissy. He was weak. He was damaged.

He was not a SPI.

Kristin hugged him when he got to chemistry class. He winced and pushed away.

"Sorry, still hurts," he said.

She looked at his face, which had been mottled red, yellow and purple in the mirror this morning.

"You okay?" she asked.

"I hurt," he replied, "But I'm okay." He'd decided to play up the pain. He exaggerated a limp, using the stiffness in his knee for inspiration. He wanted to make it clear to everyone that he wasn't a SPI, so he projected himself as weak as humanly possible. He'd gotten the idea from Buck, who had used the tactic successfully for years, apparently.

Kristin gave him a sympathetic smile, and they went to their chairs. Mr. Turner gave him a proud grin that Eric forced himself to return in an encouraging manner.

"You gave me quite the slip yesterday," Mr. Turner said in a conversational tone.

"Sorry about that," Eric said, "I just wanted to get out of there. All the attention, you know?"

"Well, next time, you should trust us." Something in Mr. Turner's voice indicated he meant "trust me." Again, Eric found himself wondering if he'd tipped the man off to what he could do.

Was Mr. Turner a SPI sympathizer?

"I wasn't thinking straight," Eric said. Which was only a little bit of a lie. His head still hurt, and there was a buzzing in his ears even now. Maybe he should have seen a doctor. Could he have a concussion?

"Don't worry about it," Mr. Turner said. Then he got on with the class, raising his voice so everyone could hear him.

Eric couldn't use the flagpole for lunch. There were too many AUSS agents wandering the front lawn of the school. It was disconcerting. Instead, he went back to the football field.

Jason was already there. Eric raised his eyebrows.

"How did you know I'd be here?" he asked.

"Dude, how'd you know I'd be here?" Jason replied. "I got here first. You looking for me?"

"There are too many people out front today," Eric explained.

"Exactly," Jason agreed.

Eric sat on the bench next to Eric. He opened his lunch bag and started in on his sandwich. Gillian was making his lunches now, so there were no M&M's. Only chips and a banana. Lame.

"It's good to see you're still kicking," Jason said in an uncharacteristically sober tone.

"Don't say 'kicking,'" Eric said, putting his hand to a particularly nasty bruise on his face. He tried a smile to show Jason that he was only teasing. "But thanks."

"Dude," Jason breathed after a few moments of silence. "I never imagined Leonard was a SPI."

"Star of every running sport in school? Hindsight says he had to be." Eric laughed, which caused a stab of pain in his stomach.

Eric finished the sandwich and chips, but he handed the banana to Jason, who wolfed it down. While Jason ate the banana, Eric reached into his pocket and pulled out the panic button Hamilton had given him. He turned it over in his hand thoughtfully.

"Whass 'at," Jason said with his mouth full.

"This scary AU guy gave it to me. He's making me carry it around in case Leonard comes back. Panic button or something. Supposed to make the storm troopers come running, I guess."

Jason dropped the banana peel to the ground and snatched the button from Eric's hand. Shocked, Eric tried to grab it back, but Jason held it away.

"Give me a sec," Jason said. He turned the thing around in his hand, testing the clear plastic cover on its hinge to expose the button. But he didn't press it. After a second, he closed the cover again. "Dude," Jason said, taking a deep breath as if to ready himself, "This isn't a panic button, not exactly. It's a tracker. They're keeping an eye on you. Following your every move. At least there's no microphone in it."

"How do you know?" Eric said, taking the black disk back. He'd never heard Jason so serious before. His entire voice changed as if the whole "dude" thing was an act.

"Du–" Jason started. He hesitated, making a quick scan of the area around them, even going so far to look beneath them under the bleachers. When he looked back up at Eric, he looked scared. "Dude, I know you're a SPI," he said, letting the words hang.

Eric let the silence fester a little too long. "What are you talking about?" he finally said, but even to him the words seemed hollow and false. He didn't want to lie to Jason. But at the same time, being outed scared the crap out of him. Even now, his heart raced in his chest and his power pulsed along with it.

"It's a long story," Jason hedged. "After you took out Leonard the first time, my parents wanted me to approach you. To keep an eye on you. To keep you out of trouble, even." He laughed at that. Then he threw his hands up. "I wanted you to tell me, dude, not the other way around."

"Your parents?" Eric asked. "What the hell is going on?"

"I told you about my cousin in California, right? Well, we're all from California. My parents work for the EUP government. I guess they're spies. Not S-P-I spies, s-p-y spies, as in espionage, you know? I've been here since I was little, but I know we moved here from California because Mental Block ordered it."

"Mental Block…" Eric said. It was the only thing that could come to his mind. He felt numb. While pain raged in his body, his mind was blank.

"Dude," Jason pleaded, "I'm sorry. You're a cool guy. You really are my friend, you know? Sure, I came to see you that first day because my dad told me to, but I stuck around cause I wanted to. I'm serious."

"I don't know…" Eric still couldn't form a coherent thought. Was Kristin a plant, too? Was this whole year a sham? Would he even have these "friends" if he wasn't a SPI? If people didn't want something from him?

"There's a bottom line here, dude," Jason said, grabbing Eric's arm to get his attention. "You're in danger. The AU knows about you. They wouldn't have planted that thing on you if they didn't. They're waiting for you to screw up, to do something stupid in public. Then they're gonna move in and take you. It's how they do it every time."

"Then… Leonard?" Jason's words were giving his mind something logical to latch on to. He worked through the steps. Leonard had gone public.

"They've probably been working him a while now, trying to get him to snap. Who knows what they did to finally make him go after you at school. It definitely wasn't the smartest move, right?"

"Wait, you said your dad told you to come interview me? How did he know? I barely knew at that point. How does the AU know?"

"You know who you are, right?"

At those words, Eric's world fell apart. He tried to get to his feet, but his leg phased through the metal step of the bleachers, and he landed back on the bench with a bang.

"Dude!" Jason cried, "Chill, dude." He reached down to pull Eric's leg out from the metal. Eric let him. Jason's face was swiveling from right to left to see if they'd been observed. The metal bleachers buzzed with Eric's power. Eric didn't care. He stared into space.

Everyone had known. Everyone. This whole time, the only person who hadn't know what was going on was him. Gillian, Buck, Jason, the damned AU. Because he was Rumble's nephew, they knew.

Everyone!

Eric's face suddenly exploded in pain as Jason punched him. The blow came out of nowhere. Not even his subconscious had seen it coming in time for him to phase through it. Then, Jason was gripping his shoulders and growling into his face, straddling the bench in front of him.

"You need to stop, Eric, now!" It was more Jason's use of his real name, rather than "dude" that got Eric's attention. His eyes focused and he found them locked on Jason's desperate, terrified blue ones. He took a breath and shut the power down.

"It's all a lie, man," Eric said. That gave him a thought that chilled him to the bone. "Does Kristin know, too? Is she one of you?" No, that couldn't be. Her parents were killed by SPIs. She might have tried to kill him if she knew.

Jason shook his head. "No. As far as I know, she's just a girl. That's why I keep getting pissed off when you screw that stuff up." He laughed and slapped Eric's shoulder. "You're friggin' clueless, dude." He sat back on the lower bench, catching his breath as if he'd just run the track.

"Yeah, I was," Eric said. They sat there for a while, just quiet. Eric's mind squirmed through the dominoes that brought him here. But he didn't have enough knowledge to place the next one so it would fall where he wanted it. "What now?" he finally asked.

"First thing," Jason said with confidence, "We need to take care of that tracker. I'm gonna get my mom to tech up something. You need to go about your day as if nothing has changed. You come to school, do your work, go home. Don't go anywhere else. Don't use your powers. Not for anything until you meet my mom. Give it a week. Then the tracker will have enough data to loop. The Security Service guys will think you've just got a regular routine. After that, we get you the hell out of Ender."

"Out of Ender…" Eric said. It was a good idea. He needed to

get away from the AUSS, from that monster, Hamilton. Hamilton knew. Hell, Hamilton probably knew more about him than Eric did. That creep had looked at him like he didn't know like he had to consult a paper to figure out who "Eric Sumner" was.

"It'll be okay, dude. We'll take care of you. We have plans for this sort of thing. You'll see."

"Yeah," Eric said flatly, "Cool." He sat on the bench, staring blankly at the Marshall High School football field until the end-of-lunch bell rang.

December 14, 2017

Kristin pulled the white cotton shirt over her head and tugged it down. As soon as her head popped out of it, Stacy's hand slapped onto her shoulder.

"You're topping today," Stacy said. That's what she called the person who was the peak of the pyramid in their contest routine. Football was over for the year, but there was still the cheer national championships to look forward to if they made it this year.

"Lin-with-an-i usually tops," Kristin said, "She's lightest." There were two "Lin/Lynn"'s in the squad, so the little Chinese girl, who was the newer of the two, had her name extended to accommodate.

"Yeah, but you're prettier," Stacy said, teasing Kristin's long curls in her fingers. Kristin batted Stacy's hand away with a grin.

"Bull," she said. "But okay, I'll do it."

"Of course you will," Stacy said in a sing-song voice. "You're awesome!"

It was a nice day for December. There was no snow on the ground, and the temps hadn't gone below fifty. Stacy decided to have after-school practice outside on the football field. The competition would be indoors, thank God, but why not enjoy the sun while it lasted?

They started practice with stretches and simple choreography. Stacy was changing it up. Something just wasn't right.

When they got to the pyramid, Stacy set Lin and Lynn to either side and stacked the remaining six girls with Kristin at the top.

As Jessica and Stacy lifted Kristin to the top, she thought for a moment that something was off. It was too simple. This was supposed to be a competition routine. They should be bringing it. She reached the top. Lin and Lynn moved to the front to catch Kristin as she came down.

In such a routine, Kristin would leap from the top with the help of the people holding her feet, in this case, Stacy and Jessica. She'd perform a flip in the air and land back down on Lin and Lynn's arms, safely caught and set on her feet.

Kristin counted the four count that the routine required, then bent her knees for the flip.

That's when it all went wrong.

Jessica's hand on Kristin's foot gave a little, then pushed up, as it was supposed to. Stacy however, gripped Kristin's foot tight for half a count too long. Kristin's leap was jarred. She tumbled through the air to one side instead of leaping straight forward. Instead of landing in the Lin-Lynns' arms, Kristin hit the wet grass, luckily flat on her back.

Instead of suffering a broken limb or a cracked skull, her breath was ejected from her mouth as her lungs flattened. Pain rocketed through her body, the bruising impact rattling down even through her legs.

She lay there for a while, trying to get her lungs to help her breathe again as the squad collapsed the pyramid and rushed to her side. Stacy bent over her, worry and shock on her face.

"Oh my God, Krissie, are you all right?" the cheer captain cried.

"What the—" Kristin tried, but then coughed as she struggled to sit up.

"Is anything broken?" Stacy asked.

"Someone get Coach Stewart," Lynn said. "Maybe we need

an ambulance."

"No," Kristin said, her breath was finally starting to return to her. "I'm okay. Nothing's broken. I'll be okay."

Stacy laughed in relief. She helped Kristin to her feet.

"You lost count, didn't you?" Stacy asked her. She didn't wait for an answer. "Maybe that'll teach you to focus on what's important. That's how you get hurt."

Kristin gaped at Stacy. Focus on…? This was all about Eric?! This had all been a setup. Even working on the field was part of it. Stacy had been planning to dump her the entire time. If this had happened in the gym, and not on the soft, snow-melt-wet grass of the field, Kristin would definitely have broken something.

She couldn't bring herself to argue with Stacy. The others were laughing it off as a near miss. Had any of them been in on it? Kristin glanced at Jessica, Stacy's BFF. Jessica showed nothing but concern on her face.

"Maybe Lin-with-an-i should be topper after all," Stacy said before turning away. "Take a break," she called out, "Five minutes, then we'll start again."

Lin and Kristin traded positions, and they went through the routine again. But for the rest of the practice, Kristin couldn't find her enthusiasm. Her smile was fake, and she was sure it showed. For the first time since she could remember, she felt like she was with strangers among her friends. But she'd never had any problems with strangers before. Strangers were never strangers for long, not for Kristin.

This was worse. This was something Kristin had never encountered before.

Was this how Eric felt around people? Scared and unsure?

She wished he was here now. Even as she was going through the motions of the routine. She wished he were out in the bleachers watching. Where was he now, she wondered?

"Kristin!" Stacy shouted, "What did I tell you? Focus!"

Kristin was glad when the practice was over.

Kristin caught up with Stacy as they left the locker room. She followed Stacy until the cheer captain broke from the other girls clumped around her and headed for her car. When they were safely alone, Kristin grabbed Stacy's arm and spun her around to face her.

"What the hell was that?" Kristin asked. Her heart thudded in her chest, but she'd decided as she felt herself floating away from the other girls that this was something she couldn't let go. Just weeks ago, Kristin would have been comfortably one of them, laughing and joking right there in the gaggle around Stacy. Now, she felt… apart. She couldn't let that stand.

"I told you," Stacy said, not even pretending that she didn't know what Kristin meant. "You need to focus on what's important."

"What does me spending time with Eric Sumner have to do with anything? You're all my friends," she paused, not sure if that was true anymore, "At least you were."

"Because you choose to socialize beneath your station," Stacy said. "He's dragging you down, Krissie. You're only as good as the people you hang around with, and right now…" she left the sentence hang and shrugged her shoulders.

"So you decided to try and kill me?"

Stacy rolled her eyes. "No one was trying to kill you."

"What would you have done if I'd landed on my head? Broke my neck? Would you have pretended it was an accident?" She was furious now. Her hand trembled so much, she crossed her arms and tucked her hands into her armpits. She watched Stacy for some kind of remorse. Stacy just shook her head.

"You're being over-dramatic, Krissie. That wouldn't have happened. Listen," she said, putting her hand on Kristin's arm. "All you need to do is let the loser go. We can all be friends again. It can all be the way it used to be." She spread her arms and smiled. "We have a championship to win, sister. We can't do it without you."

Let the loser go or be cut from the team. That's what she was saying. This was it. This was the ultimatum.

Kristin stared at Stacy. The girl was oblivious. Kristin looked back at the retreating gaggle, all heading for their cars, either their own or the waiting sedans of their parents. She wondered if they agreed with Stacy. Still, this was something a lot of them dreamed about. They had a good squad with a real chance of going all the way. It might not be this way next year, and there were only two more years after that if they made the varsity squad. Then cheer was over. No one cheered in real life, college aside. This could be the only chance her friends had of making something of their high school careers.

Kristin wanted to walk away. She wanted it with every fiber of her being. In truth, she wanted to give Stacy a punch across the face before telling her to screw herself. Stacy could rot in hell without a championship trophy for all Kristin cared. But it was too late in the year to start training up alternates. If Kristin was cut, that would leave the squad with an odd number, making choreography more difficult. This wasn't about Stacy, then. It was about Jessica, the Lin-Lynns, and the others. She couldn't abandon them. They might still be her friends, and for the sake of their accomplishments, Kristin couldn't leave them.

Stacy saw the decision in her face. She grinned. She went in for a hug, but Kristin held out her hands, pushing her back.

"I won't leave the team," Kristin said. She pointed at the others as they all drove away. "They're still my friends. I'll do what I need to do to keep it that way. You, though." She paused, not believing she was going to say this. "I've never…" she pressed her lips together, trying to hold back the tears that threatened in her eyes. "I've never hated anyone in my life. Until now."

Before she broke into tears, she turned quickly and nearly ran for her car.

AUPrimeNews Archive

(Posted: 11/2/2015)

KANSAS CITY IN FLAMES

Kansas City, MO - The AU apprehended another Super-Powered Individual today, though at tremendous cost in life and property.

An estimated two hundred are dead, and a further three-hundred or more are wounded as the EUP terrorist James Robert Gilmore rampaged through downtown Kansas City this morning at 7:30 AM. When police tried to arrest him, they discovered his enhancements to strength and stamina prevented them from manually apprehending him.

After a short standoff in an apartment complex, Gilmore exited the building, apparently ready to surrender. However, he overpowered the police, killing three officers and destroying a police cruiser in the process. His further attempts to escape escalated the situation, forcing AU police to resort to more drastic measures, including shock nets and armor piercing bullets. The resulting chaos brought Kansas City to its knees.

Gilmore was finally apprehended only when his rage and insanity brought about his own destruction. Trapped in the famous Warren Hotel and surrounded by authorities, Gilmore destroyed the support structure to the building, dropping the entire thirty-story structure straight down upon him and all the remaining occupants. Excavation activities are currently underway to retrieve Gilmore and prepare him for execution after the mandatory DNA screening.

December 15, 2017

Eric pulled up to the school building feeling the weight of the AU tracker in his pocket. He'd done as Jason asked. After school the day before he'd gone straight home. He'd spent a boring afternoon and evening holed up in his room to avoid his mother. He didn't want to tell her he was being tracked by the AU because they knew who and what he was. It was bad enough to watch the AUSS spread through Ender on AUPrime-News. The little Oklahoman town had become the center of national attention as AUPrime made the manhunt for Leonard Strange the number one story all over the country.

"Terror in the Heartland," the headline read at the bottom of the screen while the talking head played up the danger the citizens of Ender were in, while carefully deflecting any idea that Leonard might flee Ender and terrorize some other American town. It was one thing for Americans to see others in danger, but quite another for them to believe they were all in danger. The AU wanted Americans to feel safe, after all. A panic wouldn't be good for optics.

No, Ender was cordoned off. If Leonard tried to escape, he'd be captured.

Eric knew better. Leonard wasn't going to try and leave Ender, or at least if he did, he'd be back. Leonard wanted to out Eric. The bully wouldn't leave that job unfinished. He was just surprised Leonard wasn't spray painting "Eric Sumner is a SPI" on every flat surface he could find.

Kristin wasn't waiting for him at the door this morning.He hadn't really seen her since chemistry class the day before, and they'd both been busy paying attention to class.

Hoping she was in the cafeteria waiting for him, he went straight there.

She was there, surrounded by her cheer squad on a long table. The blond girl, Stacy, sat across from Eric, her eyes on the door as he walked in. She said something to Kristin. Kristin turned around as Eric reached the table.

"Hey," he said. She didn't smile at him. She seemed upset. She glanced back at Stacy, then at some of the others. They were all looking at her expectantly. A sense of foreboding touched him even before she spoke.

"Hey," she said back. "Listen, I don't think we can, um, hang anymore. You know, championships are coming up soon, and I need to, um, focus on cheer."

Eric looked from her to the others. One of the ones he didn't know, a brunette who had dyed her hair in an attempt to make it look red, sneered at him. Stacy had a grin on her face a mile long, as if she'd already won whatever championship they were competing for.

He nodded to her. After all, he'd been expecting this for a long time now, so it wasn't a surprise.

Not at all.

He turned around, not wanting to look at the cruel faces of the cheerleaders anymore. As he moved away, a chuckle went through the group. It was cut off by a hard slap to the table top. Eric suppressed the urge to look back to see who among them had done that. It didn't matter anyway.

"Well," came a voice from the table, Stacy. "He took that better than I thought he would."

Numb, Eric walked slowly through the hall. He didn't know what to do. There was still twenty minutes until the early bell. What had he done before meeting Kristin? He couldn't remember.

I need to focus on cheer. It made no sense. Surely cheer was just a couple hours a day at most. The looks of the other girls told him that she'd been pressured to break up with him. It must not have taken much pressure. How much convincing did it take for a cheerleader to realize that he was not worth her attention?

He was trapped. His body told him to walk out of here, retrieve his bike from the rack and ride hard away from here. He made his way outside, to the flagpole in front. AUSS vehicles swarmed the street, blocking the view of the sidewalk outside the middle school. Buck wouldn't be there, anyway. He'd be as far away from the AU people as he could get. While Eric went to school in the viper's nest, Buck could go where ever he wanted.

That was something Eric couldn't do. AUSS agents watched the gates. He had the tracker, too. There was no where he could hide. At least not this week. Jason told him he couldn't do anything other than home and school. He needed to cover his tracks to prepare for the day when he could escape this entire nightmare: Leonard, the AU.

Kristin.

At lunch, Eric sat quietly on the bleacher bench, watching the track girls circle the track. The air had gotten colder, even more than yesterday, and the girls ran in sweatshirts, though they still wore running shorts.

"Here we go again," Jason said. Eric didn't bother asking what Jason meant. He just watched the girls run, even though it wasn't that interesting. They weren't even that attractive, just thin and narrow-faced. "Maybe you should join the track team?" Jason suggested.

Eric shook his head slightly.

"Dude, don't worry so much. We got this. I told my mom about the tracker, and she said I did the right thing. She can loop the data and make the AU think you are where you aren't. Just a few more days."

Eric shook his head again.

"You don't want to leave, do you?" Jason said. "Now you got a girlfriend and all that."

"That's not a problem," Eric said in a dull monotone.

"What did you do this time? I told you you were gonna mess that stuff up."

Eric glanced sideways at Jason. Jason threw up his hands in surrender.

"Is that what's got you? She broke up with you?"

Eric shrugged.

"Dude, you'd have had to do it anyway. This just saves you the trouble. We'll be gone in a week. The girls in California are better anyway. You'll 'wish they all could be California Girls'." Jason spread his hands out and shook them like David Lee Roth. Eric shook his head, resisting a smile. "Oh, Diamond Dave," Jason mused. "Too bad they don't play his stuff here anymore. I loved that song when I was a kid."

"You're still a kid," Eric said. Jason slapped his shoulder.

"You know what I mean, idiot."

"Hey, you're coming with, right?" Eric asked suddenly. "I mean when I go, um, west."

"Sure, dude. I gotta show you the ropes, right? Can't let a yokel like you loose alone in L.A." Eric smiled for real now. He neglected to point out that Jason was nearly as much of an Oklahoman as Eric was.

Jason's confident answer made him feel better. He'd gotten used to not being alone all the time. The idea that he would be friendless in a strange city scared him.

Kristin stood against the wall just before the front door of the school waiting for Eric to come by to pick up his bike at the end of the day. She peered through the crowd of students heading out. He finally appeared around the corner, levering his backpack full of books onto one shoulder and threading his other arm through the strap.

She glanced around to check if any of the girls were around. They'd probably all be down at the gym getting ready for practice. She'd have to hurry if she was going to make it there on time herself.

When the coast was clear, she peeled herself off the wall and grabbed Eric's arm. She really wanted to hug him, to kiss him, to soothe the pain she'd caused him. But she held back. He probably didn't want that from her anyway.

He started when she touched him, pulling his arm from her grasp.

"What do you want?" he asked. His voice and his eyes were cool. He stopped expectantly, but he didn't seem entirely interested in what she had to say.

"I want to apologize," she said. "I had to do it. I didn't have a choice."

"You did have a choice," he said. "They told you to choose. Me or them. You chose them. But I get it. I saw it coming." His voice was steady, maybe too steady. He almost seemed like an actor saying his lines.

"Do you really?" she asked. "You don't hate me?"

Something hot flashed in his eyes for a moment. What had she said?

"I don't hate you," he said smoothly as if practiced. "I need to get home. Homework." He moved past her and through the door to the outside.

Despite her breaking heart, she had to smile. Homework. What a typical Eric Sumner excuse to escape the uncomfortable.

After the encounter with Kristin, Eric headed home, as was expected of him. The mindless ride left him with too much time to think about the events of the day and Kristin's false apology.

Do you hate me? she'd asked. She'd sounded like his mother.

Eric pedaled at an easy pace, taking his time to let his mind work. He felt beset on all sides by villains and traitors. No matter which, they all pretended to be on his side: Hamilton and his "panic switch," Gillian and her apologetic whining, Jason and his assurances of safety.

Kristin…

In a flurry of motion, Eric stood on his pedals and pushed himself forward, while turning his bike away from his destination, away even from Ender.

Screw the tracker. They knew who and what he was anyway. What was the point?

It was the first time he'd gone to the tool shed during the week. It was just as empty here as it usually was. Whatever crops had been in the field had been harvested long ago, or the field had been laid fallow this year. There were no machines working the soil, no farmers coming out to examine crops. Just an empty field of dirt and this run-down shack.

Eric dumped his bike in the dirt, not caring about the damned paint job anymore. He ghosted through a wall, and the relative darkness inside the shed enveloped him. He sank to the dirt onto his knees and put his head in his hands, trying to hold back the fear, anger, and shame that threatened to burst from him.

The pink elephant wouldn't be ignored.

He roared at the top of his lungs and jumped to his feet. He felt the stilling of his body's vibration like the blow of a sledgehammer. A pain unlike anything he'd ever felt struck him throughout his entire body as his atoms froze and compacted, hardening his skin and tightening his muscles. He lashed out with crazed fury at anything around him whether it be wood or metal. His ultra-dense fists struck anything he hit without sensation, ripping through the wooden shelves as if they were paper. Splinters flew his hands like wrecking balls. Without thinking, he hurled his arms at the wooden support beams, crushing them. The shed groaned, the weight of its steel roof making the suddenly unsupported structure sway.

Eric didn't care. He continued to lash out, the energy of his anger and sadness released through his power and the increasing pain in his arms.

Then the shed collapsed.

He didn't feel it as it did. The anger he felt washed away as he realized what he'd done. The vibration in his body roared again to life, releasing him from the pain of frozen nerves and washing through him like a chill waterfall. In the moment between the groaning of the collapsing shed and the falling of the first beam, Eric ghosted, standing in the midst of the falling debris as if passed through him. It piled around him and within him. The shed that had sheltered him from the world was now a crumbled pile of old wood and rusted metal fittings. Exhausted, he dropped down to sit among the wreckage, his body phased through the broken structure.

His rage was spent. The world was not as it once was. It would never be that way again. But that was the last time he would need to rail against the change. Now, he had to learn to live in his new reality. Or maybe he could choose not to.

Someone would come by soon and find him. Perhaps the AU tracker had already alerted Hamilton to what he'd done. They'd find him sitting half-in, half-out of the broken shed. He'd be caught. He'd be executed. Maybe that's how it was meant–

A swelling pain rose in Eric's chest. His vision swam. He tried to take a breath but failed. The muscles moved, but no air came to him. He turned over onto his hands and knees. How was he not falling through the ground? Where was his air? Why couldn't he breathe? He was still inside the shed, phased through the broken wood and iron. He'd never been phased for this long before. He'd never noticed that his lungs didn't catch air while ghosting.

He was suffocating.

His vision swam, and he couldn't shut down his power. He couldn't bring himself into phase with air in order to breathe in.

The ground in front of him dimmed, though the sun was still in the sky. A dark tunnel appeared at the edges of his vision. He was close to passing out. He desperately tried to find the off switch that had been there after Leonard's attack on him.

It was gone. His power refused to allow him to return to normal.

He rolled away quickly, getting out of the debris he'd caused with the destruction of the shed. He struggled to his feet when he was clear. Then, all of a sudden, without even a thought to turn off the power, he became solid again.

He gasped in air, dropping to his knees again. He reached out and touched the dirt in front of him. It was solid. He was solid. He breathed deeply, panting. The tunnel vision retreated as oxygen returned to his blood and brain.

Finally, he dropped onto his back next to his bike. He stared up at the sky as he breathed deeply. He was okay. He was alive. He was breathing.

When he could think again, he wondered at what happened. The part of his brain most comfortable to him kicked in, soothing him with logic and analysis. It was clear that breathing while out of phase was impossible. He'd never had to worry about that before. Anytime he'd ghosted through anything, it had only been for a moment. No more than a couple of heartbeats. Being out of phase didn't arrest his muscles as holding his breath would, so he thought he was breathing.

At the same time, one of his fears had been put to rest. He wouldn't ever find himself returning to normal while inside a wall. His power wouldn't let him. Even when he'd wanted to, he hadn't been able to. That had saved his life. In his panic for air, he could have killed himself had he returned to normal inside the shed.

But if he'd suffocated while ghosting, if he held it too long, he'd eventually pass out. What would happen then?

He didn't want to think about that.

It was easy to remedy. He'd just never try ghosting without taking a breath first. He'd make sure he was only passing through simple walls. It wasn't like he would be trying to break into a bank vault or walk through the walls of a concrete bunker, right?

Still, he realized he was running blind. One day, he would find himself in a situation that truly would kill him. He could lose control again, or he could find himself in a position where the power — his subconscious — took over and did something he couldn't recover from.

He couldn't do this alone anymore. He needed help. He

needed someone who knew what it was like to be different. To be a SPI.

Eric picked up his bike and mounted, pedaling back toward Ender.

He needed to find Buck.

Fifteen minutes after Eric Sumner left, Roger Hamilton arrived at the tool shed in a rented sedan that looked nothing like the AUSS vehicles he had access to. He didn't want anyone noting the passage of an AUSS agent out here on the heels of a random teenage boy.

He stood next to the car and examined the wreckage the boy had made of the rickety shack. It would take more of an analysis than his eyes could discern, but this didn't seem like the kind of damage they might expect of a SPI like Eric. It was localized only to the shack. There was splintered wood everywhere, but it looked like the kind of damage a demolition crew might have made to it with axes and hammers. It was not shaken apart like Rumble would have done.

Had Edward been wrong about this one? Was Sumner merely a strength/endurance SPI like Rockhide himself? If so, he'd be easy to corral and control. Yet Edward insisted that they keep their distance.

Rockhide stepped away from the road and circled the ruined shack. Almost instantly, he spotted the red metal toolbox peeking from between a pair of two-by-fours. He bent over and pulled it out. It had a shattered handle and a dent at the top, but the rusted lock was still attached. Rockhide cracked the lock open with a twist of his fingers. The lid swung open, revealing the ancient, rusted implements you'd expect from a farmer's toolbox. Completely useless. He tossed the box away and pulled his phone out to take pictures of the site. Ideally, he'd have had a forensic team out here to comb through everything, but that couldn't be risked without alerting Eric that he was being tracked.

After snapping a dozen or so pictures from every angle he

could think of, Rockhide found a broken support beam, splintered at one end. Careful not to disturb the broken end — that would need to be examined by the forensic guys — he took it back to the car and put it in the trunk.

As far as Rockhide was concerned, they should just bag and tag the kid now, but he didn't make the decisions. That sort of thing was left to Edward.

This was Exodus's show.

Always had been.

December 15, 2017

Buck seemed to have vanished since the AU arrived. Eric hadn't seen him on the sidewalk outside the middle school this morning. He hadn't glimpsed him following him as he rode through downtown.

Now, Eric rode down Main Street, scanning the parking lots outside the bowling alley and the grocery store, peering through the windows of the shops. He tried to think of every place he'd ever seen the old homeless man and looked in those places.

AUSS agents were everywhere. Some were in simple black uniforms with ballistic vests adorned with blocky white letters that said AUSS. Others were in the full body armor that made them look somewhat like robots. Eric noticed that some of the latter followed him with their facemasks as he passed. Were they just watching a kid passing on a bike, or were they keeping an eye on Eric Sumner for their boss, Hamilton?

Eric finally found Buck at Saints Drive Park. The old man was sitting on a bench, his large form hunched over as he tossed breadcrumbs to a gathered flock of birds. It was like a twisted Disney movie. The birds tweeted at Buck as if they were speaking to him of their day. They edged closer and closer to him as they sought morsels to assuage their hunger.

Eric parked the bike on the grass and sat down next to Buck. The birds scattered around him hesitantly, torn between the threat of the newcomer and the temptation of food.

"Taking the day off of stalking me?" Eric said. Buck shifted, turning his head slightly toward Eric. Though hidden by a curtain of long gray hair, Eric thought he saw a bemused half-smile pull up one corner of Buck's lips.

"Now who is stalking who?" Buck said with a chuckle. He turned back to the birds. "I thought it prudent I keep up the appearance of a feeble old man." Eric chuffed.

"Sorry, no one could mistake you for feeble. You're the size of a Mack truck."

"Fat then," Buck said. "Maybe I should put a little more waddle in my stride."

Eric looked around. The park was empty. Not even a patrolling AUSS agent moved along the grass.

"You know what's happening?" Eric asked.

"As much as I can see with my eyes. I don't really have a television. Not one that works anyway. Are they after you or me?"

"Neither. Leonard Strange. Speed enhanced."

"That where the bruises come from?" Buck waved a hand with bread pinched between the fingers toward Eric's face. Eric had nearly forgotten them. They didn't hurt unless he touched them, and he'd never been one of those people who pawed at their face all the time.

"Yeah," Eric said, "He tried to get me to out myself on camera. Just succeeded in outing himself instead."

"You finally ready to admit it, then?" Buck said. Eric nodded.

"I might as well, everyone seems to know. My mother, my friend, the AU."

Buck started at that. "The AU knows?"

"Yeah, I'm Russell Sumner's nephew."

"Rumble..." Buck said thoughtfully. Eric nodded. Somehow, he wasn't surprised to find out Buck knew Rumble's real name. His mind had been working through it all since he'd met Buck. Now, with that confirmation, he felt a certain satisfaction. For once, he knew something someone else wanted to keep a secret.

"You're Citadel, aren't you?"

Buck started as if the seat beneath him had suddenly become electrified. He dropped the crumbs he was going to toss next back into the plastic bread bag he held in his other hand. Then, he tucked that bag into his voluminous coat.

"Maybe," the big SPI said.

"Don't play with me," Eric demanded. "You're the one who approached me. You're always watching me. You knew I was a SPI before I did. How did you know if you aren't the only four-enhancement SPI that knew my uncle?"

"I'm not playing with you, Eric. I'm really not sure who I am. I can't remember anything beyond a decade or so ago. I suspect you're right, but I just don't know."

That did surprise Eric. But it fit. If this man was Citadel, and he'd survived the New York Incident, he would have been at ground zero of a nuclear explosion. Memory loss was the least that could be expected from such a traumatic experience. It was impossible to think he'd survived at all.

"Then how did you know about me if you can't remember?"

"Feelings. Flashes. I spent five years wandering aimlessly, trying to remember who or what I was. I only remembered toward the end of the Chaos Years something that had been told to me once. That led me to Ender and to you and Gillian. I was too late to save Steven from his fate. I might have been able to stop him..." Buck trailed off and stared at his hands in his lap. "When I learned about Steven and connected him to Rumble, I knew you would be next. It's genetic, you know. It's passed on from parent to child. It has been from the beginning."

"Project Brooklyn," Eric said, remembering Jason's redacted documents.

"Over the years bits and pieces of knowledge have come back to me. Not really memories, but things I knew before. Project Brooklyn was a failure. None of the test subjects exhibited enhancements. The government scrapped it. It wasn't until the survivors of the Normandy invasion, most of whom had been subjects of Brooklyn, began having children that the enhancements appeared. Brooklyn was re-opened, and those children were found and collected. They were studied and trained to be the first operatives of FORCE. The physicals were first, and they were easily controlled for the most part." Buck waved a hand generally in the direction of downtown Ender. "A lot of the tech the AU uses to capture SPIs was developed by FORCE to control their enhanced operatives. It became more difficult when mentals began to appear."

Buck was silent for a long time. Eric let him think. While not entirely mind blowing, it was interesting to hear the truth from someone who'd been there. With every word, Eric became surer that Buck was indeed Citadel. Somehow...

"Then, — and this is one of the few things I actually remember — FORCE gathered it's first third generation SPI."

"Rumble," Eric guessed. Buck nodded.

"He was uncontrollable. His powers weren't physical or mental. They were entirely new. Rumble actually tapped directly into the energy of the objects he touched. The geeks called it "potential kinetic energy." The larger the object, the more powerful the tremors were that Rumble could produce"

"Mom said there was an earthquake," Eric said. Buck shrugged.

"I don't remember that, but I wouldn't doubt it. If Russ could use his power by touching the earth itself... I don't know what he could have done."

Eric didn't want to ask the question, but he had to, especially with all he'd just been told.

"Did Rumble cause the explosion? Did he destroy New York?"

The answer was a long time coming. Buck turned away from Eric, his eyes on the birds that were still there cleaning up the rest of the bread crumbs.

"Maybe," Buck said finally. "I don't know what happened. I don't remember."

"Citadel," Eric said, his heart pounding in his chest. He couldn't believe he'd just said that word aloud to refer to a person. It was almost like calling someone "Satan" and meaning it. "Buck," he amended. He pulled the AU tracker from his pocket. "I need your help."

Eric rode home, thinking of his two detours as adding variety to the data the tracker was collecting. He leaned the bike against the outer wall of the house.

Inside Gillian sat on the couch. She was drinking, but not yet passed out. He didn't give her more than a glance. She didn't seem to notice him pass. That was how it had been between them for the last few days. Civil ignorance.

He dropped his backpack in his room, then fished in his pocket for the tracker. He dropped that next to the pack. As far as Hamilton was concerned, he was spending the rest of the night in bed.

With his burdens lifted, he headed back through the house.

Gillian stood at the mouth of the hallway, blocking the way out.

"Are you going out again?" she asked, her voice softened by alcohol.

"Yeah," he said. "I have something to do."

"It's not safe out there. Between that boy who beat you and the government, you shouldn't be going out there."

Eric thought of where he was going and who he was going to be with. "I think I'll be fine."

Gillian stood up straighter, bracing herself against either wall with her hands.

"Go back to your room, Eric," she said, her slippery voice trying to sound commanding. Eric took a step toward her.

"You can't stop me, mom," he said. "I can walk right through you."

Her shoulders slumped. "Come on, kiddo. Do it for me."

"It's important," he said, "I'll be all right."

She didn't move. Instead of walking through her as he'd

threatened, he took a breath and walked through the wall leading into the kitchen. He heard Gillian gasp as he came out inside the stove. He stepped away to the open floor quickly, so as to not lose his breath.

From the kitchen, he went through the living room to the front door. When he looked back, Gillian was still standing in the hall, rather unsteadily.

"Get some rest, Mom," he said. "Lay off the booze for a bit."

Without waiting for her response, he left, jumping on his bike and heading out of the cul de sac. He turned down opposite the direction he'd go to school and east from Ender, as Buck had told him. He followed the instructions he'd been given and found the trail Buck himself had worn in the grass leading away from the road. After just a few more yards, the trees opened up and gave Eric a view of his destination.

In the middle of a field of tall grass, a huge, bus-like RV was set on blocks. It looked like it had been brand new a dozen years ago. Now, the side graphics were faded, and exposed metal showed patches of rust. A tire stack was hidden under a green tarp that kept them protected from the elements. Eric guessed that, with Buck's strength, the tires could be re-mounted on the axles relatively easily if the RV ever had to go anywhere. If the hulking thing's engine even ran anymore.

Under the extended awning, Buck sat on a metal lawn chair. A large green cooler sat within arms reach. As Buck watched Eric approach, he reached into the cooler and drew out two scarlet cans of Coke. Eric dismounted and leaned the bike against the tire stack before joining Buck under the awning. Buck tossed him a can and indicated a carefully stacked pile of wood for Eric to sit on.

"Sorry I don't have another chair," Buck said. "Never expected visitors." Eric grinned and popped open his drink.

"It's okay, I know what you mean."

"Did you get rid of that tracker?"

"As far as the AU is concerned, I'm in my bedroom."

"You better hope so. If they come here, things will get difficult for both of us. And your mother?"

"I didn't tell her anything," Eric said. He didn't understand why Buck hadn't wanted Eric to tell Gillian anything, even that Eric was looking for help, but maybe he could see things from Buck's perspective. For a SPI everyone would want dead if it was discovered he was alive, Buck wasn't as paranoid as one might think.

"That's rule number one: No one knows about me. Not Gillian, not your friends at school. No one."

"Got it." He could be more paranoid, Eric thought.

"Now," Buck said around a sip of Coke, "tell me what you know about your enhancements."

Eric told him everything that had happened since the day in the park with Ken and Leonard. He explained his ability to pass through objects and did a quick demonstration. Then, he tried to explain the other thing, the ability to harden himself, so he didn't feel pain. Finally, he told Buck about what had spurred him to finally ask for help: his inability to breathe while phased.

"Survival Instinct," Buck said. "Every SPI has it. You might think of it as a weakness, but it's your subconscious's way of regulating your power so it doesn't kill you. A strength SPI, for example, without endurance enhancements wouldn't be able to lift a car over their head, no matter how extreme their enhancement. The car would crush them. Lifting something too heavy might break their bones if done wrong. SPIs like that are next to harmless."

"What about SPIs like you?" Eric asked. "You have pretty much every physical enhancement in the book."

Buck shrugged. "If I am Citadel," he started, "then I doubt I have any such limits. At least I didn't before New York. Now, I'm a little broken. The limp and the stoop isn't entirely an act. I hurt all the time. I haven't had to push myself since, so I'm not sure where my limits are." He sighed. "But we're not talking about me. We need to test you. Find out exactly where your limits are and what you can do. I'll have to think of some things to run you through. We're in uncharted waters with you. I'd expected your powers to be something like Rumble's, but they aren't."

Buck leaned back in his chair and took another swig from his can. The chair protested the movement, the white-painted steel groaning under Buck's weight. Buck didn't seem startled or worried that his chair might collapse under him. He pondered for a moment. Eric picked at the wood he sat on, peeling bark off the cut pieces.

"How long can you hold your breath?" Buck suddenly asked. Eric shrugged, but Buck wasn't done. "Or the real question should be: how long can you hold your breath while exerting yourself? How far can you run without breathing?" Buck smiled to himself, a grin that looked more than a little sadistic. Eric wondered if he'd regret asking for Buck's help.

Buck levered himself out of the chair with a grunt. When Eric didn't rise right away, he cocked an eyebrow at the boy.

"Well?" he said, "We're not going to find out by sitting here. Let's go!"

The answer to Buck's question was "not long." It was hard enough to hold his breath for more than three minutes. Buck had him try to do it while running across the field. He hadn't been able to make it across the length of it before his vision began to darken. Any kind of exercise while he was ghosting used him up pretty quickly.

"That is good, actually," Buck said when Eric was too spent to spend more than a few seconds out of phase. "Your weakness is tied to your lung capacity and cardiovascular system. That can be trained up. Come see me again tomorrow, and we'll do it again."

AUPrimeHistory: True Conspiracies

(Airdate: 9/11/2008)

THE FALL OF THE USA

<Archive Footage: New York City, 1994>

In the immediate aftermath of the nuclear explosion that destroyed New York City, a number of things happened all at once. Forty-Three of the world's top 500 companies were headquartered in New York City, many in the financial sector. As the shockwaves of the disaster spread around the world, foreign markets went into a frenzy. The destruction of the US Stock Market nearly obliterated all other foreign markets. The markets to arrive on top were the Russian and Chinese markets. Over the following months, Beijing opened a Pan-Asian market that quickly rose to prominence, bringing Asia onto the world stage as an economic power never before seen. Europe, with ties to the US that stretched back to World War II, was the hardest hit. Much as North America has done, Europe banded together to survive, forming a government on the American Union template: The European Union.

<Archive Footage: Quarantine Zone - September 20, 2001>

On a personal level, besides the millions that died in the initial blast, millions more were within the radiation zone. The US government acted quickly to quarantine and evacuate those affected. The immediate vicinity of Long Island, including parts of New Jersey, were quarantined. Residents there died en masse of radiation burns and sickness despite international efforts to treat them. Residents further inland and in the opposite direction of prevailing winds were forced to evacuate, many not allowed to return home to retrieve possessions or pets.

Even today, seven years later, the Quarantine Zone is still enforced in a 25 mile radius from Ground Zero. The cordon is patrolled by AU security personnel to prevent adventure seekers or looters from risking death by entering the danger zone.

<Stock Images: American Legal System>

Almost as soon as the survivors could get stabilized in FEMA encampments throughout the eastern seaboard, lawsuits began to sprout up from private citizens and government organizations aimed at anyone who could possibly be to blame for the destruction. Courts in the northeast were paralyzed by the sheer volume and complexity of the demand for legal restitution. The federal government, unprepared for a catastrophe on this scale stepped all over itself in its attempts to provide relief, assess the damage, and investigate the incident.

<Slideshow: "Anarchy in America">

Ultimately, the vaunted strength of the United States of America was broken by the legal crisis generated in part by its own convoluted legal system. The three branches of federal government, the Executive, the Legislative, and the Judicial, argued among each other. The system of checks and balances that was the foundation of US "democracy" was shattered by the efforts of one branch to overturn the other.

For three years, the United States government came to a standstill. Federal funds, those not wiped out by the destruction of America's financial center, dried up. All federal programs were canceled. The Military was downsized at the same time as it was forced into service to prevent anarchy from breaking out over all fifty states as state and local governments also broke down under the sudden pressure and surging cost of operation.

Soon, due to lack of pay and benefits, mass desertion caused severe attrition among the federal armed forces. Military vehicles were abandoned at the side of freeways or stolen to aid in the retreat of the deserters who betrayed their country in its time of greatest need.

But when the people needed a hero most, one man stepped forward to bring all of North America away from the brink of total annihilation.

<Image: Sillouhette - Andrew Marshall>

Andrew Irvine Marshall.

More after this.

<Commerical Announcement>

December 21, 2017

The week was up.

Eric rolled into school exactly a week after the AU began its security protocols, anxious for it to be over. He hadn't had a problem with the AUSS agents who checked in each student as they entered school property, but he was still hyper-aware that they knew who he was. Even after several days, he trembled with perfectly normal fear every time he turned the corner onto Wall Street. He was afraid that one morning, they'd all be lined up to meet him with electrified nets or some other tech that might possibly hold a kid who could walk through walls.

He just wanted them gone.

That they were still here was proof that Leonard was still at large. Every day, AUPrimeNews gave updates that were full of speculation and dire warning. A curfew had been implemented, curtailing the time Eric could spend with Buck and the endless cardio the old SPI forced on him. Gillian continued to watch the developments on TV. She didn't say anything to Eric when she was coherent enough to say anything at all, but he knew she was worried.

Leonard had apparently holed up somewhere, waiting for the AU Security Service to go away. One thing, at least, Eric could respect—Hamilton and his people were tenacious.

As instructed by Jason, Eric went through his day as he had the last six days. He didn't do anything other than go to class. When lunch came around, he went to the football field bleachers where he'd gone every day this week. The flagpole out front was too close to the AUSS people. At least here, there was only one, walking back and forth between the bleachers in the field. The same two girls were running the track again today, and Eric noticed the AUSS agent was watching them more than anything else.

Jason arrived just moments after Eric, noticeably waiting until the AUSS thug was on the opposite side of the track before climbing up to Eric. Jason had become more and more withdrawn as the AUSS spread through town. He'd admitted to being afraid that they'd begin searching houses soon. He was worried about what they'd find if his own house was searched, even though he claimed his parents had everything under control.

They sat for lunch in silence. Jason didn't say a word, only tracked the AUSS agent with his eyes.

"Kristin isn't here today," Eric said. "She wasn't in chem. She called in sick or something." Jason just nodded. "I keep thinking, what if they took her? What if they're gonna use her to get to me?"

"I don't think so," Jason said, "You two aren't a thing anymore, remember?" But his tone wasn't very convincing, too sober for the excitable kid.

They fell back to silence. When the after-lunch bell finally rang, both of them rose together and descended the bleachers.

"Today's the last day, right?" Eric asked, patting his jean pocket to indicate the tracker there. Jason glanced toward the distant AUSS agent before nodding.

"I'll meet you after school," Jason said. "We'll go to my place. They're expecting us."

They walked. Eric rolled his bike along beside him. Jason led him away from the school, eyeing the agents that peppered the streets. He even went so far as to delay crossing streets until the AUSS people had moved away.

"You're being a little over-cautious," Eric warned. "They'll notice."

"Naw, I've been doing the same thing every day. They're used to it now. They stopped me the first day, but I gave them my best clueless teenager act, and they bought it."

Eric gave his friend a sidelong look. He didn't believe that for an instant. "So you acted like yourself?" he asked.

Jason glared at Eric in mock offense. "Dude, I thought we were friends." They both chuckled.

The Williams house was just a few blocks away from the school. It was a nice, two-level craftsman style house with a wide front porch and a peaked roof. It's siding was painted the color of wet sand. It looked as normal as any other house in the neighborhood. It was a lot bigger than Eric's house, and it made him wonder if Jason had siblings. How much space did they need otherwise?

Eric leaned his bike on a post that held up the porch roof. Then, Jason led him into the house. Eric gaped at the interior. It looked right out of a TV show. Framed pictures dotted the neutral-tone walls and sat on narrow shelves along with nick-nacks of every type. Unlike Eric's house, the front door opened into an entry area instead of directly into the living room. Jason indicated Eric should take his shoes off.

After they'd removed their sneakers, Jason took him into a kitchen bedecked with chickens and cows. As if the residents were Midwestern farmers, there wasn't a surface that didn't hold a wooden carving of a milk cow or a stuffed rooster of every size and shape. Even the refrigerator magnets were farm animals with the cow and chicken dominant. It was so different than the plain white kitchen at home, and a shock to Eric's senses.

"Mom! Dad!" Jason called. "Eric's here!"

Instantly, a little woman with curly blond hair the same shade as Jason's rushed into the room. She took an instant to regard Eric, then she held out her hand. Eric took it and shook it. She pulled it away coldly and held it out again.

"The tracker," she said. Embarrassed at his misstep, Eric reached into his pocket and produced the tracker. Jason's mother snatched the little plastic disk and disappeared back into whatever part of the house was beyond the far door.

"Come on, Mom," Jason called after her. "Really?" He got no response. "Sorry, dude. She takes her work seriously."

Eric nodded. They took a seat at the kitchen table. Eric reached out and pulled at a chicken-shaped napkin holder to see it better.

In another moment, a tall, narrow man entered the room. His face resembled Jason's, narrow and almost feminine, but the years he had over his son had chiseled it into a more manly shape. His hair was sandy brown and cut short. He wore a thin beard that could almost be a five-o'clock shadow but was impeccably groomed at the edges.

"Dad," Jason said as the man entered, "You need to talk to Mom about her manners." Jason's dad smiled.

"Well," he said in a surprisingly deep voice, "You know her." He turned to Eric. "Eric, nice to meet you. I'm Zak." He held out his hand, which Eric shook, confident this time that it was what Zak intended. "Let's get you boys something to eat."

Zak went about making sandwiches. Eric waited for the inevitable questions about his power. Surely Jason had given them details. They knew he wasn't normal, even for a SPI. But Zak didn't even mention it, even as he placed the biggest sandwich Eric had ever seen in front of him. It had some sort of multi-grain bread with big chunks of seeds or grains or something in it. Between the bread slices was probably half a pound of roast beef, cheese, a big clump of dark greens — fresh spinach? — and tomatoes.

"Go big or go home, right?" Jason said as he dug into his own sandwich.

"So, what now?" Eric asked as he tried to flatten his sandwich into something that might actually fit into his mouth. Zak took a seat next to Jason and fixed his eyes on Eric.

"Now, we wait to see what Ashley can do with that tracker," Zak said. "AU tech can be tricky, at least that's what she tells me. I couldn't turn on a computer without help." He smiled.

"Aren't you worried they'll know I'm here?" Eric asked. Zak shrugged.

"There are risks we take," Zak replied. "I'm guessing they're just in observe-and-report mode. They don't know you know they know." Jason groaned, and Zak chuckled. "So as far as they're concerned, you're just visiting a friend's house. You'll go home after this in case anyone is physically watching. Then we'll contact you with plans to get you and your mom out of here."

And your mom.

Eric hadn't even told Gillian this was happening yet. Was he going to just spring it on her as he walked out the door? Hey, mom, come on! We're going to California. Chances were she was already passed out on the couch.

"When do we leave?"

"That depends on—"

The doorbell rang, breaking into Zak's sentence. Almost as if another person had taken his place, Zak's warm, positive expression turned dark and cold. He held out a hand to tell the boys to stay in their seats. Then he got up and stalked toward the front door.

Eric glanced at Jason, who shrugged and shook his head.

There was a brief exchange at the door. Then Zak returned ashen faced. Jason started and opened his mouth to ask his dad what had happened. But his question stuck in his throat as Zak was followed by three men. All of them wore the uniform of the AUSS.

One of them was Roger Hamilton.

December 21, 2017

"It seems there has been a miscommunication," Hamilton said by way of greeting. He broke away from the others and approached Eric. "I came here thinking there was trouble." He looked around the kitchen. His gaze returned to Eric. "Is there trouble, Eric?" He held out his hand. "Someone pushed the button. You didn't sit on it, did you? Let's see."

Eric squirmed in his seat and consciously held back his power. Something in him perceived the held out hand as a threat. He felt the push of his power in his chest as it tried to break through his resistance.

"You can't just come to my house and make demands of my guests," Zak said, suddenly. He approached Hamilton and poked a stiff finger accusingly into Hamilton's sleeve. Hamilton turned to him and casually brushed Zak's hand away.

Jason suddenly pulled away from the table. The two AUSS agents near the door started, hands going to tasers at their hips. But Jason just bent down to the floor. He came back up, the black tracker between his fingers.

"Is this it?" he asked. His face was pinched in consternation. "I'm sorry, I must have stepped on it."

He held out the tracker. The casing was intact, but the clear plastic cover was cracked. Hamilton took a step toward Jason and snatched the tracker away. He examined it.

"I must have dropped it," Eric said, glancing at Jason. Jason's mother must have slid the tracker across the floor to Jason from out of sight. The damage was her fault. She must have triggered the panic switch when she was tinkering with it. It would be best for Eric to play along with the ruse.

Hamilton cocked his head at Eric, a scowl on his lips. Was Zak right? Did Hamilton really not realize that Eric knew what was going on? Had this incident just sparked his suspicion?

Hamilton handed the device to one of the agents, who produced a tiny tool which he inserted into a tiny hole in the casing. The red button on the tracker popped up. The agent tested that the cracked cover still prevented accidental triggering and handed it back to Hamilton.

"Be more careful, Mr. Sumner," Hamilton said. "After you're done visiting your friend, go straight home. I'll leave a car outside for your protection." Hamilton paused. "And to prevent further false alarms."

Eric's stomach lurched, but he just nodded. Now, he wouldn't just be tracked electronically. He'd be followed.

Hamilton spun on his heels and led his agents out of the house. Zak followed them at a distance until the front door. When the door was safely closed behind them, Zak returned to the kitchen, but instead of resuming their conversation, he held his finger to his lips. He bent to a cabinet and pulled at a drawer. The drawer was full of odds and ends: old electronics, batteries, office supplies. Instead of rummaging through this drawer, he pulled it all the way out and reached into the cavity behind the drawer.

Eric glanced at Jason, who was biting into his sandwich, a lazy gaze on his father.

Zak eventually drew a long, flat device from his stash. It had a round handle, but flattened at the end, almost like a cricket bat, but much shorter. Zak flicked a switch on the handle, and two green lights appeared on the end of the device.

Zak grinned as he showed off his new toy. He came over to Jason and put the tracker on the table. He waved the device over the tracker, and one of the green lights turned red. Zak gave a thumbs up.

Then, Zak walked over to where the two agents were standing just minutes before. He waved the wand anywhere that could have been reached by one of the agents. Over a lamp, both lights turned red. Zak pulled at the shade to peer into it. He pointed to his mouth, then to the lampshade.

Eric watched the display and furrowed his brow.

"Well," Zak said finally, putting his finger back to his lips for silence. "I'm glad those guys have your back, but they do come off kind of creepy, yeah?" He rolled his finger toward Eric.

"Yeah," Eric said uncertainly. Then Zak pointed at Jason, then a finger down.

"Let's go back to my room," Jason said on cue, "I want to show you my collection."

They all gathered, Jason and Eric holding their sandwiches on the plates. Zak jerked his head and Jason guided them out of the kitchen and around the corner. When he opened a narrow door, they were greeted by a staircase down and Jason's mother, Ashley. Her face was creased with worry, but when Zak nodded and smiled confidently, she relaxed visibly. They all went down the stairs then.

The room at the bottom of the stairs was cavernous. It must have been the size of the house itself. It was unfinished, the concrete foundation of the house serving as walls, and concrete support beams as separators for the various sections of the space. On the far side of the room was a workbench with hundreds of tools of all sizes, most of which Eric had never seen before. In another section was a trophy case full of gold and bronze plaques. The prominence given to this case was strange in the otherwise bare room.

As soon as his foot touched the bare concrete floor, Zak said, "That man is a SPI."

Eric, Jason, and Ashley all turned to stare at Zak in shock.

"Which man?" Ashley asked.

"The big one," Zak replied.

"Roger Hamilton," Eric supplied. "He's the head of the AUSS here."

"A SPI in the AUSS?" Jason asked, incredulous. "What the hell?"

"Jason Zachary Williams! Language!" Ashley snapped. Jason blushed and nodded.

"His arm was as hard as stone," Zak said. "It felt like poking a concrete wall." He demonstrated by poking his finger into a nearby column.

"Endurance SPI," Ashley mused. "Maybe strength too, given his size?" Zak nodded in agreement.

"Why are neither of you surprised?" Jason demanded. They gave him a sympathetic look.

"We've known for a while now that the AU recruits SPIs to work for them," Zak said. "They use them to do their dirty work. We don't know where they get them, though, or who they are. Now we know one of them. We need to send a report to Mental Block."

"You've known, and you haven't told me?" Jason asked. Eric took a step away, uncomfortable to be witnessing an argument between Jason and his parents.

"We don't tell you everything, Jay," Ashley said. "This was sensitive information."

"So what does this mean for me?" Eric asked. "The tracker...?"

Ashley shook her head. Her blond curls fluttered around her head like ribbons. "I accidentally triggered the signal," she said. "I can't find the carrier to loop the data. I don't think that one uses the conventional tech. I haven't seen anything like that before. It's new." She shrugged.

"Looks like you're stuck with it," Zak said, mimicking Ashley's shrug.

Eric's heart was dashed to the floor. Not only was he stuck with the tracker, that meant he was stuck in Ender. Zak confirmed that much in the next instant.

"We needed that week's lead time to prep and move you far enough west to throw off any search. At most now, we'd have a day. If you dropped that thing on your bed and were somehow able to slip your new shadow, they'd investigate why it was in one place for so long in less than twenty-four hours. Then they'd start looking for you."

"So I'm stuck," Eric said. He dropped back against a support column as there were no chairs nearby to sit in. The soft feel of the concrete tipped him to his power even before he felt the hum in his chest. He shut it off and slammed his back against the pillar again just to feel the solid thump against his back.

"Not so fast," Jason said. "We can figure something out, right?" He looked from Zak to Ashley expectantly.

"We'd need to give the AUSS a public reason to leave Ender," Ashley said.

"So we need to make sure they capture Leonard," Eric said.

"In public with AUPrime media covering it," Zak said. "So they'd have no public excuse to remain."

"They've been drawing the search out for a lot longer than usual," Ashley said, "They're probably stalling to give them time to figure out how to out you and capture you, too."

"Why don't they just take him?" Jason asked. "They've snatched people before with no one being the wiser."

"Rumble," Eric said. "They don't know what I can do. My uncle was dangerous. So dangerous that FORCE didn't know how to control him if he ever decided to break from them. They think I might have the same power set." Zak's eyes narrowed. Eric had probably said too much. Had what he'd said all been in Jason's documents, or had he used too much of what Citadel had told him?

"Do you?" Ashley asked, apparently not as suspicious as her husband. "Are you that dangerous?" Eric shook his head.

"No," he stopped himself from explaining that he couldn't possibly have the potential to destroy an entire city like Rumble had. That would definitely be too much. He couldn't reveal Citadel's existence, even to these people. It was what the big SPI had demanded of him in return for his help.

Instead, he demonstrated his power, backing through the

concrete column he'd been leaning against. In the act, he discovered that the concrete had a steel core. The materials felt like opposites and the steel dragged at him for a moment before his body adjusted.

The two SPI sympathizers stared at him, their eyes wide. Even Jason looked a little stunned, though he'd already seen a little of what Eric could do.

"I can also do the opposite, harden parts of my body, so they are really dense. I don't know how to control that, though. I have a feeling that does actual damage to my body when I do it."

"So that's how you broke Leonard's jaw?" Jason asked.

"Yeah."

"How does that even relate to Rumble's powers at all?" Ashley asked. She seemed eager to find out everything she could about what Eric could do.

He shrugged.

"Okay, folks," Zak broke in. "This is all nice and interesting, but Jason is right. We need to figure out an alternative plan. How do we get the AU to leave Ender?"

"We draw him out," Jason said. "Leonard."

"We get Leonard to face me in public," Eric said, nodding. "I push the panic switch, and the AU swoops in for the win."

"So, use you as bait?" Zak asked. He shook his head. "We can't do that. Mental Block would have our balls."

"Zachary!" Ashley scolded. "Language." Zak nodded sheepishly in apology.

"Besides," Jason said, "that's something Mom doesn't need to worry about," His grin opened ear to ear under Ashley's glare.

"Let's work this out," Zak said. "There has to be another way. Ashley and I can brainstorm. You better be getting home, Eric. We'll have Jason invite you over again when we have something."

Eric nodded reluctantly. He and Jason started up the stairs.

"And be careful what you say on the way out," Zak said. "I'll have to figure out how to get rid of that bug without tipping off the AU guys."

Outside, a black AUSS sedan was parked across the street. When Eric and Jason stepped out the front door, the car started. Eric couldn't see its occupant past the dark glass.

"Let's do this again soon," Jason said cheerily. Eric gave him a sideways smile.

"Soon," he responded soberly, unable to put up appearances like Jason did.

As promised, the AUSS car followed Eric all the way home.

When he was hungry, he ate. When he was thirsty, he drank. Steak, beer, whatever he wanted he took.

No one noticed until they turned around and found their stuff had vanished. The slight breeze that blew by them was a good distraction to get their eyes off their treasures.

Leonard became a ghost. Rockhide was right. He'd never really pushed his power. He'd never really tried to go as fast as he could. It was dizzying how fast he could move. Somehow, he was still able to see it all, as if time slowed around him. His muscles obeyed his commands at blindingly fast speeds, allowing him to snatch whatever he wanted from whoever he wanted.

As long as he stayed away from the school.

Rockhide must have had his people staged in McAlester, with how fast the AUSS had responded to what he'd done to Sumner. They'd clumped around Marshall High the first day, no doubt grilling the student body about what had been seen and watching the footage from the security camera.

Then, they reached out their black, jack-booted tentacles, searching the town for him. They shut down the town, setting speed traps on the roads heading out of town and patrolling the fields, searching for some sign that he'd left down.

He hadn't. That would have been too easy. Now that he knew what he could really do, he wanted to prove Rockhide right. They were going after him because he'd failed to out Eric when he'd had the chance. Rockhide had warned him. Now,

Leonard wanted to turn it around on them, to challenge the AUSS to find him. He would get to Eric Sumner through the net they'd set to catch him.

Sumner had taken that beating like a champ, refusing to out himself. Leonard was pretty sure he couldn't do the same. It almost made him respect the kid.

Almost.

Before doing anything, he had to find out how to get past Eric's power for real. He'd beat the kid pretty good, but that wasn't what he'd planned to do. Eric had only taken it because he didn't want to be outed. The real challenge would be to force him to use his powers in front of everyone. To pit speed against whatever it was that Eric could do.

It was the last thing Leonard had left.

He'd ruined whatever life he'd had when he used his powers in front of that camera and those people. All his fame had turned to infamy. He was sure even now his records were being expunged, and all the wins he'd racked up for Marshall were being taken away and given away to the second best school in Oklahoma.

He could never return to the life he had. He could never go back to what he was before everyone knew the truth. His picture was probably all over AUPrimeNews. The entire Union would know who he was now. There was nowhere to hide.

Which was why he was sitting on his dad's recliner in his own home, drinking his dad's beer, and thinking in the silence of this familiar place.

His dad, the great Sheriff Reginald Strange, would be running himself ragged looking for his outlaw son. The AUSS would have commandeered his resources, deputies and all. For once, Reggie Strange would be forced to center his attention on his hometown and his son. No more ignoring either. Since he'd been elected, Reggie had used his position to stay as far away from Leonard as possible. The Sheriff's office was in McAlester, yet Reggie had refused to move there, claiming the position was only temporary and eventually he'd be voted out. But even two election cycles later, Reggie still kept his son in backwater

Ender and spent almost all of his time away from Ender in "service to the whole County."

Leonard drained the rest of the beer can. He added it to the others on the coffee table. He considered turning on the TV to see what AUPrime was saying about him. He decided against it. Instead, he went to his room to look at the trophies and plaques that lined one wall. He touched each of them, remembering the moment they'd been awarded and the pride he'd felt. Even after realizing his powers were helping him win, he still loved every one. His powers were a part of who he was. Why not use what God had given him to be the best at what he loved to do? If only he could have shown them what he could really do.

He could show them now.

A key rattled in the lock of the house door. Leonard sighed. It was time to go. He'd been hoping that his dad would be too busy to come home tonight, that maybe he could get some real sleep in his own bed. He set himself to slip out the door when his dad opened it. Maybe he'd give dad a "love tap" on the way out.

Then, his eyes alighted on the aluminum bat that leaned against the wall nearby. He'd tried baseball once before his powers manifested. He'd been pretty good at it, but it was boring. It didn't move. You were either standing out on the field waiting for something to happen, or you were sitting in the dugout waiting for your at-bat. The fun moments came infrequently and not enough to hold Leonard's interest.

But the bat was there, and it gave Leonard an idea — the old sheriff's cruiser battered to a lump of steel in the driveway.

He picked it up and, holding it by the knob, spun it in circles in the air. His mind drifted for a moment.

That moment made him miss the opportunity to leave unnoticed. The next thing Leonard knew, the front door clicked shut. Instead of being mad, Leonard nodded his head. It felt right. This was how it should be.

He remembered an old song lyric, "Jeremy spoke in class today."

Reginald paused while unbuckling his gun belt. His steel-gray eyes were on the coffee table and the beer cans that littered it. As he turned his haggard and unshaven face up toward Leonard's room, where Leonard hid behind the half-open door, Leonard made his move.

The television exploded as Leonard swept by with the baseball bat. As fast as he was moving, it didn't take much of a swing to completely destroy it. The coffee table was next. In the first pass, Leonard batted through the collection of beer cans. They were still in the air, rocketing toward the wall when he came around again and turned the thick wooden table to splinters. He came to a stop to appreciate his work.

Reginald only had time to put his hand on his service pistol before the living room exploded in metal, glass, and wood. Leonard stood opposite him in the living room, breathing heavily from the exertion. The beer cans hit the wall behind Reginald, causing the Sheriff to flinch aside. The wood shards scattered around Leonard's feet.

"What the hell, Lenny?" Reginald roared. Leonard leaned on the baseball bat.

"That was as fun as I thought it would be," Leonard said. "The look on your face."

"Of course the 'look on my face'!" Reginald said, his face reddening, "You just destroyed our living room."

"'Our'?" Leonard asked. "It's yours, dad. Or was." He laughed. "I don't live here anymore."

"You could, Lenny. I can get you out of this. I have pull at County." Leonard laughed again.

"You got pull with ASS, too?" he asked. "Maybe I'm the one with pull this time. But that's not gonna keep me living here." He put every ounce of disdain he had in that last word. Then, he took a deep breath, trying to get some energy back. He'd pushed himself on that one, akin to a full sprint. Just three passes through the living room had worn him out.

"Just come home, Leonard," Reginald said. He didn't often use his son's full first name. That either meant he was mad or drunk. "I'll stand behind you the whole way."

Leonard's eyes narrowed. Reggie was offering to sacrifice himself along with Leonard. Standing with a SPI was a prison term at least. It might be seen as full-on treason from a government employee. Reginald was offering to stand next to him in front of the firing squad.

No, not really. He was setting Leonard up to be betrayed. It was a trap. The great Sheriff Reginald Strange wouldn't sacrifice everything he had for his son.

It was the first life lesson Leonard had learned.

"I'm leaving," Leonard said. He started for the door, passing his father at a normal walk. He was still breathing hard.

The snap of his father's holster strap warned him, but he didn't react the way he might have if it had been anyone else. He didn't spin around and snatch the gun out of his father's hand before it could be raised. He gave his father the time to raise it if that was what he was going to do.

"Don't go," Reginald said, his voice hard. Leonard turned slowly to his father. Reginald held his service pistol, a black 9mm, toward Leonard's face. The barrel was shaking. Leonard wondered how many times the man had drawn the weapon, if ever. Now, he was pointing it at his own son. Leonard might have felt sorry for the man if he was someone else's father.

Instead, the idea that his own father wanted to shoot him snapped something in him. He moved, causing Reginald to reflexively pull the trigger. The sudden bang of the gun almost disoriented Leonard, but the bullet was never a threat. He was already out of its path by the time it left the barrel.

Leonard took the gun away from his father, then brought the baseball bat up in his other hand, the speed of the strike giving him the power to knock his father onto his back. Without waiting for his father's stunned body to settle, he jumped on top of Reginald and battered the man's head with the grip of the pistol. In a blink of an eye, Leonard had dealt nearly a dozen blows.

By the second blink, Reginald Strange was dead.

AUPrimeTV - Fridays 8pm

CSI - CHICAGO

The nation's capitol is rocked by a series of murders.
But the victims are all SPIs.
Is the killer a villain or a hero?
Could it be one of the CSI team?

December 22, 2017

The grisly result of Leonard's attack on his own father was displayed on the television the morning after Eric's visit to the Williams house. It was the first time Leonard had truly surfaced since his attack on Eric and AUPrimeNews was milking it for everything they could.

Eric stood at the mouth of the hallway, staring at the screen, listening to the anchor describe in detail how Leonard had run through the house, destroying everything that could be destroyed, then battering the Sheriff's head with the butt of his own pistol until nothing was left of it but a red pile of mush on the floor. The anchor speculated that the entire event had taken less than a minute.

"I want you to stay home today," Gillian said. Eric shifted his glance to find his mother sitting up straight on the couch. Her gaze hadn't wavered from the TV screen. "I wish you'd come home straight from school yesterday. I worry."

"I was visiting my friend Jason," Eric said as he joined her on the couch.

"Who's Jason?" Gillian asked. "I thought you'd be out with Kristin."

Eric considered hiding the truth about Jason and his parents, about the tracker and what had happened over the last week. But she deserved to know. So he told her. About Jason, about Kristin breaking up with him, and about the tracker and the black car that would, even now, be parked somewhere in the cul de sac waiting for him to go to school. The only thing he skipped was Citadel.

After he was done, Gillian sat silently, not even paying attention to the TV. She took a deep breath. It was then Eric noticed she was sober. She hadn't yet started drinking this morning.

"This is my fault, isn't it?" she said finally. "I was going to yell at you for not telling me any of this sooner. But it's my fault. I should have been the one talking sooner." She slid over and hugged Eric tight. "I'm sorry, kiddo. I'm sorry you've had to do all of this by yourself."

Eric returned the hug as tight as she did. A wave of relief washed over him as if she'd taken a weight off him. His logical mind had no idea how this apology was different than the others she'd given him, but somehow it was. Maybe he was just ready to accept it now.

"I want to meet this Zak Williams and his wife," Gillian said when they parted. "I want to know what they have planned for you. Not just now, but when we get to California."

Eric cocked his head. "What do you mean?"

"You don't think they'll just drop you off in Los Angeles and let you go, do you? Eric, you're the most powerful SPI out there since Rumble. You may not think that, but you are. They surely think that, too. They are not going to let a SPI like you go. Russ got sucked into FORCE because he needed help. But they didn't offer that help for free. The EUP won't be any different. They're either going to want you to help them fight the AU, or they're going to put you in a lab and study your power until they crack what makes you tick."

"Hum," Eric said in an attempt at levity, "I hum, not tick."

Gillian chuckled despite herself. She reached out and touched his face.

"You better get to school, I guess. They're watching you."

Eric got up and headed back toward his room for his things.

"Just be careful, kiddo," she said as he stepped out the front door.

Gillian was furious. Not at the AU, or the EUP, not even at her son or his friends. She was mad at herself.

When Eric was gone, she went to the window. She watched as he sped off on his bike, then she saw the black car pull out to shadow him. When they were both gone, she turned and stared at her home.

For weeks, she'd kept the place clean, using the work as a distraction from the urges and withdrawal of a recovering alcoholic. Now, in just a week, the place had fallen to pieces again. It wasn't that bad, just the accumulated disarray of a week's living.

No, she wasn't mad at herself, she straight-up hated herself. She'd had one job. She was supposed to protect her son. She should have prepared him for what he now faced. Now, he had no one to help him except an organization that wanted either to use him or study him.

She'd failed her son.

She tore her eyes from the mess of the living room and headed for the kitchen. There, she opened the drawers and cabinets and extracted all the bottles she'd accumulated over the week. Eric hadn't been at them. He'd probably been too busy with his own problems to try and solve hers. Or he'd been mad enough at her to stop trying.

Taking a play from Eric's book, she dumped all the alcohol down the sink and dropped the empty glass containers in the trash can. The first one shattered and made such a satisfying sound that she threw the rest hard into the can after it, breaking every bottle and building a pile of broken glass in the bin.

Then, she went into her bedroom and found the one bottle she kept for "emergencies." After draining the first one, she'd replaced it, in case Eric got to the others. She stared at it for a long moment, feeling the pull it always exerted on her. She gripped the neck hard in her hand and rekindled the flame of her anger and self-hatred. She stalked out of the room, through the hallway and into the living room. Without stopping, she walked out the front door of the house and stood next to her ancient, red Ford Tempo.

With a savage cry that might have been loud enough to wake the neighborhood, she smashed the full bottle of rum onto the asphalt driveway. Liquid splashed over the asphalt, and the aroma of rum assailed her nose. Her stomach turned with the smell, repelling her and sending her back into the house.

After emptying her stomach into the toilet, Gillian returned to the living room and looked at the mess again. Somehow, the house no longer felt like a black hole that sucked away her energy. Even during her attempts to stay sober over the last couple of months, she'd found that escaping the house was sometimes the only way to resist temptation. Now, she felt energized. She felt like she had a new purpose.

For the first time in years, Gillian Sumner felt free.

December 22, 2017

E ven though the football season was over, the cheerleaders still wore their blue and gold uniforms on Fridays. Unlike other schools, basketball hadn't been popular enough to field a team, so most sports were done for the year, not counting the geek sports like chess club or indoor track, neither of which rated cheer squad participation.

But having the girls in their bright blue outfits traipsing through the halls was a distraction. Even when Eric tried to turn his attention inward, a flash of blue would draw him out. His gaze followed the girl until she disappeared from view. But each time, it wasn't Kristin.

Only at chem class, it was Kristin. Her flash of blue was especially dazzling, and for once he was glad she sat at the back so he couldn't reasonably look at her the entire fifty-five minutes. Mr. Turner took pains to call on Eric every chance he got, it seemed. Eric answered every question with the responses he'd read in his chem book weeks ago. He hadn't even cracked the book open in the last week, but still, he remembered much of it word for word as if he'd read it last night.

After class, he rose from his desk only to have Mr. Turner's hand land on his shoulder. For an instant, he almost ghosted through it on impulse, but he resisted the urge.

"Is everything okay, Eric?" Mr. Turner asked. "It's nice to see you've got all the answers again, but you're reciting them verbatim from the book like Ben Stein. I'm afraid you're not really learning it."

"I'm okay," Eric said. "It's just been a long week."

"Must be tough with all the attention on you," Mr. Turner said. Eric started. How did Mr. Turner know he was being hunted. But no, that wasn't it. There was legitimate attention on him, as he was the first victim of Ender's newest SPI. "But that's not your only problem is it?"

"I feel like I don't have control of my own life. Like all I can do is roll with the punches. I get things, then those things are taken away." He paused, "Or they come at a price I don't know if I can pay."

Mr. Turner nodded. He seemed to be thinking seriously about his words. "When you're young sometimes you think you don't have a choice. That you have to be what others want, do what others want." He paused, his lips twisting as he shaped more words in his head. "But everyone has a choice. It's part of growing up. At your age, you need to start taking control. It won't be that long until you're on your own and you'll be responsible for yourself no matter what happens. Your life is about to begin for real, Eric. You have to start making your own choices. You have to start fighting for yourself, even if the outcome seems inevitable."

Mr. Turner blinked as if surprised that he'd said so much. He smiled sheepishly at Eric.

"If it's inevitable, why fight it?" Eric said.

Mr. Turner shrugged. "Nothing is really inevitable. You have the power to guide your own life. There is no force in the world that can stop you, or change you, or force you into a circumstance you don't want. There are a lot of forces that will try: Parents, friends, situations. But the human mind, the human will is stronger than all of that. If you apply it in the right ways, if you fight," He clenched his fist. "Nothing can stop you."

Eric glanced back at the desks, his eyes going naturally to the one Kristin used.

Mr. Turner sat on the edge of his large desk. His face showed that his mind was going back into the past.

"I haven't always been a teacher, Eric. In fact, being a teacher was probably the last thing I wanted to be. Before New York, I was a government scientist. Nothing really cool. That wasn't what I really wanted to do either. But I was smart, I liked to read. I was pushed by my parents and my schools toward science. My parents wanted me to be a doctor. My school counselors told me that if I was good enough in physics and math, I could be an astronaut. I could go into space."

"What did you really want to do?" Eric asked. Mr. Turner laughed.

"I don't know. To this day, I don't. No one ever asked me what I wanted, probably until this very moment. Everyone wanted to choose for me, and I let them. I went to the colleges they wanted me to go, I took the classes they wanted me to take. I got recruited to work for the government." He shook his head, "I spent days and days, month over month, doing nothing but solving equations. When it all ended, I had nothing. Teaching is all I could do."

"You never fought for yourself," Eric said, trying not to sound accusing. "How do you know it works?"

"Because I know what happens when you don't." Mr. Turner said, his voice hard. "When you roll with the punches, you end up on the ground. When you live by reaction, you get nothing.

"Did you know that Ender was the only town in Oklahoma not sacked during the Chaos Years?" Eric's shook his head. He hadn't.

"Its people stood together in the face of danger. They didn't hide behind walls like McAlester. They fought. They repelled the gangs and militias. They made an example of themselves, and they made it clear to everyone that trying to attack this town would be a huge mistake.

"So, now, Eric Sumner, I'm going to do you the favor no one ever did for me. I'm asking you: What do you want? What are you willing to fight for?"

Kristin broke away from the others as they hit the parking lot. Practice had almost been fulfilling today. She felt herself starting to get back to the place she had been at the beginning of the year. She found humor in the girls' jokes and banter again. Some of her old energy was coming back.

Maybe she was faking it a little bit still, but she'd get there, eventually. She loved these girls. She owed them her best effort.

Things were still tense between her and Stacy, but that didn't alienate her from the others. In fact, with the exception of Jessica, who would always take Stacy's side of things, the others seemed supportive of Kristin. Of course, they'd all heard what had happened between Kristin and Stacy in gory detail, no matter how both girls had tried to keep their falling out private. There was no privacy in gossip.

At least it hadn't spread through the entire school. Yet.

When she reached her little green Tic-Tac of a car, the Mini Cooper, the button on the keyfob deactivated her alarm and unlocked the doors. She dropped into the driver's seat and slammed the door behind her. Her hand was reaching the key toward the ignition when she saw movement out of the corner of her eye. She turned her head.

Eric Sumner sat in the passenger seat, waiting patiently for her to notice him.

Kristin screamed and jumped in her seat.

"What the hell, Eric!" she cried as she slapped him repeatedly with her keychain. He raised his arms to protect himself.

"Sorry, sorry, sorry," he said, repeating the word until she stopped hitting him. "It seemed like a good idea at the time," he groaned when she let up.

"A good idea?" she said. "How the hell did you get in my car in the first place?"

He stared blankly at her as if he didn't know how he got there either.

"Um," he started, "The door was unlocked."

"What the hell?" she repeated. She couldn't think of anything else to say. Her heart was calming down now, no longer trying to leap out of her chest with every beat. Her lack of words was more than just the surprise of her finding him in her locked and alarmed car. She felt a little fear. He was a SPI. She'd broken up with him, and more than a little cruelly. Was he here to exact his vengeance on her? Had his powers taken over his mind like Leonard's had?

"Sorry," Eric said, not at all angry or vengeful. "I just wanted to talk to you somewhere private, and this seemed like the only place." His face was flushed, and she could see his embarrassment written plain there. Maybe her fears were unfounded. She couldn't help but know that he meant her no harm. Still, the chemicals in her brain that had ignited due to her sudden terror weren't done with her yet.

"Well?" she said. She jammed the key into the ignition, then crossed her arms, mostly to hide the trembling in her hands.

Eric swallowed hard. Kristin had read a book on social anxiety before going to Eric's house to ask him on that first date. It had explained a lot about his behavior at school and why he always demurred when asked to go to football games. That understanding had led her to make the first move, and why she'd always chosen relatively quiet or private places to go on their dates. This right here was probably the hardest thing he'd ever had to do. Sure, he was doing it all wrong — scaring the crap out of her — but he was trying. It had to be important to him if he was taking this leap.

"We've made a decision, I think," he said. He took a breath. "My mother and I. We're leaving Ender."

The news wasn't surprising. Between Leonard and the AU, life must be a living hell for him. Still, her eye twitched when he said it. She had to blink really slow and press her lips together to suppress the emotion that rushed through her.

"When?" she asked in a whisper.

"I don't know. We have to set things up first. Probably a week or two. I didn't want to leave without... telling you." He hesitated before the last words. Had he been about to say something else?

"I'd have understood if you did," she said, "but thanks."

"What do you mean?" he asked.

She didn't want to burden him with the knowledge that she knew what he was. She thought she'd already proven that she'd never tell anyone, but she didn't know if he would trust her not to. Besides, this really wasn't about that.

She turned to him, the edges of her vision blurred as she fought tears.

"I've treated you like shit, Eric. You don't owe me anything. You were completely right. I chose this over you." She fingered the yellow fringe of her blue cheerleader skirt. "That was a mistake. I didn't see how much I was being manipulated until I couldn't make any other choice. For what? A championship? A thing." Her words spilled out, surprising even her with a truth she hadn't completely internalized before now. "I've never been a 'thing' person, Eric. I couldn't care less about trophies and ribbons or whatever. It's people I care about. I thought Stacy was my friend. I thought those girls were my friends. They might like me, but none of them really care about me as much as they care about competing in that damned championship. I cared about them too much, what they thought and how they would feel if I abandoned them. But then I abandoned you."

She was crying in earnest now. She couldn't even see him anymore. Her own words surprised her. Just minutes ago, she thought she was getting better. She'd begun to enjoy herself again. But it had been a lie she told herself.

She wiped her fingers over her eyes, trying to clear them up. When she looked at him again, he was sitting there awkwardly, completely unsure what to say or do. She nearly laughed, he was so predictable. She took some deep breaths to get herself back under control, then wiped her eyes dry.

"It's okay," she said. "I'm okay." She smiled at him to prove that she was indeed okay. "I made a mistake, Eric. I didn't see what was really important. I saw something," she paused unsure if she wanted to go down that road. She veered off a little bit. "I saw something in you that day in the park. You are stronger than even you believe. If you think you need to leave, to get away from all this," she gestured out the window. By coincidence, or maybe inevitability, there was an AU armored vehicle parked on the street next to the middle school in front of them. "Then that's what you need to do. But I think you can survive this. I don't want you to make the same mistake I did, Eric. Remember what's important better than I did."

Why did she say that? She instantly regretted it. She'd all but begged him to go out there and fight Leonard and the AU with all his super-human power, whatever that was. He was smart, probably inhumanly smart. He'd realize what she knew sooner or later.

For now, he didn't seem to. He stared at her, his face open in some sort of shock or wonder. She imagined what he might be thinking: Damn, that's why I fell for this girl.

The idea almost made her laugh. Her lips even twitched up in a smile.

Instead of replying, he reached over with his right hand and opened his door. He nodded to her silently and retreated to the parking lot.

When he was gone, when he was out of the view of even her rear view mirrors, she slammed her back against her chair.

"Damn it!" she cried.

Leonard sat in the giant maroon sedan he'd broken into and watched, wishing he had some popcorn. Eric's face was priceless as he walked away from the green Mini. He'd either had his heart broken, or needed to go number 2 real bad.

When Eric was almost out of the view of the Mini, he turned around to watch it as it backed out its parking spot and drove away. Whatever had just happened in there, it was clear Sumner wasn't over the cheerleader.

Perfect.

Leonard started the car and pulled out after the Mini.

Maybe he'd finally found a way to touch the untouchable kid after all.

Alec Gunn

(Posted: 10/13/2016)

A CLOSE CALL

AU Security forces apprehended an EUP SPI today in Pittsburgh, PA. Investigators discovered the SPI before an attack could be perpetrated. It is believed an attack was planned for this weekend's NFL football match between the Pittsburgh Steelers and the Chicago Bears, last year's Super Bowl champions.

The villain is Chistopher Ronald Blake, 24, a Strength/Agility SPI. He will be executed on Saturday at 6:45PM by firing squad pending the obligatory DNA screening.

The execution will be live-streamed right here on AUPrime-News.com at 6:45 pm (CDT).

232

December 22, 2017

A fter leaving Kristin, Eric returned home to find Gillian out. That was either a good sign or a very bad sign. He guessed she had gone to find Zak and Ashley. Maybe the three of them could do something that the Williams couple could not.

Either that, or there was going to be a huge dust-up between the parents.

There was one upside to Gillian being gone. She wasn't there to keep him from going out again. Eric set the tracker on his desk and changed into a black sweatshirt and black jeans. He tightened the hood over his head and slipped out of the house through the wall opposite the cul de sac. After checking his surroundings to be sure he wasn't being watched, he ran across the bramble infested open space behind the house and crossed the shallow stream to reach the road circuitously.

It took him longer than normal because he was jogging and not riding his bike, not to mention the round-about path he was forced to take to avoid the AUSS, but he eventually arrived at Citadel's RV. Before ducking into the trees on the track that led to the RV, he looked all around for observers. There were no cars on the road in either direction and no one walking or watching. When he deemed that he hadn't been followed, he raced along the track and arrived at the RV's parking spot.

"Running now?" Buck asked. Eric couldn't think of him as Citadel when he was looking at him. It just seemed wrong somehow. "What happened to the bike?"

"Being watched," Eric said. He filled Buck in on what had happened with Hamilton and the Williams, and how he'd reconciled with his mother. Citadel liked the story even less than Gillian had. He rose from the creaky metal chair.

"You weren't followed coming here, were you? If you brought them here, I'll…"

"It's okay!" Eric cut in, not wanting to hear what Buck would do. "I was real careful. They don't even know I left the house."

"Turning into a real Ghost, are you?" Buck asked with an uncertain smile. "Fine. That's what I'll call you. You need an alias anyway if you're going to hide." He gestured for Eric to take a seat on the pile of wood, then ducked into the RV. He returned a minute later carrying what appeared at first to be a shallow white bowl. When Buck held it up, Eric saw that no, it was an old-school hockey mask.

"If you ever need to act in public, use this." He tossed the mask into Eric's lap. "Might work well with that getup," he added, gesturing to Eric's current, black attire.

"I'll really look like a ghost," Eric said, examining the mask. It has some breathing holes near the mouth and two large eye holes. Otherwise, it was hard white plastic. "Or a serial killer."

Buck shrugged. He returned to his seat and looked carefully at Eric.

"Your power work okay in that sweatshirt?" Buck asked.

"Yeah, why?" Eric replied.

"You said you couldn't bring anything with you when you 'ghost'. The clothes you wear, the t-shirts and jeans and such, live sort of close to your skin, so it makes sense that you don't fall out of them when you ghost. But that sweatshirt is rather loose." Eric noticed that his assurances that he hadn't been followed hadn't completely soothed Buck's paranoia. The man often glanced out toward the trees behind Eric as he spoke.

Eric pulled at the sweatshirt. Buck was right. He hadn't even thought of it when he'd used his power to leave the house.

"My subconscious must know the difference. I haven't been able to do it consciously."

"But just the fact that you can means you can spread your power outside of yourself. So it must be possible that you can take something with you when you phase out."

Eric nodded in agreement. "I don't know how, though."

"This means that the full extent of your power may be unknown," Buck mused. "Who knows what else you can do that you just haven't discovered yet."

"Mom said something like that," Eric said. "She thinks that's why Jason's parents are helping me."

"Might be. No one really does things completely selflessly. Very few, at least. I can't imagine the EUP being any different."

"Zak and Ashley report directly to Mental Block," Eric said hesitantly. "Maybe if I tell them about you, Mental Block could help with your memories. He at least knows you well enough to remind you who you were."

"No," Buck said with a sense of finality. "I don't know enough about Mental Block or anyone else that I can trust them. For all I know, New York might have been Mental Block attempting to kill me."

Eric was shocked to hear such a theory. Why would anyone kill millions of people like that just to get rid of one SPI? How could anyone live with himself after doing that?

"That's why you haven't gone to the EUP," Eric guessed. "You're afraid someone — Mental Block — might try again?"

Buck shrugged. "That's the point, Ghost. I don't know. I don't know anything. I'm not safe anywhere, even here. Any moment, someone could find me, and more people will die because of me."

"Then why stay here? Surely you're a little safer on the move."

"I'm here because at least here I can do some good." Buck gestured to Eric.

"You just said no one does anything selflessly," Eric argued.

Buck scowled at him. Then he breathed a sigh.

"I was hoping that helping you might help me remember

my past. Why do I feel this obligation toward you? What kind of hold does the Sumner family have over me?" He threw his arms up helplessly. "I still don't know."

They sat in silence for a while. Buck retrieved two Cokes from the cooler and tossed Eric one.

"You should take the EUP up on its offer," Buck finally said. "Get out of Ender."

"We can't until the AU leaves," Eric said. "They need to capture Leonard. Then they won't have a public reason to stick around. They might leave a few agents here to keep watch, but Hamilton and most of the others will be gone. We have to wait."

"That could take a long time if the AU wants it to," Buck said. "They could capture the speedster and put him in a deep hole somewhere, only to bring him out again when they're good and ready. They could spend months or years in Oklahoma 'searching' for this SPI." Buck held his Coke can with his pinky finger as he made air-quotes with his hands.

"Not if we draw Leonard out into the public and take him out." Eric fingered his new mask. Would it keep his secret for him? Could he "safely" go out in the open in order to lure Leonard out?

"That's such a bad idea. We aren't superheroes like in the old comic books. A simple mask won't make the AU ignore your actions if you out yourself. It'll just give them another reason to stick around."

"But we have something they don't know about," Eric said, the hint of a smile forming on his face. He pointed to Buck with the hand holding the mask.

"What the hell are you talking about? I thought I made it clear I'm not going out in the open!"

"You're going to let me do this alone?"

"I'm not going to let you do it at all," Buck argued. Eric's smile vanished. There was very little anyone could do except wait. That wasn't an option. Eric had to act.

"How are you going to stop me?" Eric asked. He respected Buck's power, but he was a Physical. There was nothing Buck could do to him. He was untouchable.

He held out his Coke can and clenched his fist. Instead of crushing the can, his hand passed through it, sending the can falling to the ground. It was just bottom-heavy enough to stay upright when it hit the dirt. "I'm getting out of Ender," he said flatly. "Whatever it takes."

"Then do it yourself," Buck growled. "Now, get the hell out of my home. I won't be responsible for your death." With that, Buck rose from his seat, stomped into the RV and slammed the door behind him.

Shocked at the sudden dismissal, Eric sat on the wood pile a little longer. When Buck didn't re-emerge, he stood and left, returning home at a walk, giving him time to think.

Eric walked his bike toward home. The air had a cold chill that told of winter coming in earnest. It was about that time of year. It had been a warm fall and winter was coming quite a bit late this year. When the snow started coming, Eric would have to garage his bike and walk to school every day.

But then, he'd probably be in California by then. He could ride his bike all year round.

Kristin had used a word Eric thought of often: "Abandoned." Eric knew what that was like. He'd been abandoned by his father, the suicide. He'd even been abandoned by his mother, the alcoholic. He'd spent much of the last few years afraid. He'd lived his life alone, secure in the idea that he could never be abandoned again if he didn't have anyone that could abandon him. Then, he'd had friends thrust on him: Kristin and Jason. He'd come to appreciate them, and for a time, maybe he thought he'd been wrong. Then, he'd been betrayed by Jason and, yes, abandoned by Kristin.

Oh yes, he knew what it was like to be abandoned.

He didn't want to do that to Kristin, who as much as admitted she wanted him back. He didn't want to do that to Mr. Turner, who wanted him to join his AP science classes. He couldn't tell himself anymore that he had no one who cared about him, that he had nothing tying him to Ender.

He didn't want to be his father. He didn't want to be "that guy."

To an extent, he was responsible for Leonard. He was the one who had hurt the bully first. He'd triggered an anger in the young SPI that Leonard couldn't control for whatever reason. It had been that anger that had caused Leonard to out himself and draw the attention of the AU in Ender, a town that had always thought of itself as somewhat separate from the troubles of the world, including SPIs, like Mr. Turner had said.

When you came down to it, this whole thing was Eric's fault. Like his father, he was responsible for what came after, the consequences of his actions. Now all of Ender was paying that price.

If he wanted to be better than his father, he couldn't run from this.

What are you willing to fight for?

He'd gone to Kristin's car to tell her everything. He'd wanted to be honest with her. Instead, he'd chickened out. That was how it was. How he was.

No. Mr. Turner was right. He couldn't place blame on anything or anyone, even himself. All he could do was fight.

And he knew the place to start.

Charlotte Matthews noticed the difference as soon as her granddaughter opened the door. The girl had never been troubled before. The last couple of weeks, since discovering one of the football players was a SPI, Kristin had been on a rollercoaster of emotions. It didn't help that she was of that age when nothing made sense and no trauma was needed for something to feel traumatic. Charlotte herself hadn't fared well during those years.

The little storm cloud that was Kristin Matthews passed through the kitchen and would have kept walking if Charlotte hadn't spoken.

"Anything you want to talk about, hun?" she said. Kristin dropped into a chair at the table as if that was her destination the entire time. Charlotte retrieved a tall glass, ice, and iced tea and placed the filled glass on the table. Almost roboticly, Kristin poured sugar into the tea that Charlotte liked better unsweetened.

The older woman watched silently as the young woman got the tea to her liking and drank. Patience was something Charlotte had learned a long time ago, mostly by dealing with her taciturn husband and equally stubborn daughter, Kristin's mother. Kristin might have drawn a little of that into herself, but it only manifested when she was sad. She'd never been a crier, even as a baby. When her mood was low, she only grew silent. You never got her to stop talking otherwise.

Charlotte looked at Kristin now: really looked at her. Her cheeks and eyes were red. She had been crying. This in itself scared Charlotte more than anything. She leaned across the table toward her granddaughter.

"What's wrong, Kris?"

"It feels like I've lost everyone I love, Nan. The girls hate me. All my friends are leaving me. And..." she trailed off. Charlotte wanted to cry out that she hadn't lost anyone. That everyone who loved her still loved her. How could they not? But Kristin had more to say.

She waited.

"There's a SPI at my school," Kristin said as if it were news. Charlotte nodded.

"We know, hun," Charlotte said. Kristin shook her head.

"Not that one. This one is a good guy. A really good guy. He helped me. He..." Tears glistened in her eyes again. Charlotte frowned. She'd never been a hateful woman. She'd always taught Kristin to judge a person by who they are, not on the color of their skin or whether they were rich or poor. It was a lesson Kristin had taken to heart, a lesson that shaped her very being.

But this was too far.

"You're hiding him?" Charlotte asked her. Something in her tone made Kristin look up. Kristin's freckled face had gone from flushed to pale in an instant. She pressed her lips together as if the mere pressure would seal them shut forever.

Charlotte's little girl was dead because of those people. Millions of people. Thousands more since that day. Now, her granddaughter had befriended one, was hiding him from the authorities.

"Who is he?" Charlotte asked. Her voice was as calm as she could make it, though she still heard a tremble.

"Nan," Kristin started. "Nan, he's a good guy."

"I'm sure your mother would have said the same thing."

Kristin drew back as if struck. Her chair drew across the floor in a shriek that echoed through the kitchen. Charlotte stood, then rested her palms on the table, leaning toward Kristin.

"You are going to tell me his name, then you will sit here with me as I call the authorities. We will do together what you should have done alone."

Kristin stood and shook her head. Her eyes teared up freely now. "Nanna, this isn't you," she said through a constricted throat. "Don't do this to me."

"To you?" Charlotte asked. Her mind had stopped working when she'd found out her granddaughter had been consorting with one of them. All she could think of was that she needed to get the girl away from him or she would lose Violet's daughter as well.

Charlotte opened her mouth to say more, but Kristin whirled around and fled back out the door, sobbing audibly.

Kristin fled, hating herself even more than she had when Eric had run away from her. She'd always been able to tell her Nanna everything. She'd never before gotten anything but support and love. Now, she'd found the one thing that would turn Charlotte against her, and it could cost Eric his life.

How could she have been so stupid?

She had time to notice the strange car pulling up into her driveway — an old maroon sedan so square and angular that looked like it had been chiseled from stone. Then her world exploded in motion.

Hands grabbed her all over, mostly around her arms and legs. Her uniform tore at the force of the attack. She started a scream, and the world blurred as she was moved.

Suddenly, as quickly as it started, it was over. She found herself reclined awkwardly in the back seat of the big sedan, her arms and legs bound in several yards of electrical tape. She silenced a scream that seemed like it had barely started struggled against her bonds. The rubbery tape strained but didn't break. It was wrapped too many times around her.

Leonard.

That was the only explanation. She levered herself up to get a better view of the front of the car. The driver's and passenger's seats were empty. A ballistic pistol lay on the dashboard, an official-looking revolver. It was a service weapon like those carried by the County Sheriff's deputies. It had flecks of what looked like rust on the white plastic handle.

Okay, not rust.

Her trembling eyes rose to look out the front window. She adjusted her body so she was sitting properly in the back seat, though her bound ankles made the position awkward. Beyond the car, the driveway looked peaceful. Her car and her grandparents' car sat still and undisturbed.

Then she saw the house.

As if a tornado had formed inside the building, curtains whipped on their rods. The windows shook. First, only the ground floor was affected, then, the second floor went into motion.

Leonard was going for her grandparents.

Just as she was about to ask herself what he was going to to with them, the horror of whatever was going to come with her imagination not yet creeping up her spine, the front door of the house whipped off its hinges. The car doors in front and one in the back all opened in quick succession, and the bodies of Charlotte and Henry Matthews fell into the car.

Charlotte dropped against her shoulder. Kristin grabbed at her awkwardly with her bound hands. The old woman's skin was still warm to the touch. When Kristin was able to get her face close, she heard Charlotte's breath rasping from her lungs.

She was still alive.

Kristin peered over the front seat to see Henry struggling stubbornly against ties similar to those that bound Kristin. He squirmed and worked at the electrical tape, trying to escape despite being long past his young and strong days. It was a futile effort for the old man, but Kristin loved him for it.

Then, Leonard occupied the driver's seat. His door closed with a decided thunk.

"That about does it," he said between panting breaths. "Had to leave a message for your boyfriend."

"You shouldn't push yourself so hard," Kristin said, drawing every ounce of hate she could muster into her voice. It felt strange to her, and she really did have to force it.

"I'll be fine in a minute," Leonard said. "By the time he reaches the arena, I'll be just perfect." He tossed something back to Kristin. It landed on her lap. It was her cell phone. Carefully, she worked her hands around enough to be able to pick it up. Flipping it around, she saw that the screen was on the texting app. The last text was to Eric, but it wasn't one she'd sent.

It read:

Come by my house. Find me at the Bowling Alley.

"You're an idiot," Kristin said. "He'll go to the bowling alley first."

Leonard shrugged and started the car.

"As long as he goes. It'll be better if he sees what I did in there, though." He giggled like a kid excited to see the results of a carefully planned prank.

Kristin's thumbs hovered over the screen of her phone. She considered texting Eric again to warn him not to go. But he would anyway, especially if he thought she was in danger. There was only one way to keep him away.

She closed the text window and opened another. She scrolled through the pre-loaded emergency numbers on the phone, finding the one for the County Sheriff. She typed in a simple text.

Leonard Strange. Ender Lanes. Now.

Then, she dropped the phone on the floor and slid it under the front seat with her foot.

"Lenny," she said to him when she was done. "You are a complete idiot."

December 22, 2017

Eric was half-way to Kristin's house when his back pocket buzzed, and the chime that said he had a text came to his ear. It was the first time he'd gotten a text from Kristin since the break-up. Had something about their conversation earlier spurred her to add something by text?

He didn't look at it right away. Only when he pulled into her driveway and dismounted from his bike did he pull the phone out of his pocket and look. The words baffled him. Her car was in the drive way. If she was here, then she wasn't at the bowling alley.

Then, he saw the front door. It was shattered and hung off the frame by broken wood and a twisted metal hinge. It reminded him of the tool shed before he'd destroyed it.

The text hadn't been from Kristin.

With long strides, Eric left his bike and rushed to the house, just barely keeping himself from breaking into a sprint. He needed to be calm, he needed to keep his logical mind. If he rushed in with his emotions, he'd walk right into whatever trap Leonard had set for him.

He entered the house carefully, ready to trigger his power if there was anything in the least threatening — besides the broken door.

He'd been here once, but he'd never gone inside. Kristin had just stopped here once with him when they were on one of their dates. She'd forgotten her credit card and had to go in quick to get it.

He expected a rich girl's place with all the amenities, not unlike the Williams house.

What he got chilled his blood and drove him back to his bike at a dead run.

Eric sped up to the RV to find Buck sitting in his usual spot. Something was different. It took Eric a moment to notice. The RV's wheels had been mounted. The RV was off its blocks. Buck could leave at any moment.

He hit the brakes and skidded to a halt just short of the covered area outside the RV. Reclined in his chair, Buck stared at him from under lidded eyes.

"I'm still mad, Ghost," Buck said before Eric even dismounted his bike. "You need to leave."

That sure wasn't going to make this any easier.

"I need your help," Eric said. He didn't get off his bike. He was in too much of a hurry to do so. Instead, he straddled the middle bar.

"All of a sudden, you need my help a lot." Buck didn't look at Eric as he spoke. "I told you, I'm not going to help you do anything stupid that will get people killed."

Eric tossed his cell phone onto Buck's lap. The old man's eyebrow rose as he looked at the text on the screen.

"Who is this?"

"Kristin. She's sort of my girlfriend."

"The cheerleader?" The comment reminded Eric of how Buck had been stalking him for the last several weeks.

"I took pictures of the house," Eric said. Buck tapped through the menus and found them. He showed no reaction as he swiped through them.

"That's one sick kid," Buck said. He lifted the phone and showed Eric one of the pictures. It was the living room. The furniture had been trashed, broken beyond recognition. On the wall was written: "Eric Sumner is a SPI" in some thick red substance. "Whose blood is this?" Buck asked.

"Dog," Eric said, "Or cat. I couldn't tell." He hadn't taken a picture of that. He hadn't wanted any record of it in case Kristin looked at his phone at some point.

"You destroyed it?"

"I wiped it off the wall best I could."

Buck turned back to the pictures.

"Why do you need my help?" The big SPI asked. "You've handled Leonard before. You're more than qualified to get in and get your girl out. Probably better than me. You're the ghost. I'm a tank."

Buck's voice had taken on a soft quality, not the angry refusals he'd given Eric before. Eric took that as a good sign.

"It's not just Leonard. I went by the bowling alley first. The AUSS is already there. Their boss, Roger Hamilton, is a SPI. Like you."

Buck glanced up at him, glowering.

"Well then," Buck said. "Looks like the situation is handled. They'll have Leonard in no time."

"At what cost?" Eric demanded, a flash of heat rushing through him at Buck's careless words. "Kristin's life? You're the one who said you didn't want anyone else to die!"

"Then get her out of there, Ghost," Buck rumbled. "The longer you argue uselessly with me, the closer she comes to being collateral damage."

Eric stared at Buck with shock. He'd thought that if lives were on the line, he could convince the old man to help.

"Fine," he said, hopping up onto the seat of his bike and lifting the hood of the black sweatshirt over his head. "Don't expect me to help you anymore, Citadel." He spat the name like the curse it was. "Your memory can rot in hell for all I care."

He spun the bike around and pushed his way down the trail toward the road.

He rode hot, pushing for speed back toward town. He was

alone now. Everyone had left him behind, now with Citadel adding himself to the list. He had no one he could turn to. Jason and his family were just people. Their job had been only to get him out of Ender. That wasn't on the table anymore. They would fade into the background now. Gillian wouldn't be a help in this either.

There was only one way to save Kristin now. A public confrontation between SPIs. Something to wet the appetite of AUPrimeNews and settle up the reason for the AUSS's presence in Ender. They'd get both Leonard and Eric when it was done. All that was important was that Kristin and her family make it out of that bowling alley. It wasn't exactly how he'd planned it, but without Citadel, there was no other option.

Leonard would finally get what he wanted.

Eric steered himself around Main Street, not wanting to get caught out around the bowling alley. He approached from behind, hiding the bike in bushes a block away. He sneaked closer to the huge building and saw that the AUSS was still building up their resources. Armored agents moved through the parking lot. At intervals, they knelt and placed a device on the ground. Those would be the speed traps, electronic mines that would detect any object moving faster than a jogger's pace and explode in an electric shock designed to stun the speedster long enough for the armored agents to move in and restrain the SPI.

There was no flurry of activity, at least not the kind that Eric expected. Because of the mines, everyone moved at a sedate walk in an overabundance of caution. Agents did move nonstop, walking from here to there to make reports or conduct patrols. Eric noticed one of the vehicles, a black panel van seemed to be the hub of all activity. That would be the command station where Hamilton was.

Almost as soon as the thought occurred to him, Eric saw the large black form of Hamilton emerge from the van's side door. His hand was held up to his ear. He was on the phone with someone. Hamilton shrugged, responding to whoever was on the other end of the line.

As if the shrug were signal, every single one of the speed traps ignited in quick succession. Ringing the bowling alley in crackling light that immediately faded away.

Eric stared in shock as Leonard ripped his way through the AUSS.

What did you do? Edward asked Rockhide.

Rockhide held his dead cellphone to his ear.

"I gave him a push," Rockhide said. "That's what you wanted, right?"

What if he kills the boy?

"Sumner?" Rockhide said as he pulled open the van door to examine the preparations in the bowling alley's parking lot. The speed traps were set. His people were ready. "I'm still not sure he is what you think he is. I don't see it. But no matter what happens here, both these kids will be outed and we can take them."

You are not to take the boy, Edward said. Even if he is outed. He's too dangerous to take by force.

Rockhide shrugged and nodded reluctantly.

"Whatever you say, boss." He lifted his head and brought his eye up to watch the front of the bowling alley just in time to see the shit hit the fan.

The door to the bowling alley flew open, and a blur of motion burst from the building. Rockhide had an instant to register the motion before the speed traps triggered.

Every one of them.

Rockhide's eyes widened in genuine surprise as he realized what had happened. Leonard had run fast enough to beat the electrical fields of the speed traps. By the time his motion triggered the sensor, and the command went from the processor to the payload, he was already out of its range.

Rockhide had never experienced a speedster so fast.

Before the flash of the speed traps had even dimmed, his men were in disarray. Weapons flew into the air, seemingly of their own accord. Many of them discharged into their owners, dropping several agents before any of them could react.

Then, the armored agents began to drop. In one moment, they were reacting to the sudden movement, the next they were bleeding from knife wounds. The blade Leonard wielded sliced between armor plates into the flesh beneath.

Rockhide had time to take one step forward before it was over.

Leonard let himself catch his breath. That had been a gamble. He'd pushed himself harder than ever. It was exhilarating! He'd felt a little bit of a shock when he'd run across the speed traps, but he'd gotten out of the way just in time.

He'd only had enough strength in him to take out a few agents, using their own weapons against them, when he'd seen the KA-BAR knife at the belt of one of the agents, he'd used it to take out a few of the tougher ones that bullets wouldn't.

It was amazing. Letting out his frustration in such a way was its own reward. A rush of what he could only describe as "freedom" slid through him now. That would make them rethink their reluctance to give him what he wanted. Eric would come. And when he did, it would be Leonard Strange who took him down.

He could make another run when he caught his breath. With the speed traps gone, he could take it easier next time. Give him ten minutes, and he'd finish this, leaving that prick Hamilton for last.

He turned to his hostages, sitting in chairs against the wall. His hostages, Kristin and her grandparents, stared at him. Only Kristin didn't show fear when she looked at him.

That would change when she watched him kill her boyfriend.

"There he is!" came a shout. A pair of agents, one armored, one not, was coming around the corner. The armored agent was pointing at him.

Eric leaned against the wall of the bar attached to the bowling alley. He adjusted the hockey mask that hid his face from them. They knew who he was of course, but any proof they might have from body cameras or other surveillance wouldn't be able to convince anyone that he was Eric Sumner. Right now, he could only be "Ghost."

As they rushed forward to capture him, he took a breath and pushed himself back through the wall and into the bar.

The electricity had been cut some time ago. The bar was dark, lit only by light filtering through the frosted glass windows. The expected smell of stale alcohol that Eric had expected from such a place wasn't present. Instead, the place smelled of fried food and cigarette smoke. Chairs and stools littered the floor, tossed aside as the patrons fled Leonard's appearance. Glasses of bear and baskets of chicken strips, fries, and cheap hamburgers still lay on the tables and bar.

Eric's head swiveled back and forth, scanning the shadows and cursing the limited vision the mask gave him. He had nearly no peripheral vision in the thing, and the thick plastic over the bridge of his nose was always visible no matter where he looked.

He ghosted through tables and furniture, being careful to breathe in between when he was solid. He tried to picture how the bar opened into the bowling alley. It had been years since he'd been here on a school "fun" field trip in fourth grade. Obviously, the bar wouldn't have been part of the activities. A single door separated the two, an attempt to put a barrier between the all-ages entertainment center and the adult drinking establishment. A round glass window frosted like the outside window so eager teenagers couldn't peek in was the only break in the dark wood door.

He ghosted partially through the wall closest to the door to peer into the bowling alley to see what he would be walking into.

The huge room beyond the wall was mostly dark. Ancient emergency lights running off batteries lit the space in spectral yellow pools of light. In the shadows, the indistinct shapes of tables, chairs, lane consoles and other odds and ends lay like black Lego blocks waiting to be stepped on.

Eric spotted Kristin in a pool of emergency light near the first lane. Leonard had tied her and her grandparents to chairs and set them like spectators to a game. They were close to the wall, but about a dozen yards from where he was now.

He stepped back into the bar and glanced in the direction the chairs were set. The bar's kitchen was that way. They'd be on the other side of the wall from there.

Eric turned in circles, trying to figure out how he was going to get them out.

If Leonard was in the bowling alley, he'd hidden like a hunter who'd set a snare and was waiting for the prey to trip the trap. He'd be watching the Matthews.

Eric had to figure out where he was waiting and try to find a way to sneak Kristin and her family out.

Carefully, Eric pushed through the wall and solidified so he could breathe again. Ducking low, he crept through the dim light. Hiding behind shelves of bowling balls, he made his way toward Kristin and her grandparents.

Where was he?

Eric peered over one of the shelves and looked down the line of lanes. Some still had pins racked. Others were cleared of them. The entire place was deathly silent. The normal bowling alley noises, the cracking of pins, the rolling of balls, the churning of the lane machinery, was absent. The last time he'd been here the only sound that had interested him had been the jingling sound of arcade games.

He glanced toward Kristin. She was the furthest from him. Her grandfather was closest with her grandmother between them. Eric judged he might be able to able to reach the old man while staying hidden by the bowling ball shelf. Kristin sat stiffly, her head swiveling around, eyes searching for something. Her cheerleader uniform was torn, and there were bruises on her face. The sight of them stoked a fire in Eric's chest that had nothing to do with his power.

As he got closer, her eyes swept over him. Though he should

have been perfectly visible to her, she didn't show any indication she saw him. Eric froze. When her eyes brushed over him again, she blinked. It was just a casual blink, but it occurred right as their eyes met. That couldn't have been a coincidence. When it happened again, he was sure. She knew he was there, but she didn't want to give away his location.

That meant Leonard was in a place that he could see her.

He watched her eyes as they slowly swept away. When they pointed toward the far lanes, she blinked again.

Smiling behind his mask, Eric took a deep breath and ghosted into the bowling ball shelf. In the shelf, he had a view from within an empty ball cubby. In a shadow between emergency lights, Eric saw him. Leonard crouched in the darkness, his vantage giving him a clear view of the entire room, save the space Eric had been creeping through behind the shelves. He was over a hundred feet away, but Eric was sure he could reach Kristin in a blink.

There was no way he was getting them all out unnoticed.

But if Eric judged it right, Leonard was at just the right angle to mostly hide Mr. Matthews from his line of sight. Eric could at least get one of them out before risking both.

He pulled back once more in to the space between the ball shelves and the wall. He approached the chairs until he was nearly to the end of the shelf. Mr. Matthews' attention was drawn to his motion. When the old man saw him, he started. Fearing that the man might call out, Eric put his finger quickly to the breathing holes at the bottom of the hockey mask. The old man calmed, and Eric waited a few seconds to see if the movement had alerted Leonard.

"Nanna," Kristin said suddenly, her voice soft, but in the large echo chamber of the silent bowling alley, it must have carried across to Leonard. Kristin's grandmother looked away from the horrified stare she had pinned on Eric. "It's going to be okay," Kristin said. "We'll get out of here. Just trust me, okay?"

Eric smile again in his mask. She was diverting the attention of both Mrs. Matthews and Leonard. Now was the time to move.

A stab of doubt hit him. How was he going to do this? An image of the red toolbox flashed through his mind. The tools in it hadn't phased out at his command. But Citadel had pointed out his clothing. Even the mask he wore phased out with him when he ghosted through walls. How did he do that? He didn't even think about it.

A lot of Eric's power ran off his subconscious. It acted irrationally. It acted of its own initiative. It took something of a wrestling act to wrangle control of it. Eric had read about the idea of the subconscious, or unconscious mind, but he didn't understand much. There was nothing logical about it. Where the conscious mind was one of reason, the subconscious was one of feeling. Where the conscious mind thought it words, the subconscious thought in images.

When Eric ghosted, he did it by feeling his power. Feeling the buzz of it in his chest and spreading through his body. There wasn't a conscious word thought, like "abracadabra" or something. It was a feeling. It was a visualization.

Slowly, so as not to attract attention, Eric reached out to Mr. Matthews. He touched the old man's skin and squeezed his arm in what he hoped was a reassuring way.

This was going to be awkward.

Eric started his power, feeling it course through him, ghosting his flesh and bone, his clothing and his mask. He "felt" it spread out from his hand and through Mr. Matthews, starting at where his hand touched the old man's arm. He imagined Mr. Matthews sinking slowly through the chair, through the tape that tied him to the chair.

Mr. Matthews ghosted, his body blurred. He started again and struggled. Eric had to reach out with his other hand to hold on and catch him as he fell through the chair.

"It's okay, it's okay," Eric whispered as he drew Mr. Matthews to him. "I'm going to get you and your family out of here, trust me."

Mr. Matthews stared through the holes in Eric's hockey mask, searching his eyes.

"Shh," Eric said. "Come with me. Don't fight me."

Mr. Matthews got his feet under him, and they moved together toward the wall. Mr. Matthews hesitated when it became clear they were going through it. Eric pushed at the man's back. They went through the wall together, emerging into the kitchen of the bar. When they were clear of the equipment and on the open tile floor, Eric made them solid again.

Mr. Matthews gasped, drawing in air and leaning a hand on the counter to steady himself.

"Are you okay?" Eric asked.

"I will be. Get the others."

Eric nodded, not wanting to tell him that in order to get the others he'd have to confront Leonard directly.

AUPrimeHistory: True Conspiracies

(Airdate: 9/11/2008)

THE MARSHALL COUP

<Interview with President Andrew Marshall: 2007>

Andrew Marshall

"The administration at the time didn't want to look any deeper into this than we already had. I hoped that with the incoming admin- istration in 2005, things would change. We needed better leadership. When things didn't change, I decided that if no one else could, I would."

After the 2004 election, then-senator An- drew Marshall gathered his things and left the Capitol. He didn't leave because he'd been de- feated. He left to seek assistance in finding a new way forward for America. He took trips to Toronto and Mexico City to seek the aid of those countries in helping the United States of America survive.

<Slideshow: "Anarchy in America">

What came of those meetings would forever change the course of North America. At the time, the Federal government of the United States had very little sway outside of the District of Co- lumbia. Anarchy and lawlessness ruled in all but the strongest states. Refugees flooded both the Canadian and Mexican border seeking a safer home for their families. Armed gangs and out-of-work police officers warred for control of rural areas where food was more plentiful, and government security presence was lacking.

<Slideshow: "Chaos in Congress">

In D.C., the government continued to squabble amongst themselves, seeking political advantage instead of looking out for the welfare of the people. So when the time came for a formal summit of the leaders of the three major North American countries, D.C. was intentionally left out of it. The meetings were held in Chicago. There, a draft was completed for a new coalition government for all three countries to strengthen what had once been the most powerful region on Earth. On April 4th, 2005, the American Union was effectively born.

<Archive Footage: "Siege of Washington, D.C.">

On the strength of Andrew Marshall's leadership, a security force was established with the ability to restore order to the majority of the former United States. After three months of conflict, gangs were suppressed, criminals were arrested or executed, and the former government in D.C. was brought to heel. The US Court System, legislature, and executive administrations were disbanded in favor of the American Union constitution. Finally, the disparate branches of the US military apparatus were absorbed into the AU security force or released from service.

Andrew Marshall

"I regret what had to be done, but I would do it again if I had to. We were facing a

complete dissolution of civilization in this country. If we had let the administration in Washington continue on their course, more people would have died. The thousands that were killed during the Coup - mostly criminals and opportunists - would have been millions of innocents dying of starvation or as the victim of organized oppression in the form of cartels and bandit gangs. I believe we made the better - but by no means good - choice."

<Commercial Announcement>

December 22, 2017

Eric backed into the wall as Mr. Matthews left the kitchen, heading for the back door of the bar.

He emerged back into the bowling alley. There was no more hiding. There was no way he'd get Kristin or her grandmother out without a fight. He moved through the bowling ball shelf and exposed himself in the same pool of light that illuminated the Matthews.

Leonard rose from his crouch. A shadowy form rising into the half-light.

"Are we going to try this again?" Eric called out into the huge, silent room. "You gonna try and beat me down? I promise I won't disappoint you like last time."

"What's with the getup, Sumner?" Leonard replied. "You think that mask is fooling anyone?"

Eric reached up and pulled the hockey mask off, letting it ruffle his hair as the straps pulled away from his head. The black hood of the sweatshirt also fell away. If Kristin didn't know who he was already, she did now.

"There are no cameras here, Leonard. No one to care what we do." Leonard pointed toward the Matthews.

"There's them."

Eric looked back to Kristin. She showed no emotion on her

face as she gazed at his face. Mrs. Matthews had a strange look on her face, something like interested confusion.

"Sorry I lied to you," Eric said to Kristin.

"So am I," she said. "I know how you got in my car."

Eric let his eyebrows rise. She'd known this whole time?

There was no time to dwell on it.

Leonard rushed forward. Eric braced himself, calling up his power. But at the last moment, Leonard veered away. In another blink, he stood next to Kristin's chair. In his hand, he held a police service pistol pointed at Kristin's head.

She jerked in her chair, her eyes trembling in sudden terror.

"You're not quite as untouchable as you thought, Sumner."

Eric froze. His heart leapt into his throat at the moment Leonard had settled. The gun's hammer was already pulled back. A touch of the trigger and Kristin would be dead. She struggled in her chair, unable to stay calm as she helplessly faced death.

"You see," Leonard explained, "I know I can't kill you. But I've outed you. The AUSS outside? They know all about you now, thanks to me. When they come in here, you'll be weeping over the blood and brains of this cutie here."

He stabbed the barrel of the gun against Kristin's head. She squealed, holding back a full-throated scream.

"They'll take you away," Leonard continued in his taunting tone, "and I'll watch your execution on the Prime Time news." He smiled. "I'm sure they'll figure something out. It might take awhile. Hell, you're better than one of those Endurance freaks they have to drown for three hours. It might take all night to find what works for you."

Leonard stepped back to take his shot. Eric screamed.

"No!"

The gun went off. Eric's power roared audibly in sympathy with the explosion. Both sounds reverberated through the empty bowling alley.

Mrs. Matthews' chair tipped, and the woman fell over onto the ground. The hole that had been drilled in her head by Leonard's bullet spilled her life onto the slick hardwood floor.

"Nana!" Kristin screamed. Her tear streaked face turned violently to Leonard. "I'm going to kill you!" She fought against the tape that bound her to the chair with renewed vigor, no longer a panicked response to the gun, but a furious effort to attack her assailant. Her right hand came free of the bonds. As she reached out to him, fingers bent like claws, her chair overbalanced. Leonard calmly steadied it with his free hand. Setting it back on all four legs while moving casually out of the way of Kristin's reaching hand.

Eric used the distraction to move. He took a deep breath and leaped forward, ignoring the obstacles between himself and Leonard, ghosting through them.

Leonard's arm was up and firing in a blink, a startled reaction to the sudden rush. The bullets passed harmlessly through Eric. Leonard may have had super human speed and reflexes, but his mind didn't quite work as quickly.

Leonard Strange was physically superior to Eric in every way, even without the super speed and agility. Eric had only one weapon against him.

Air.

As his shoulder struck Leonard, Eric let go of his logical mind and focused everything he had on the rage that burned in his chest. For everything Leonard had put him through. For every person Leonard had harmed or would harm. Leonard Strange must die.

His anger rewarded him with a hammer blow of pain that accompanied the reverse of his power. His entire body changed. His fury took the pain and fed off it, leaving Eric with nothing but the fire inside him.

He landed on top of Leonard. He saw but didn't hear the breath escape the older boy's body. Leonard's lips flapped and nostrils flared. In that instant, Eric took the rage into his mental fist. He only had moments. He had to stifle it, bring it under control and bury it under a concrete slab of logic. He wrapped his arms around his enemy as if Leonard were that rage personified.

His body flipped from ultra hard to ghost thin in that instant.

Leonard came with him.

In the transition, he had no time to take an extra breath. If he could, then Leonard could. They both had to fight with whatever oxygen was in their system.

Leonard struck at him with feet and fist as Eric fought to hold on and keep them both ghosted. Suddenly, Eric felt a cold pressure at the side of his head.

The gun had come out of phase with them!

His attention shifted to the cold solidity of the weapon, trying to figure out in an instant how to remove it from the equation.

Again, the gun went off.

Kristin screamed as Eric practically flew across the ten feet of distance between him and Leonard. His body passed through a bench, the bowling ball return machine, and the dark console that controlled the scoring computer for this lane. He might as well have been sprinting through mud. Leonard's arm flashed up, his gun barrel flashing at the same instant.

The sound pounded like tiny fists into Kristin's eardrums and echoed in the cavernous room. But the bullets passed through Eric, puffing through his body like it was smoke. To Kristin's tear streaked vision, Eric's form was a blur, as if her eyes couldn't quite focus on him even as it focused on everything around him.

But in the instant he connected with Leonard, Eric's body suddenly came into hyper-focus. He went from blurry apparition to high-definition-on-black-and-white-TV in a snap. Both of them hit the floor with a too-loud thump. Air burst from Leonard's lungs in an explosive gasp.

Eric changed again, his black-clothed form blurring out once more. But this time, Leonard's body did the same thing. Both of them wrestled on the floor, blurring. They rolled over into the second lane, passing through the gutter and the barrier that kept balls from jumping the lanes. Leonard threw punches into Eric's side with his free hand, then seemed to realize he still had the gun in the other.

Leonard pressed the gun against Eric's head. Kristin saw her boyfriend's eyes widen in shock as he felt it. Both combatants slowed in their struggles. Kristin saw Leonard's finger tighten on the trigger.

She cried out as the barrel of the gun flashed. The sound of it seemed somehow out of sync with the ejection of the bullet.

The gun clattered to the floor and became just another object for the two wrestlers to pass through.

Kristin's eyes widened as a fiery pain ripped through her stomach. She looked down, touching her middle. Her hand came away bloody.

The damned gun shot her!

Eric felt the gun drop away and redoubled his efforts to hold onto Leonard. He thought of how Buck had wanted him to do breathing exercises to increase his lung capacity. He'd never really gotten around to doing them. How many minutes did he have before he passed out and Leonard was free?

All too soon, Eric's vision dimmed. His struggling with Leonard had used up almost all the oxygen he'd stored from his last breath. His lungs were pumping, trying to get air, but coming up empty. He didn't have long.

But then, Leonard hadn't had any breath in him. He was still struggling, but the punches and kicks were becoming less painful. Was that because of Leonard's weakness or Eric's power?

Then, as his vision darkened almost completely, Eric heard a muffled voice, a thick vibration against his ear.

"Let him go, Eric. Let him go," The voice sounded similar to Kristin's, but off. "You'll kill him!" she cried.

Yup, that was Kristin. So what if he killed Leonard. Wouldn't that be better for everyone?

But he was pushing himself too far, too. He couldn't feel his surroundings. What if he passed out and came back into phase in the middle of a wall, or bench, or something?

At last, he rolled over so he was on top of Leonard, then shut off his power. Solidity came back with a snap of feeling and air. He gulped in air and felt every bruise Leonard had inflicted on him as if they were just now being inflicted. He dropped back to the floor with a low moan.

Leonard lay unconscious beneath him. They were in the middle of Lane 3. They'd gone so far?

Panting, he looked up to Kristin. She gave him a weak, relieved smile, but her face was pale. She pulled her hand away from her stomach and showed him the blood.

"Oh God!" Eric gasped.

He stood and rushed to her, slipping on the slick wood of the bowling lanes. His own pain and exhaustion were forgotten. The blood was seeping out of the wound, not gushing. That meant it hadn't hit anything vital, right?

"You'll be okay," he said to her.

"I can feel it in there," she said. "Every time I breathe."

Eric ran a hand behind her and didn't find an exit wound. She was right. The bullet was still in there. He carefully phased her remaining hand and feet out of the tape that bound her to the chair. Then, he pulled her chin up to him so she was looking at him.

"It'll be okay," he assured her. "I've got this, don't worry about it." As he spoke, he ghosted his free hand through her stomach. It felt squishy, but he was sure he wasn't harming anything. Well, reasonably sure. He'd passed through flesh before without any bad consequences. After a bit of feeling around, he could feel the difference between flesh, bone, and the metal of the bullet. The slug was intact inside the abdominal muscle just to her left side. It hadn't penetrated to her organs.

When he drew his hand out, he had the slug in his palm. "See?" he said.

She lowered her head and gasped when she saw the bullet in his cupped hand. It was almost entirely intact, having lost almost all of its momentum somehow. Eric had nothing that would fix the damage already done, but the bullet wouldn't do anymore internal damage.

Just then, the main doors to the bowling alley burst open.

"Get out of here!" Kristin hissed at him. Eric nodded. She'd be safe enough with the AUSS. They'd get her to a hospital.

He stood, found his hockey mask and was about to slip through the wall into the bar when he heard a familiar voice.

"Ghost?"

December 22, 2017

"What now, sir?" one of the surviving armored agents asked Hamilton. He couldn't tell who it was, but the voice was female. Agent Strauss maybe?

Hamilton glared at the front of the bowling alley. Just a few minutes ago, a patrol had brought back Henry Matthews, unconscious but alive, and reported that they'd seen a man in dark clothes and a hockey mask walk through a wall into the bowling alley.

Eric Sumner? But what the hell kind of power was that? Surely nothing like his uncle Russell.

Hamilton glanced back at the rest of the set up here. Two AUPrime news vans had parked courageously close to the AUSS vehicles lined up in a blockade around the bowling alley. They'd be broadcasting, one in English, one in Spanish, for the entire country to see and hear. Surely even now, they were speculating on the power of the speedster that had successfully evaded all of the speed traps and killed the majority of the agents under Hamilton's command.

He didn't care what they reported. It wasn't his job to control them. Whatever came out was only what Exodus would want them to say.

The rest of the black AUSS vehicles parked in a line through the parking lot, blocking both access and view of the bowling alley from the street.

Suddenly, the interior of the bowling alley thudded with the sound of gunshots. First one, then a quick succession of them.

Sumner!

Well, the speedster was getting what he wanted. He hoped Leonard would appreciate that once this was all over. Maybe they could recruit him after all.

He turned to Agent Strauss if indeed it was her.

"Get ready. I want breach in two minutes."

Strauss nodded and jogged the short distance to the others and began forming them up for a breach action. Hamilton noted almost subconsciously that he only had half a dozen agents remaining. The rest were laid out on the ground near the vehicles.

Hamilton turned to get the completely redundant body armor he'd have to wear during the breach. He'd just started to throw his shoulders into it when the crash of a car accident slammed through the air. Something crunched into his van, and he reached out instinctively to hold the car still. The metal around his hands crumpled when the force of the impact shivered down his arms.

"Fuck it," he growled to himself. He dropped the armor and ran around the van to find out what the hell was happening. The scene that greeted him was startling in its strangeness.

The AUPrime vehicles had been turned on their sides. The broadcast dish on each had been ripped from their mounts, all the wires pulled. One of the media vans had come to rest against the side of his operations van.

The man who had done this emerged from behind the media vans. He carried one of the big cameras AUPrime used to record footage. He pulled it apart piece by piece like it was Hallah bread, dropping broken shards of it to the ground in a trail behind him.

The man was big, taller than Hamilton by about a foot. His large frame, indicative of the strength SPI he'd proven himself to be, was mostly hidden by a long, voluminous coat, torn and dirty. The huge pockets seemed to be weighted down, the trailing edge of the coat didn't move right when the man walked. Though he walked straight-backed, he had an obvious hitch in his step, probably from an old wound.

But it was his features that were most interesting. Long gray hair had been pulled back and tied into a tail atop his head like he was some ronin from an Asian martial arts movie. His face was rippled with horrible burn scars, his nose looked melted. His eyes were bright, but gray and colorless.

The man turned those eyes on Hamilton.

"Where's the kid?" the man said in a gravelly voice. "Eric Sumner?" Hamilton grinned.

"He's a popular brat," he said. Just then, another gunshot went off inside the bowling alley. "My guess is you just missed him."

The man strode forward, but Hamilton moved into his path.

"Move," the man said simply. When Hamilton didn't budge, the man placed his hand on the SUV opposite the operations van. He seemed to be resting against it. Was he injured? "I know what you are, Roger Hamilton," the man said with resignation soaking his voice. "Don't make me show them." He jerked his head toward the agents caught in uncertain stances, awaiting orders. Hamilton would give them none. They hadn't come prepared for a strength SPI. The one S.E.A.S. power armor they had to counter this man was lying dormant in the back of the big rig parked just beyond the SUV. It wouldn't be ready to fight before it got torn apart.

"Let us go in," Hamilton said. "Neutralize the situation, then we can talk about the disposition of Eric Sumner if he's still alive."

The old man sighed. His body flexed — just flexed — and the SUV he leaned against lifted from the ground like a kicked skateboard and slammed into the tractor trailer hard enough to knock the entire rig on its side. The agents standing nearby screamed and fell back. Those that still had wits left raised their Tasers and launched a barrage of darts at the man.

Hamilton had seen Endurance SPIs shiver at the touch of an AUSS Taser. They were much more powerful than any standard law enforcement Taser. A hundred thousand volts of electricity passed from weapon to target. Enough energy to set hardwood aflame.

Three Taser darts made contact with the old SPI's skin. Two through his shirt in the space between the flaps of his big coat and one in his bare cheek. Hamilton heard the snapping and buzzing of the weapons at work.

The burned man didn't even wince.

He picked the darts off his skin as if they were slivers, letting them drop to the ground uselessly. One of them arced off his metal belt buckle as it fell, proving to Hamilton that the weapons had indeed been charged.

"Let me through," the man said.

"It doesn't look like I can keep you from doing anything, does it?" Hamilton asked. "So why not just walk through me?" He wanted it. Hamilton hadn't gone one on one with a SPI like himself in a very long time. He'd once been assured that no one could match his strength and resilience. He'd tested higher than anyone since Citadel himself.

"I don't want to hurt anyone," the old man said. Hamilton laughed.

"You're the one who just wrecked four vehicles," Hamilton said. "I'm not the bad guy here."

"I'm going in there." With that, the man took another step forward. Hamilton shook his head incredulously. Then, he grabbed the man's arm and slammed him into the operations van. The van rocked back, nearly folding around the old man's body. It crumpled and fell over onto its side.

"No," Hamilton said, "you're staying here with us. I think we know what's on TV tonight. If we're lucky, it'll be a triple bill."

The SPI's eyes blazed at Hamilton's words. He shrugged and the bent metal pinning him to the van screeched and ripped away from the car in sharp, ragged sheets.

"It's been a long time since I've pushed myself so hard," the old man said, "I'm a little rusty." He gripped the edge of one of the car panels and tore it off the body completely like it was a sheet of construction paper. In the same motion, he swiped it edge-wise toward Hamilton.

Hamilton blocked with his forearms. The sharp metal cut through his shirt sleeves but merely scraped against Hamilton's skin, curling the edges of the metal sheet up.

The SPI's eyes widened in surprise.

"You didn't see that coming, did you?" Hamilton asked, his lips straining into a grin. "There's a reason they call me 'Rockhide.'" He stepped closer to the old man, batting the sheet of metal out of his opponent's hand. Then, with his other arm, he threw a punch with all his strength behind it.

The force of the blow hammered the old man back into the van, knocking it over. A shocking stab of pain jolted up Hamilton's arm at the impact. He might have broken something in his fist or arm. Regardless, it was quickly absorbed by his Endurance enhancement. Any wound he might have inflicted on himself vanished in moments.

Hamilton rarely experienced pain anymore. The last time he'd felt such a thing was during his testing when he'd struck a three foot thick titanium panel with all his strength. The titanium had dented.

The old man had not.

He rose from the wreckage of the van, his clothing torn but not looking too much different than it had before. His hair had been pulled from its topknot. It fell across his face, but he didn't seem to care. His face held all the determination he'd had before. Not a lick of fear or uncertainty.

"They didn't call you 'Citadel,'" the old man said. Hamilton had time for an instant of shock before the old man returned his punch. Then, he was thrown from his feet and into the surface of the parking lot. Asphalt crumbled around him, dirt from beneath scattered into the air.

When Hamilton came to a stop, his breath had left his body. He sucked in dirt-clouded air to get it back and coughed. Throbbing pain spread through his chest. He couldn't tell if it was from a collapsed lung, or if his chest had been bruised. This pain vanished as quickly as the other.

"Stay down," Citadel said. Citadel! How was that possible? No, it couldn't be. There was no way.

But whether this old man was truly Citadel or not, Hamilton was done. The old SPI had proven himself more powerful. He could have the damn kid. Hell, he could have both of them.

He gestured with a wave of his hand, hoping his agents didn't try something stupid.

Citadel nodded and stepped past him toward the bowling alley.

"I'll be right back," he said. "Don't go anywhere."

When the old SPI reached the front door of the bowling alley, he kicked it in.

Then, Hamilton felt the buzz in his head that meant he was in shit-tons of trouble.

"Ghost!"

Eric froze and turned, the hockey mask limp in his hand.

Citadel strode in through the open front door of the bowling alley. He walked tall, without the stoop he normally used to disguise himself. His hair was in disarray, and his clothing was even more disheveled and torn than usual.

"What are you doing here?" Eric asked. "Did you go through them?" Eric found himself searching what he could see of Citadel in the emergency lighting for blood. How many had died?

"Calm down, kid," Citadel said. "Nobody got hurt. Except maybe Rockhide."

Eric shook his head. Rockhide? Hamilton?

He was too tired to ask for details. He'd get them later. He pointed toward Kristin, who was staring at the big man in shock. She'd expected Hamilton and the jack-boots. She had to have put the pieces together enough to realize this man had to be a SPI. He'd spare her the full truth until later.

"She was shot. We need to get her to the hospital."

Citadel nodded and approached the girl. Eric winced as Citadel hesitated. The big SPI had glanced at the floor where Mrs. Matthews lay. His eyes were frozen there for a moment. Eric saw Citadel's jaw work, then he turned to Kristin.

With more gentleness than Eric would have imagined, he lifted her from the chair. She suppressed a groan of pain as she was moved. Cradling her in his arms, he smiled reassuringly at her and carried her toward the front. "Come on, kid," he said. "I have to make sure our uninvited guests are behaving."

The girl in Citadel's arms barely felt like anything. She laid her head against his shoulder, and a glance showed she'd passed out. The blood loss didn't seem severe, but the pain of being moved combined with what she had lost was probably more than her relatively frail body could handle.

The old woman on the floor hadn't fared nearly as well. The image haunted him. He'd let one die. He'd hesitated before rising from his chair to follow Eric into town. He hadn't moved fast enough, and someone was dead.

The girl would be okay. There was a clinic up the street that could probably help her. If not he'd take her home and her parents could take her to the hospital in McAlester.

Ghost trotted nervously along with him as they emerged into the light of day from the dark bowling alley. The AUSS agents bustled around the parking lot, removing equipment and spent speed traps from the asphalt.

Rockhide sat on the edge of the wrecked operations van. He seemed to have recovered from their fight, not surprising given the level of his endurance enhancements. Citadel hadn't pulled any punches with the man, unsure of how tough he was and how much strength he'd lost over his years of inactivity.

But the stare Rockhide gave him was strange. It didn't match with the way the brute had looked at him before. It wasn't the hot glare of the angry government agent nor the stark terror in the man's eyes when he'd lain defeated three feet under the surface of the parking lot. This was a cold calculation, doubt changing to surprised certainty as Citadel and Ghost approached.

"Citadel," Rockhide said. He stood, clasping his meaty hands in front of him. Citadel stopped, keeping some distance from him, hoping the man wasn't eager for another fight. "A little worse for wear." Rockhide waved his hands over his face, "But that… is a face I will never forget. Heh." Rockhide shook his head with a chagrined smile.

The cadence of the voice wasn't Rockhide. It seemed familiar, though the gravelly tone of Rockhide's voice disguised the speaker's identity. It was clear that this was not Rockhide.

"Who are you?"

Rockhide's brow crinkled as his eyebrows shot up for a moment.

"It's been awhile, but it can't have been that long. Who else do you know that can do this? Mental Block never had the focus for this sort of thing." Rockhide's hands gestured to his body.

"You're the fifth member of FORCE!" Ghost blurted out. Citadel held out a restraining hand for silence. A strong impression came to him. It was vague, but he saw shadowy figures in his mind's eye: friends, companions. Mental Block, Jitterbug, even Rumble. Yet there was another who loomed over all of them. Citadel couldn't remember his face, or anything about him, really. Thinking about this shadow, he felt only hatred and betrayal, emotions almost as powerful as he was. The fire of those emotions burned away a portion of the curtain that hid his memories from him. Behind that curtain lay a single word. One that surged through him until his eyes teared and he feared he would drop the girl in his arms to leap at the man who was telepathically controlling Rockhide.

"Exodus…" Citadel whispered. Even speaking the name felt like an assault on his heart. He hated this man more than anything. Why?

An image came of a carpeted hallway, walls painted white lined with doors. On the floor before him lay the bleeding body of a man dressed in black military garb. Above the man stood an indistinct figure holding out a handgun. The gun in his memory shone with a strange light.

"What have you done?" Citadel spoke, both in the present day and in that memory. Rockhide's eyes, controlled by Exodus's mind, narrowed, his brow furrowing. "Edward, what—?"

A flash of light seared his mind. Crying out, he fell to his knees in the bowling alley's parking lot. Ghost was suddenly there, scooping the girl from his arms and laying her on the ground. Citadel braced himself on the ground with one hand as the world spun around him. All the pain in the universe ripped through him. He threw his head back and screamed.

Kristin groaned as Eric set her hastily on the ground several feet away from Citadel.

Citadel screamed. He knelt on the ground, one hand laying flat, supporting him. His head flew back, and a thundering cry of agony rattled the air. The hand on the ground clenched, tearing into the asphalt.

Rockhide — Exodus — stared patiently at the display, a look of intense interest on his face. Eric looked on helplessly, trying to think of some way he could help his friend.

Exodus was a telepath powerful enough to take control of another's body. He was now exerting some sort of control over Citadel, causing him intense pain. Eric had never heard of anything like this. As far as he knew, telepathy was only good for reading minds and speaking into them. What level of power did you need to have in order to take over someone's nervous system?

Eric only had one option. He needed to stop it.

There was only one way to do that.

Eric charged Hamilton.

Exodus turned Hamilton's head as he came on. The change of attention didn't stop the torture he was applying to Citadel. But now, the telepath knew he was coming as well.

Eric's head exploded in a cacophony of buzzing as if he'd stuck it in a hornet's nest. He recognized the feeling, it was like the headaches he got when Hamilton had interrogated him. Exodus had been there then, as well, reading his mind.

But if Exodus was trying to hack his brain now, it wasn't working. Despite the pain and discomfort, he was able to think and move. He pushed past the pain and moved forward.

When he was within arm's reach, Hamilton reached out and wrapped a hand around Eric's throat, cutting his breath off.

"What the hell—?" Exodus started. But Eric wasn't going to be talking. He grasped desperately at Hamilton's arm.

Then he started his power up like a lawn mower.

There was something different this time. Pushing his power into Hamilton was a struggle. His flesh was too dense. He felt the vibrations rattle through his hands, shaking Hamilton's thick skin, but not pulling it out of phase as he intended. The buzzing in his head intensified.

He was in a struggle with Exodus for control of his own power.

"I could pop your head off your body, boy," Exodus snarled. Hamilton's voice burred as he spoke, Eric's power humming through his vocal cords.

For whatever reason, Exodus didn't follow through with his threat, but Eric was still choking. He couldn't get a breath through Hamilton's vice-like grip. He needed to stop that buzz in his head. He needed to at least phase himself free of the choke hold.

He turned his attention to that buzz. It was a vibration. It shook his teeth like an electric shock. But as with any vibration, any sound, there was always a counter frequency.

He remembered the physics experiment he'd seen in Mr. Turner's class the year before. The same one that he'd used to produce the sonic fractals in sand. Mr. Turner then set another speaker on the other side of the tray of sand. After a little fiddling with the sound frequencies, he produced a cancellation wave, and the sand became smooth again.

Eric imagined those waves in his head, visualizing the experiment to command his power to do his will. He focused that image on the buzzing in his head.

Almost at once, the buzzing vanished.

Able to concentrate again Eric focused his power on Hamilton. He felt himself go out of phase, and sure enough, Hamilton came with him.

But it didn't last more than a moment. With a jerk of his arm, Hamilton threw Eric away from him. Eric's power cushioned him from the worst of it, but he still hit the ground hard, adding to the bruises he'd have when this was all over. When he'd settled on his back, he became fully solid again.

Citadel roared again, not in pain this time, but in terrible anger. Eric looked up and saw the big man getting to his feet. He rushed at Hamilton and took him by the throat as Exodus had done to Eric just moments before.

"No no no! It wasn't me!" Hamilton cried, his voice no longer hinting of Exodus.

Citadel ignored Hamilton's pleas. He lifted the man from the ground and slammed him down again, making the parking lot shudder with the impact. Asphalt crumbled under Hamilton's body.

Twice more, Citadel slammed Rockhide into the ground. The ground tore apart more with each blow until Hamilton lay in a shallow crater of brown dirt and black asphalt. Then, Citadel knelt over the groaning form of Roger Hamilton. Citadel was breathing heavily, but not from exhaustion. The big man's face held an anger he seemed to be trying desperately to hold back. Finally, he relaxed his hold on Hamilton.

"Get out of Ender," Citadel told him. "Every one of your thugs, every piece of equipment, every computer and technician, every damn bug and tracer. You're done here. Ender is off limits to the AU. If I find any trace of Exodus in this town, I am coming for him. I'm coming for you. I will tear Chicago apart, I will crush the capitol until I sift that… creature from the rubble." He stood, leaving Hamilton staring up at him in terror, perhaps expecting a final crushing blow of Citadel's boot. But Citadel just sighed and turned away. "You have 24 hours."

Eric watched Citadel walk away, stunned at the vehemence of his words. This was his fault. He never should have pressured Buck to help him. Now, the frightened, paranoid, mild-mannered Buck was gone. There was only Citadel, the man who may have been responsible for destroying New York City.

SPI ROUNDUP - 2015

Chicago - 2015 was a big year for American Union efforts to quell the Super-Powered Individual (SPI) uprising. A record eight EUP operatives were captured and executed this year. Only two incidents of SPI related terrorism were recorded in North America with a total casualty count of 387. Televised executions had the record-high viewership, as well, up 5.4% from the previous year.

The following is a detail of AU arrests since 9/12/2014:

1. 10/24/2014 - Jeremy Rice Mitchell (38)
   Enhancements: Telekinesis
   DNA screening: Confirmed
   Execution: Electocution (10/26/2014 - 6:45PM)
2. 12/13/14 - Marwan Khoury (34)
   Enhancements: Strength
   DNA Screening: Confirmed
   Execution: Firing Squad (12/14/14 - 6:45PM)
3. 12/13/14 - Reda Khoury (34)
   Enhancements: Endurance
   DNA Screening: Confirmed
   Execution: Firing Squad (failed), Drowning (12/14/14 - 7:34PM)
4. 3/11/15 - Massen Pascow (86)
   Enhancements: Agility
   DNA Screening: Confirmed
   Execution: Electrocution (3/13/15 - 6:45PM)

5. 4/15/2015 - Kevin Andrew Lourde (42)
   Incident: Jackie Robinson Day Massacre - Wrigley
   Field, Chicago, IL
   Enhancements: Speed, Strength
   DNA Screening: Confirmed
   Execution: Hanging - Enhanced (4/31/15 - 6:45PM)
6. 6/18/2015 - Elizabeth Henrietta Greeley (17)
   Enhancements: Agility, Endurance - Extreme
   DNA Screening: Confirmed
   Execution: Firing Squad (failed), Drowning (6/22/2015 -
   10:28PM)
7. 8/4/2015 - Nicholas Robert Marsden (38)
   Incident - Mass Suicide - Starbucks, Jacksonville, FL
   Enhancements: Telepathy
   DNA Screening: Confirmed (posthumous)
   Execution: First Responder - Gunshot (8/4/2015 -
   2:35PM)
8. 8/22/2015 - Amanda Regina Vera (25)
   Enhancements: Strength
   DNA Screening: Confirmed
   Execution: Firing Squad (8/24/2015 - 6:45PM)

December 2017 - January 2018

With Citadel effectively cutting Ender off from the rest of Oklahoma and the AU, there was no hospital to safely take Kristin to. It was too much of a risk. Instead, Eric called Jason. Surely his parents had some sort of plan for emergencies like this.

Fortunately, they did. Zak had been a paramedic in Los Angeles before making the move to Ender. They came to pick up Eric and Kristin. Zak treated her right there in the parking lot, closing the bullet wound and taking her back to the Williams house to recover. She didn't regain consciousness until later that evening. By then, her grandfather was there to comfort her in their shared grief of Charlotte's loss.

Exodus must have been convinced of Citadel's sincerity. The AUSS unit was gone by the next day without a trace they'd ever been there. Even after a week, the incident did not appear on AUPrimeNews. No mention of Ender made the news at all. The AU was hiding their defeat. Jason's mother said it was because they were afraid the incident would attract the wrong attention. People would wonder why the AU wasn't sending in a force large enough to kill them all. Why would the government let such an act pass? Of course, they couldn't report that it was Citadel himself that had forced the AU Security Service to give up. That would have nullified their entire story about New York City — how Citadel had been there and had been responsible — the whole reason Citadel had been demonized in the first place.

Citadel didn't show his face in Ender for weeks. Not as himself, and not as the homeless man, Buck. Eric went to visit him after a week at the RV. The tires that Buck had mounted on the RV were again stacked in a pile nearby.

It wasn't going anywhere.

"I'm sorry," he said when Citadel wouldn't acknowledge his presence. The big man was sitting on the creaky metal lawn chair, drinking Coke out of a can. His eyes were unfocused, staring at nothing.

At Eric's words, Citadel turned obliquely toward him.

"For what?" he asked.

"You wouldn't have been put in that position if I hadn't pressured you."

"No, you would have just let me forget my obligation."

"What obligation?" Eric said. He sat on the wood pile across from Citadel. "I don't understand that."

"I didn't either," Citadel said. "But I think I'm beginning to." It took several moments for Eric to ask the big question.

"What did he do to you?"

"He took the worst memory I'd lost and gave it back to me." He took a deep breath as if reliving the memory again. "I experienced the moment the bomb went off."

Eric drew in a breath. It was all the response he could muster.

"It was nothing but pain. My body was being torn apart, but my enhancements kept me together. When the initial flash was over, I was nothing but... I don't know. Nothing but pain, I guess. I don't know how I survived. But as soon as it was over, my enhancements began healing me. I shouldn't have been able to remember that, but somehow Exodus pulled it out of me."

"I wish I could have helped," Eric said. "Nothing I did seemed to do anything. It was like Exodus disabled my powers somehow."

Citadel shook his head. "Kid, it was you that stopped him."

He shifted and dug a cold can of Coke out of the cooler at his side. He tossed it to Eric. The can chilled his hands. How did Citadel have such a seemingly unlimited supply of this stuff? "Whatever you did to Rockhide, your Roger Hamilton, it disrupted his connection with Exodus. Exodus should have been able to shut you down. With a thought, he could have rendered you unconscious. You must be resistant to telepathy."

Eric remembered the buzzing in his head, the headaches that had nearly crippled him before he was able to free himself of them.

"Telepathy must work on a vibrational frequency," Eric said. "When I used my powers to cancel out the sensation in my head—" Citadel stopped him with a wave of his hand.

"Save it for someone who understands that science crap, kid."

Eric smiled and took a swig of his Coke.

After the New Year, school resumed. The people of Ender, ever resourceful, found a way to keep the local government running. They'd taken similar steps during the Chaos Years when Ender was the only successfully self-sufficient town in Oklahoma. Citadel was asked to come meet the town leaders, probably to explain himself or probably to come to some sort of agreement on how this all was going to work without the support of the AU. Citadel went. Eric didn't know what happened during that meeting.

He was in school.

Kristin was fragile for some time. Eric stayed by her side whenever he was able. He felt responsible for what happened to Charlotte. Kristin assured him that he wasn't and that she was grateful for getting her grandfather out when he did. Still, he couldn't abandon her in her time of need. And he didn't want to.

She kept his secret, as she had since September, he came to discover. No one else knew of Eric's part in what happened at the bowling alley. Only Jason and Kristin knew the truth, and only because they'd been a part of it. As far as anyone else was concerned, it was Citadel that had stopped Leonard and prevented the AUSS from making Kristin and her family collateral damage in their efforts to stop him. Word went out that Citadel had saved Ender from becoming a permanent AUSS outpost. Talk against the AU increased, and Citadel found himself something of a celebrity in Ender. People remembered how, as Buck, he'd helped when asked and had never lifted a finger against them. Then, he'd saved one of their own and Ender itself from both the AU and Leonard Strange.

As for Leonard, the AU took him with when they left. His execution was televised on AUPrimeNews. They called it Enhanced Hanging — Leonard was hung by the neck with weights tied to his ankles so he couldn't use his powers to escape. It was the last thing AUPrime broadcast into Ender.

Eric didn't watch.

After that, all signals from AUPrime TV were cut off. No cable, no satellite, no over-the-air broadcasts. The repeater stations must have been switched off. Electricity was shut off. Water stopped flowing through the pipes. It was part of the AU attempt to urge the people of Ender to abandon their home and Citadel.

But after all was said and done, Ender surprised everyone who thought the AU would eventually wear the town down. As they had during the Chaos Years, Ender tightened its bootstraps and made it work. This was their home, after all. This time, there were no gangs knocking on the door, no concerns but themselves to take care of. There was a river nearby for water. Gasoline could be rationed to run generators where electricity was needed. Security and law enforcement, when it was needed, was left to the people who had always looked out for each other before.

And to Citadel.

The big SPI became ever present after his meeting with the town council. If tempers flared or fear made someone do something stupid, Citadel was there to create peace. Not with strength, or any of his other enhancements, but with calm authority.

Eric was beginning to appreciate home, probably for the

first time. Gillian stayed sober with a new determination. Eric didn't fear going home anymore. He didn't fear being discovered anymore, though he didn't openly use his powers. Most of all, he didn't fear what he had become. He accepted it. He knew it wasn't going to force him to make bad choices or become an evil person. If that happened, it would be his own fault.

For the rest of that school year and into the next summer, Eric and his friends found a sort of peace in the little town of Ender.

AUPrimeHistory: True Conspiracies

(Airdate: 9/11/2008)

CONCLUSION: A BRIGHTER FUTURE

<Archive footage of 'pristine America'>

Now, over a year after the completion of the Marshall Coup, The American Union is healing.

<Footage: The 'rainbow' of the AU - Diversity and Unity>

The people of the American Union are our strength. Together, we are bringing a nation from the ashes to create a new, stronger collective.

We are no longer just Canada, just Mexico, or just the United States.

We are one.

<Animation: waving American Union Flag>

We are the American Union.

<End Credits>

<u>Epilogue</u>

The plaque on the desk read "Edward Bradley." But those under his command knew him by another name.

Exodus.

In the sixteen years since he'd taken over the DSA, Edward had been working to rebuild the American continent. The loss of New York City had been the death-knell of the United States of America. Edward knew that on Sept 12th, 2001. The city had been not just the center of American finance, but the center of everything American. Its destruction had been worse than if it had happened to the District of Columbia with all its politicians and so-called leaders. The nation could have recovered from that. There were always more people willing to take the reins of power.

After two weeks of planning, his efforts had begun that day in the conference room, when he'd shown the investigative committee and the president the doctored video of what had happened in New York. The subtle cues he'd planted in their minds that day were designed to draw out the man who would someday return America to its former glory. Edward had thought it might be Chuck Grassley, or even President Gore, who had once been a strong man. But Grassley had proven resistant to Edwards manipulation, and the death of those millions had broken the back of the once powerful Al Gore.

No, it had been Senator Marshall, the young man from Missouri, who had come to him with the idea of merging the three powerful nations of the Hemisphere and creating a grand new state. Marshall had been willing to do what needed to be done to topple the United States and build something better.

Every day, Edward was heartened by what he was building. It was by no means finished, of course. The AU was by no means perfect, but just its existence was a light shining on the resiliency of man for the world to see.

All his work was finally coming to fruition.

He'd hit some stumbling blocks along the way, most recently the events in Ender, Oklahoma and the return of Citadel. But those types of things happened behind the scenes and could be dealt with. The more worrying issue was the boy. In the blink of an eye, that boy had ripped him from Rockhide's mind with such viciousness that his power had been blacked out completely for nearly twenty minutes.

Plans had to be laid to neutralize the Sumner boy.

As if the name was a spell of summoning, Edward felt the tug on his mind as a powerful SPI approached the door through the dark corridor, disdaining the light in lieu of secrecy like a good-boy. The man could see in the dark after a fashion after all. What use was light to one such as him?

The door opened without a knock. The SPI paused to let his eyes adjust to the light. He was a few years younger than Edward, but he had just as much gray in his black, wavy hair. He wore a long, billowy trenchcoat over a black tactical suit, the type special forces operatives wore on night missions. Edward knew that the military uniform reminded the man that he was nothing more than a soldier in Edward's employ. He wore it with disdain, bitter that he no longer had a say about how or where he lived his life.

"Ender?" Edward asked before Sonic blinked his vision clear. Sonic was not the type of man to be oblivious to world events, even when Edward tried to keep such knowledge from him. Edward would have to have a talk with Rockhide about operational security.

"What else?" Sonic said. *I wouldn't bother coming to this shithole or to be near you if it were anything else*, Edward heard him think.

"It's taken care of," Edward said, ignoring Sonic's treasonous thoughts. "We'll process Leonard Strange as usual. I'll have Rockhide evaluate whether he's worth keeping on, he might become a valuable asset."

There had been an "execution," of course. But that mattered little. It was the number one rule of the new Department of Supernormal Affairs: All SPIs die. All SPIs stay dead – At least in the view of the public. Operatives like Sonic were all dead in the eyes of their friends, their families and the world at large. It was how order was maintained and the populace controlled.

"You know what I mean," Sonic said. The thought that accompanied his words was too filthy for words.

"Watch your tone, Sonic," Edward growled, putting a touch of coercion in his voice. It didn't take much anymore. After so many years, Sonic belonged to Edward completely. Edward had even taken Sonic's body for a spin, running missions beyond covert that even Sonic wasn't aware of.

"I want to bring him in," Sonic said after a moment's hesitation as he fought the urge to obey. His voice did take on a meeker aspect. An image of a small child flitted through Sonic's thoughts.

I want. Those weren't words Edward heard much from Sonic anymore. It wasn't good to allow him such freedom of desire.

"No," Edward said. "Let it be. Even if you could get past his protector, we don't practice extraordinary rendition. It draws too much scrutiny and could alert Mental Block's agents. He's already being shadowed by them. No need to bring us more problems than we want to handle right now."

Sonic nodded reluctantly. Edward felt a twinge of uncertainty. When it came to Ender, Oklahoma, Sonic was dangerous. It was one of the few limitations of Edward's control over the man. If Edward were to let his control slip over that damned boy…

"I've got something else for you for the time being," Edward said. He had to give the man something to do. "Miami. There are reports of an emerging SPI. I want you to give her a push, then bring her to Rockhide for intake."

"Two in one month?" Sonic said. Edward nodded. They needed to draw any undue attention from Ender and quickly. After Leonard Strange, thoughts would be on the little town he'd come from. They needed another to shift focus away. Sonic returned the acknowledgment and made to leave.

"And Steven," Edward said, using his real name to draw his full attention. "Stay away from Oklahoma."

Steven Sumner's eyes narrowed, but he jerked his chin down as he whirled back toward the door, his coat billowing around his legs. A burst of sound rocked the room, sucking the air from it and changing the air pressure so violently that the door slammed shut.

Edward rubbed his ears, suppressing a cough until he was certain Sonic was out of earshot. Even alone in the room, he didn't want to show weakness. He forced the cough to be a simple clearing of the throat and the struggle to regain his breath a simple deepening and slowing of his breathing. The room was far from airtight, so the air pressure quickly returned to normal.

When he recovered, he smiled. He could trust Steven to be Steven. In fact, he counted on it. It was all setting up so perfectly.

If he wasn't careful, he'd get everything he wanted.

Alec Gunn

The Greatest Gift

The greatest gift you can give an author isn't your money. Yeah, we love money just as much as other people, but the true currency in the literary world is and al¬ways has been

THE REVIEW

If you enjoyed this first adventure of Ghost and Citadel, and you want to show your appreciation, head on over to the on-line store where you purchased it (or the online version of the physical store where you picked it up), and leave a positive review. Feel free to reveal the flaws and give your honest opin-ion. I hope you'll write good things, but I want you to be honest above all (in reviewing this book, and in life in general).

I am grateful for every review. Every review means some-one will make an informed decision whether or not to buy this book (and thereby give me money — see how that works?).

Stay True, Believers!

—ALEC GUNN

Untouchable

<u>The Truth is HERE</u>

The Heroes of FORCE were once American Legends.

Now their legacy burns in the nuclear fire that engulfed New York City.

Discover the truth about FORCE! Read the
Top Secret Project Brooklyn Documents
featured in this story and discover the secrets of FORCE.

Find it now at:

pencastlebooks.com/alec-gunn-heroes-of-force-force-feed/

Alec Gunn

Sneak Peek: Unbreakable
Heroes of FORCE #2

Prologue

Mr. President, this is Subject Alpha.

The first time Alpha met President John F. Kennedy, he'd been at least as impressed as Kennedy was with him. It had been 1962, a year after he'd broken the back of George Hudson during the Virginia state wrestling finals. Alpha had flipped the two-hundred-thirty-pound teenager onto his back and slammed him to the mat hard enough to shatter bone.

Mr. President!

Why had he been in Dallas that day? Dr. Morrow had instructed him to follow the motorcade along with the Secret Service detail. He was just a kid. Still barely sixteen. But he'd done it. And when the report of the gunshot had reached his ears, he acted without thought. He threw himself at Kennedy, the only obvious target. He'd been fast enough. Just fast enough. The 6.5mm round hit his shoulder and broke into 37 pieces, none of which had penetrated his flesh. One ricocheted and struck Governor Connely in the front seat of the car, grazing the side of his head.

By the time the sniper had time to fire his second shot, Alpha's tall, lanky form completely obstructed Kennedy. That shot cracked against the back of Alpha's skull and ricocheted into Secret Service Agent Clint Hill who was standing on the side of the car behind them. Hill fell from the car, his stricken right knee giving way.

Someone had known that Kennedy was in danger that day.

Someone had ordered Alpha to Dallas, even though he lived and trained in sub-basement 3 of the Pentagon building in Virginia.

You want me to do what, Jack?

When you saved someone's life, President Kennedy had told him, you earned the right to call him by his first name.

It was April 22, 1964. Alpha strode along a winding riverbank in a hot, wet, foreign land. He wore loose camouflage pants and a brown, sleeveless shirt. The shirt was ripped in several places, flaps torn from the shirt flopped wetly at his side.

Alpha didn't feel the shirt. He didn't feel the heat. He didn't sweat. He hadn't felt normal heat or cold against his skin in almost three years.

He did smell the smoke. It smelled of diesel fuel and oily rags burned with too much heat. Behind him, the plumes of it rose into the damp air in billows that fought the humidity to rise into the sky.

In front of him, weapon emplacements tracked his progress, waiting for him to get close enough for their .50 caliber rounds to do damage. If he could speak Vietnamese, he might have told them the barrels of the weapons would have to be two feet from his skin for those rounds to penetrate, let alone kill him.

When the jungle trees to either side of the river opened up wide enough, Alpha could see the buildings of Hanoi rising on the horizon. He was almost there. Almost to his target.

The thump of a mortar came to his ears. A patch of dirt to his left exploded and rocks pelted him. The .50 cals opened up on him, peppering him like golf balls thrown by seven year-olds. Those he felt, but only as ripples on his flesh akin to the quick strikes of an Asian masseuse.

The mortar was a bigger problem. He'd never been struck by high explosives before. He was pretty sure he would survive, but his wounds might hamper him for too long before they healed.

Rest break was over.

His eyes spied the two machine-gun nests a hundred feet away. The mortar would be nearby, but he couldn't see it.

He rushed the nests, reaching them in three leaping bounds. The operators couldn't track him fast enough, so their rounds went wide of him. On the final leap, he landed in the midst of one. The two operators shrieked in alarm.

Alpha snatched the gun up by its barrel, the red, glowing metal hissed as it evaporated the moisture on his skin in an instant. He swung it like a scythe, the metal of the receiver ripping through sandbags and flesh with equal effect.

Blood spattered on Alpha's skin unnoticed.

After the operators were dead, Alpha twisted the weapon in his hands until it was a useless coil of metal.

He threw it at the other nest.

That nest went up as if he'd thrown a grenade into it. Sand exploded everywhere. The screams of the operators were cut short. One of them climbed up onto the remains of the sandbag wall, his face covered in blood and one hand a mangled stump.

Alpha ignored the wounded man. He shut out the screams of agony as he scanned the jungle for the mortar nest.

The mortar thumped again. Alpha noticed a shifting in the foliage as the round jumped into the air. He leaped out of the machine gun nest just before the mortar struck it and exploded, destroying whatever Alpha had left behind.

He landed ten feet away from the mortar. The two operators, perhaps having seen what happened to their comrades, screamed and fled in opposite directions. Alpha moved to the nest and crushed the mortar tube in his hand. For a moment, he considered tossing it after one of the fleeing NVA soldiers. Instead, he left the ruined mortar where it was and moved on, heading northwest toward Hanoi.

On the river behind him, miles back, American and South Vietnamese boats would be following him. He had to be swift now, or surely they would catch up to him. They'd only given him two days head start. Clearing the NVA defenses along the river had taken time.

He picked up the pace, turning his long-legged stride into a pace he thought of as a jog, but his trainers considered an Olympic sprint. It was hard here. Foliage threatened to tangle up his legs. Despite his strength and agility, tripping was still a danger over this terrain. He concentrated on bringing his legs up high and straight down as he moved.

Alpha might have been the most physically powerful human being on the planet, but he was still a seventeen-year-old boy who had spent the last three years mostly cooped up in a concrete training facility. Sometimes, he became overconfident. Sometimes he didn't think things through completely.

Sometimes, he didn't consider landmines.

The explosion combined with his momentum threw him high into the air and a dozen yards into the brush.

He hit the muddy earth face first and slid several feet until his head thumped against a thick vine or root. He rolled over onto his back, thankful there hadn't been anyone else around to see such an ignominious stumble. He sat up and wiped mud from his eyes.

Then, he looked down at his legs.

His boots were gone. About three inches of black leather and frayed laces remained on his right ankle, but the left boot, the one he'd landed on, was completely gone. His legs were peppered with shrapnel, blood rimming the wounds. Already his enhanced endurance was closing the wounds around the shrapnel.

His left foot was bare, bloody and about half the size it normally was. The shock of the explosion combined with his natural pain suppression ability had made the amputation painless. As he watched, the shattered bones were mending and growing. Give it a couple of minutes and the foot would be back to normal.

But that was a couple of minutes Alpha had to spend sitting on his ass. The explosion would draw the attention of the NVA. They'd see his wound and put two and two together. Put together a large enough explosion, and they might finally kill him. He imagined the dozens of grenades they'd throw at him.

He pushed himself back, sliding on his butt down toward the riverbank. There was only one way he could think of to both hide and give himself time to heal.

By the time he reached the river, he heard shouts from above, toward the jungle. His toe bones were just beginning to form and become recognizable. He felt a buzzing in his foot as nerves further up were knitting back into place.

He fell back into the water, pushing himself along the silt toward the middle of the flow.

Taking a deep breath, he let himself sink, heavy despite the air in his lungs.

He held his breath as he sat at the bottom of the river. His wounded foot tingled, a good sign, he supposed. His eyes were shut against the muddy brown water.

He spent the time waiting for his foot to heal plucking the shrapnel from his leg. It was only a momentary sting when the metal shards were pulled out, then a brief tingle and the skin was whole again.

When that was done, he waited. His lungs were generating oxygen for him or some such thing. He could hold his breath indefinitely if he wanted to. His body would keep him going.

When he thought his foot was whole again, maybe five minutes after he'd dropped below the surface of the water, he reached down to feel it.

That was a mistake.

The toes bones were whole. Tendons had formed and the muscle was beginning to regenerate, but it was far from finished. In his fingers, his toes felt like odd sticks of gelatin in the water. He drew his hands back, grimacing.

Then, the NVA found him.

The water exploded around him as the NVA soldiers emptied their weapons into the river where his trail ended. Some of the bullets tapped against him harmlessly.

He needed to take care of this. When the American boats came through here, this pack of soldiers would be sitting here waiting.

Injured foot or not, he had to move.

He crawled along the riverbed toward the shore and the NVA soldiers. When he was shallow enough, he pushed himself out of the water.

He stood gingerly, aware that the river silt was probably getting inside his still healing foot.

The soldiers' eyes widened as he came back up into the air, Water sluicing off him as he rose to his feet. In shocked reaction, some opened fire on him. The bullets shattered against his chest and face.

Standing knee-deep in water and with a wounded foot, he couldn't move with the speed he was normally capable of. He limped forward. The nerves in his toe must be forming now, because he felt them dig into the silt.

Beaches would never hold the same allure for him as they did for others after that moment.

The soldiers backed away from him as he approached them. They kept firing until their clips were spent, then they reloaded and fired again. When Alpha was out of the water, he glanced down at his foot. The flesh was red, inflamed. The skin was intact, but his body still needed to fight the infection caused by the open wound in the dirty mud and water.

But he could move now.

There were thirteen of them. Only three got away.

They weren't running toward Hanoi, so Alpha let them go.

In the distance, Alpha heard the buzz of motors. The boats were coming. With the defenses down, their progress was unimpeded.

Alpha picked up his pace.

You are nothing but a coward!

Ho Chi Minh's English was surprisingly good. Alpha had expected a string of expletives in Vietnamese. He got those, too, but Ho Chi Minh stared up at Alpha as the large American reached for him to do what he'd done to the others.

At the insult, Alpha paused. He was doing this to save lives.

Thousands of lives. Seven Vietnamese lives, not counting the soldiers he'd had to kill to get here, in exchange for thousands of Americans.

The lives he would save, both Vietnamese and American, were worth this.

Jack Kennedy had said so.

You did good, son.

Alpha would have preferred those words to come out of the mouth of his own father, but hearing them from Jack was as good as he was going to get.

Upon his return, Alpha had been told that all record of his existence before 1961 was being expunged. His father had been ordered to stay away, and like a good soldier, a veteran of the second World War and Korea, he'd obeyed.

Alpha would never see him again.

But Jack Kennedy would become a constant companion until his death in 1986 from pneumonia. He would become the father figure Alpha never really had. And there were worse people than a US President to look up to.

There had been a small ceremony in the Oval Office after the Vietnam operation. Jack, Vice President Johnson, and Dr. Morrow, the head of Project Brooklyn were the only people who could know about what had happened. Even the Americans and South Vietnamese on the boats hadn't known how they'd gotten up the river without opposition. The raid on Hanoi had been a cover for Alpha's mission, the assassination of Ho Chi Minh and the Central Committee of the Communist Party of Vietnam.

"The United States owes you a debt we cannot express," Jack said as he brought Alpha a small, thin box. He lifted the lid and showed Alpha the contents, a gold star-shaped medal with a blue ribbon bedecked with white stars.

The Congressional Medal of Honor.

"No one will ever know you have this," Jack continued.

"There is no paperwork, no certificate. But I want you to have it, a feeble attempt to show you how much what you did means to this country."

Alpha lifted the box out of Jack's hands. He nodded his understanding, though he was speechless.

Jack turned to Mr. Johnson and Dr. Morrow.

"This boy... this man, has proved himself this nation's defender. He is our strong wall, our impenetrable fortress. He is our citadel."

Dr. Morrow smiled. "Then that is how he'll be known from now on, Mr. President. He needs a better name than 'Alpha' anyway."

"Welcome home, Citadel."

www.ingramcontent.com/pod-product-compliance
Lightning Source LLC
Chambersburg PA
CBHW052023240626
47153CB00006B/1923